# CODE OF HONOR

## CIPHER SECURITY BOOK #2

## APRIL WHITE

*To Maria, Happy birthday my lovely friend. ♡ April White*

WWW.SMARTYPANTSROMANCE.COM

# COPYRIGHT

"Maybe love, at its essence, is being a mirror for another person—for the good parts and the bad. Perhaps love is simply finding that one person who sees you clearly, cares for you deeply, challenges you and supports you, and subsequently helps you see and be your true self."

- PENNY REID

# [ 1 ]
## ANNA

*"That awkward moment in a fight with my twin sister when one of us calls the other one ugly."*

- ANNA COLLINS

"If you can't seduce him wearing this dress, I'm taking your woman card," Colette said as she adjusted the hot pink silk evening gown lower on my chest.

"That's a thing? I was clearly absent the day they handed those out." I batted her hands away and hiked the straps up. "I don't know how you wear this without boob-spillage. I've worn more substantial things to the beach."

Colette scowled at me in the mirror. "You wear a wetsuit at the beach. And speaking of, why do you have a tan? It's March."

Even glaring at me, she was elegant and feminine and everything I wasn't. It was a ridiculous thought for an identical twin to have, but facts were facts, and mirrors did not lie.

"Did you forget I just got back from a surfing trip to Australia?"

She sighed. "Sorry I don't keep track of your *surfing* trips." Colette was seven minutes older than me, but to her, I had all the

1

sophistication of a ten-year-old tomboy. To be fair, I *was* a tomboy, but I was also a fully functioning adult who had been around the world a couple of times and occasionally went toe-to-toe with bail-jumpers.

"My point," she said, finally smiling at me, "is that you look gorgeous, and if you'd stop fussing with the straps, no one would ever know you're not me."

I scoffed. "As long as I don't try to walk, talk, or laugh, or do anything that requires coordination or grace."

She shook her head. "I have no idea how you climb mountains or ride your motorcycle or jump out of planes. Honestly, Anna, for someone so athletic, you're totally hopeless."

I shrugged. "I bounce."

And just like that, my boob popped out.

I shoved it back in and hiked up the strap again. "Seriously, how do you wear this thing? There's no way I can seduce Gray if I'm constantly worried about falling out of your dress."

"Good thing for you he's been troweling on the charm for two months, so an actual seduction would be overkill," my sister said with a smirk.

"An actual seduction requires looking seductive," I grumbled as I adjusted the dress yet again in a futile attempt to hide the cleavage. "There is no part of me that is remotely comfortable or confident in this thing."

Colette turned me toward her and put hot pink gloss on my lips. "Well, if I'm the one who goes to the party, then you have to trust me to set everything up."

"Uh-uh. No way. I do my own recon, and that way I always get out," I said as I studied the oil slick on my mouth with a grimace. I touched my lips together and tried to open them, watching in revolted fascination as they stuck to each other.

"Then you have to be me, and you have to be sexy, and you have to make him invite you to stay so I can come back and be your alibi." She slicked the pink goop on her own mouth and studied her reflection critically.

How was it possible that Colette, wearing jeans and a linen shirt, could look so effortlessly female, while I looked like a confused boy playing dress-up in his sister's closet? We had exactly the same long, curly hair, courtesy of our mother, and the same weirdly long lashes on gray eyes, courtesy of Dad. We were genetically identical, and yet my body was awkwardly athletic while hers was willowy and slender. My laugh was loud and startling, and hers made fairies sigh and small woodland creatures come out and sing. She walked like a supermodel in stiletto heels while I teetered around like a drunk toddler in anything higher than Doc Martens combat boots.

It was humiliating to be Colette's sister.

And I wouldn't trade it for the world.

My sister watched me in the mirror. "Are you sure you don't want me to go in and set things up? You can trust me, you know."

I scowled at her. "I know I can trust you. I also know I have to do this part myself. Your photos were brilliant for planning this thing, but I've never been there, and if I'm going to be creeping around this guy's place later, I want to walk the floors first."

She sighed like a long-suffering older sister and tucked the pink lip slime into the pointless little evening bag that went with the dress. She handed it to me, along with the embossed invitation printed on super-swanky Italian paper, and then gave me her stern, big-sister look.

"Gray invited me because he knows I'm not seeing Mac anymore, and now that he's done supervising the remodel, he doesn't have to worry about pissing off his architect. He's going to get you alone, and he's going to hit on you. It's what he's been trying to do since we met, but I had Mac to shield me. My sweet-but-clueless boyfriend is now out of the picture, and Gray knows I wouldn't come tonight unless I was prepared to hook up. I'm stating the obvious here so you remember that *you don't have to try too hard* with this guy. Just set the meeting time and then stay the hell out of his way so he doesn't wonder why you're acting so weird." Colette spoke completely without irony, and it made me wince just a little – not a lot, because I was a realist, but a little.

She must have seen something on my face, because her tone softened, like she was sorry for me. "You don't have to try so hard with guys, you know. You're beautiful and funny and wicked smart."

I smirked, because she was describing herself and she knew it. "And awkward and dorky and way better than you at strategy games and plotting perfect crimes, so at least I've got that going for me." I adjusted the dress one last time, then kissed her with a big, hot pink, goopy smack on the cheek. "Love you, sis."

She cringed away and rubbed the oil slick off her cheek with a scowl. "Don't do anything dumb."

I turned back to look at my sister with a look of disbelief on my face. "You mean like make a date for you to sleep with Richie Rich so I can steal back the painting that his dickhead dad stole from our mother?"

She smiled infectiously, and I returned the grin when she said, "Yeah, like that."


Sterling Gray was actually more like Richie Rich's entitled older brother. But his entitlement came with a great house. It was technically the "family" mansion, which meant it was owned by Dickhead Dad, but Gray had supervised every aspect of the extensive renovations for his father, who apparently spent most of his time on the East Coast.

Colette had dated Gray's architect a few times, which was how she had gotten into the old Prairie District mansion while it was being renovated. Colette had been able to tour the house right before inspection, but then Mac met someone else, and things like furniture layout and security systems could have changed since then.

A uniformed butler opened the heavy leaded glass door and took my invitation. "Welcome back to the manor, Ms. Collins," he said in a soft, Southern drawl. It was a strange voice to hear in a Chicago mansion, but it added gentility to the austere entry hall.

I had my hand out to shake the butler's before I remembered I probably shouldn't do anything to make myself memorable. "Nice to m—see you again," I said, with a smile Colette would've called 'toothy.' I remembered just in time that Colette had said Sterling used a butler for parties, but she hadn't told me his name.

No one in Chicago knew that Colette had a twin sister – honestly, if I had such an unsophisticated tomboy sister, I'd keep me on the down-low too. But even if I wasn't a liability, I traveled so much for work that we were rarely in the same city at the same time – and we never went out in public together. Basically, she was Bruce Wayne and I was Batman, because of life hack #323: *Always be yourself, unless you can be Batman, and then always be Batman.*

The butler's expression was pleasant and polite. "It's nice to see you again too, ma'am. Shall I take your wrap?"

"No, thanks," I said, pulling the thin cashmere shawl around my shoulders. It was the only thing that would save me from all the potential boob-spillage of the evening and was therefore as necessary as the mask and bat ears.

I stepped into the entry hall and nearly tripped at the sight of all the fanciness. The room was painfully elegant, with white marble tiles on the floor and warm wood paneling on the walls. There was a fireplace surrounded by an exotic stone mantle, and a real wood fire that warmed two chairs which had been artfully placed in front of it. It wasn't even a room; it was a space designed to intimidate and impress guests into feeling honored that they'd been graced with an invitation.

No amount of architectural plans could ever do justice to a space like this, and I had to remind my awe to sit down so I could pay attention to the details. Figuring out the story from the details was what I did best, which is why I had the mind of a master criminal – without the inclinations of one. Mostly.

I knew I'd lingered in the hall too long when I heard the butler greet someone else at the door. "Come in, Mr. Masoud. Mr. Gray will be glad to see you."

I turned instinctively to see who else Gray had invited to his inaugural house party, and almost tripped again at the sight of the

Disney prince who had just entered the hall. Seriously, the guy was a dead ringer for Aladdin, and he was *beautiful*.

"Thank you, Marcel. It's good to see you." Mr. Masoud's voice sounded exactly how a Disney prince would speak, too – in a vaguely accented, probably educated in Europe, quietly cultured tone.

"I'll just take your coat, sir?" The butler said with quiet dignity.

Mr. Masoud smiled wryly as he handed over a topcoat that was probably made of cashmere. "Please call me Darius."

Fancy name for a fancy man, and interesting company for a guy like Gray to keep.

Maybe I was painting the son with the brush of the father, but I had my doubts about Sterling Gray. The man had installed a panic room in his thirteen-thousand-square-foot mansion, and he'd told his architect to wire a wall for an art alarm. The panic room ID'd him as a man with enemies, and the art alarm was almost certainly for the painting I was there to steal. Neither of those things inclined me to be charitable toward him.

I turned to avoid Darius Masoud's gaze as he entered the hall, and found myself looking at the elaborate stone fireplace. I tried not to notice him when he stepped up next to me, which was approximately as successful as not noticing a scorching flame. The man radiated heat, and I almost fanned myself when he spoke.

"The stone looks as though it has rivers of blood running through it. A bit disconcerting, isn't it?"

I turn to stare at him, and I'm pretty sure my mouth fell open too, just to complete the expression of *WTF* on my face.

The Disney prince sighed when he saw my face. "As am I, no doubt, for having observed something so morbid. Right. I'll just go then," he seemed to say to himself, "before she has me removed from the premises."

"Talking to yourself isn't helping the serial killer vibe," I said, because I have the subtlety of an elephant in a hot pink tutu.

He didn't immediately bolt, so I must have surprised him, which was novel. I usually inspired something closer to fear with a side of self-preservation. Men were especially susceptible to this, probably because I looked so much like my sister at first glance, which didn't prepare them for the utterly inappropriate things I said.

He seemed to actually look at me then, and his gaze gave me sweaty butterflies. I've determined they're a thing, since I don't get simple, fluttery, girly butterflies like most straight women do when a ridiculously handsome guy notices them. My butterflies flap around so hard they make me feel slightly nauseated, which inevitably leads to a mild case of the sweats. Ergo, sweaty butterflies.

"I can promise I've never referred to myself as Precious, if that helps," he said in his low, accented voice that made the little bastards flap harder.

"I don't know. Are you more of a Buffalo Bill 'Precious,' or a Gollum 'Precioussssss?' Because that might determine your creep-factor." I seriously needed help. The sheer nonsense I was spouting in the face of such pretty Disney royalty was staggering, and if the look of confusion on his face was any indication, Mr. Darius Masoud was about thirty seconds away from making his polite excuses and beating a hasty retreat. So I got there first.

"Sorry, I just remembered I have to pee." Oh, that was *much* better. His expression was morphing from confusion into amusement, and I pressed my lips together to keep from upping the mortification factor any further. "Excuse me, please."

I hurried down the corridor toward the sounds of conversation and wondered if the laughter came from behind me or ahead. I was clearly not fit for polite company, much less gorgeous, rich, high-class company. I entered a reception hall the size of a ballroom, thinking I'd be able to lose myself in a crowd, and then practically screeched to a halt. Chandelier people – the kind who dripped glittery things and tinkled with laughter – filled the room. They were that special breed of people who chatted easily, laughed at all the right moments, and moved gracefully from group to group like best friends. My feet felt rooted to the thick silk carpet that was covered in an elegant vine pattern and looked far too expensive to walk on.

Then my imagination kicked in, as it always did, and I pictured tendrils of ivy creeping across the carpet to wrap around my ankles and hold me fast. And because that image was so compelling, I began to feel the silken leaves weave themselves around my legs. I pictured thorns budding from the vines to prick my skin and send a deadly neurotoxin sliding up my veins to paralyze my lungs until the lack of air made me black out and fall to the ground, which would tear Colette's hot pink gown on the thorny vines and send boobs spilling out everywhere.

"You're not breathing," the Disney prince said quietly in my ear.

*Oh no, no, no, no, no*! I actually tried to press my lips together again to stop the words, but they slipped on the pink oil slick and opened of their own accord. "Of course not. The neurotoxin from the deadly vines around my ankles has paralyzed my lungs, and I'm pretty sure I only have a few moments left to live," I said.

Out loud.

My sister *hated* this about me. She despaired of my imagination because she was also pretty sure I had an undiagnosed case of Tourette's syndrome – this despite being *genetically identical* to her – and the combination inevitably resulted in unfiltered fantastical nonsense spewing forth with horrifying regularity.

The silence at my right ear was deafening for the space of several exceptionally loud heartbeats before a low chuckle sent my sweaty butterflies into frantic flight.

"It's a cat," he purred.

A cat?

The cat purred? No, the man purred. Men didn't purr, did they?

I threw the switcher on my brain-track and wrenched it back to the situation at hand. The silken ivy I'd pictured wrapped around my ankles was, of course, an actual cat winding itself around my legs.

"I knew that," I said. "You purred when you said it, though. Are you some relation?"

"To the cat?" Darius Masoud stepped around my shoulder to look into my face. The sweaty butterflies hung suspended in mid-flutter, and I grinned because they weren't making me sick at the moment, which was reason to celebrate.

Darius seemed to think the grin was for him though, and his slow, answering smile started the fluttering right back up again. "Don't do that," I said with a scowl.

"Don't smile?" A look of confusion dimmed the smile down to something the butterflies could manage, and I nodded.

"Thank you. The sweaty butterflies were making me a little ill."

Now, I'd always been totally conscious that I sounded like a fruitcake when I spoke in situations like this. The problem was that a: I didn't care, and b: I didn't often have much to say in the matter. The filter between my brain and my mouth had always been tenuous at best, but it completely disappeared whenever sweaty butterflies got involved.

The Disney prince's expression had begun to shift to something much more familiar. The "this one's a whackjob" face that started looking for the exits. And as pretty as his face was to look at, I didn't have time or attention for sweaty butterflies or Disney princes. I had a house to scout, its owner to seduce, and a panic room to find. I pulled on a benign smile – the one Colette said made me look dim – and waited for him to find an excuse to run away.

# [ 2 ]
## DARIUS

*"Unexpected things take your breath away. She wasn't just unexpected, she knocked the wind out of me and ran away laughing."*

- DARIUS MASOUD

S he was waiting for me to run away.

The woman in front of me, with whom conversation was akin to playing barefoot hopscotch on hot asphalt, who walked like shoes confused her, and who smelled of a spring breeze through a field of wildflowers, expected me to turn tail and bolt.

I rarely did the expected, however, and often made choices that flew directly in the face of convention. And as nothing about this woman or this conversation was conventional, I stayed.

And I laughed.

This startled her, and she suddenly dropped to the floor in what seemed at first to be a defensive maneuver, but was actually a crouch in order to pet the cat. Her posture put her face at approximately groin height, and for the space of exactly one half-second, I considered remaining in place to see if she would notice. But chivalry got the better of me, and I knelt down beside her.

Her face flamed bright red, and for a moment I thought she was ill.

"I was just staring at your penis, wasn't I?" she said in a tone of complete chagrin.

Rarely did I meet someone even more straightforward than myself, and I attempted a benign expression. "Were you?"

The delightful girl sighed. "I was. I'm sorry." But then a mischievous glint came into her eyes, and she said in a perfectly benign tone, "So, what do you think about my pussy?"

I choked on a startled bark of laughter, and she allowed herself a small grin as she deliberately ran her hands through the fur of the very contented cat.

"On that note, I believe it's time for me to find something red to drink to match the color of my face," she said, as she rose to her feet. She wasn't graceful about it, but she was strong and didn't wobble until she tried to take a step. She'd managed to stand on the hem of the pink silk gown she wore and winced at the sound of her heel tearing the fabric.

"Well, now I've officially hit my humiliation quota for the night. Enjoy the party, Mr. Masoud," she said brightly, as she hurried away across the room. I let her go without further comment, though my eyes tracked her as she plucked a glass of red wine from a passing tray and finished half of it in one large gulp.

Sterling Gray chose that moment to greet her. She smiled at him and said something that turned his expression predatory. My eyes narrowed at the way Gray touched her arm, and I wondered where her blush had gone. She smiled brightly, despite her pale cheeks, and he leaned in to whisper something into her ear.

Another Sterling Gray conquest, albeit an odd choice for him. Gray was predictable in his companions – slender blondes with long hair, small waists, and high breasts were favorites. And though at first glance, this one fit the requirements, her hair was unruly and verged on wild, her arms and shoulders had the kind of muscle that spoke of outdoor fitness rather than polite gym sessions, and she seemed uncomfortable with the amount of skin her dress revealed. And all of that was before she even opened her mouth.

I smirked at the memory of the least conventional conversation I had perhaps ever had. This woman was far too unfiltered and odd to be an obvious match for one of Chicago's richest, most eligible, and most image-conscious bachelors.

I had no desire to observe the mechanics of Gray's hook-up and turned to the bar for a mineral water. Gray's dates were not my problem, his father's security systems were, and I made a mental note to speak to Marcel, Gray's butler, about the guest list. That the woman's name was sure to be on it was not a motivating factor.

When I turned back to observe the room, Gray was standing with a couple who wore the approximate net worth of a small kingdom in clothes and jewels, and the blonde woman in the pink dress had disappeared.

# [ 3 ]
## ANNA

Hot pink was not a stealthy color, and stiletto heels were approximately as subtle as gunshots on the long marble hallway that led to a back staircase. I paused to slip off the shoes, for which my aching feet thanked me in ALL CAPS, and then had to wipe the smudge of my handprint off the high-gloss walls.

Who did that? Who used high-gloss paint on walls? People who didn't clean their own walls, that's who.

The marble floor was cold under my bare feet, and I had to hike the pink silk up over one arm so I could run down the empty hall. The sounds of the party receded when I reached the staircase, and the carpeted steps even felt quiet as I climbed them.

All the art in the public rooms was large-scale black and white photography – iconic images that were probably numbered and signed by people with names like Leibovitz, Beard, and Avedon. The walls of the back staircase were paneled in warm-toned wood and opened up to a second-floor landing that overlooked the garage. The space was a pass-through, with pretensions declared by a couple of small landscape photographs in gilt frames hung on the walls and a decorative hall table sporting a nude statue of a ballet dancer.

Yeah, right. Keep the toe shoes, lose the tutu. Like that would ever happen in real life.

I slunk down the hallway as a mental conjuring of the naked ballerina stepped off her pedestal and whirled past me in her toe shoes. I admit, I checked out her butt-to-thigh junction with a degree of envy that would've made my sister laugh and everyone else shake their head and look worried for my sanity.

I wasn't worried, though. I mean, who would want to live in a world where naked statues *didn't* step off pedestals and dance away? Besides, this naked dancer stopped and pirouetted in front of a built-in bookcase that fit the approximate location of the door to the panic room.

I *loved* secret bookcase doors. I'd had to drag a bail-jumper out from behind one once, and solving the puzzle of how to open that door had been the best thing about the whole job. That had been an old Victorian house, and even though the bones of Sterling Gray's mansion were old, the remodel was all high-gloss and tech. I doubted this secret door puzzle would be quite so easy to solve.

I glanced at the floor first, then the ceiling. Nope, no metal tracks. The thing about bookcase doors was that they were incredibly heavy when they were full of books and generally required a track on which to slide open and closed. The fact that this one didn't have a visible track meant that the door opened *into* the panic room, which placed the door pin inaccessible within the undoubtedly steel door-frame and made it infinitely easier to bar from the inside.

I'd been watching for cameras since I slipped away from the party, and so far I'd counted six, which meant there might be eight or nine between me and the ballroom. According to the wiring schematic, this panic room was the hub for all the optics cabling, and was therefore the logical place to put a control room. One of the primary reasons I'd come to Sterling Gray's party was to find out whether that room was manned by a security guard, monitored remotely, or was just a place to record the footage for later review. There was one unscientific way to find out.

I stood in front of the bookcase and searched the book titles as if I were just a regular guest who got lost on the way to the bathroom and decided to bring some reading material in with her. Because taking a book into a stranger's toilet was how I rolled.

I tilted a couple of the books toward me, choosing titles at random. They were leather-bound classics for the most part, with gilt edges and uniform heights. The gray leather bindings marched along the shelves in alphabetical order like Virginia Military Institute schoolboys with their brass buttons and gold trim, and names like Scott, Shakespeare, and Shaw called out with a sharp "here!" with each tug of my hand. If the latch was book-operated, a wire would be strung up through the shelf and attached to a plate inside the book, but the spines gave no indication of any differences in construction from one book to the next.

The uniformity was like an itch I couldn't reach to scratch, and I had the sudden urge to rearrange the perfectly ordered books. First, I switched Orwell and Huxley next to each other, because a dystopian debate among the books might liven things up. Then I put Mary Shelley next to Octavia Butler so they could discuss all the things. And finally, humming *I like big books and I cannot lie* under my breath, I decided to group Jack London, Rudyard Kipling, and Herman Melville together. It was when I tugged on *Moby Dick* that the latch finally clicked open.

"No!" I whispered gleefully as the heavy bookcase slid open on soundless rails. Either Sterling Gray was the most insecure pinkie-dinkie on the planet, or his security guy was laughing his butt off at him. I knew the camera had already caught my literary mischief, so I donned a look of stunned surprise worth the year of acting lessons Colette had demanded we take when we were kids, and leaned forward to peek inside.

The room was longer than it was wide – sort of like a double-sized walk-in closet – and it was empty of anything with a heartbeat.

17

A dim light glowed from one long wall where a large screen television displayed the various security camera views. Below the TV was a long cabinet that included an under-counter refrigerator, an espresso maker, a stocked bar, and several computer hard drives. A low sofa that probably converted to a bed was pushed up against the opposite long wall, and a plush carpet and a coffee table filled the middle of the floor. I had the impression of luxury and comfort, but my eyes lost all focus on anything other than the gilt-framed painting on the wall behind the sofa.

It was a portrait of two sisters in the style of the Chasseriau painting that hung in the Louvre Museum. The women were dark-haired and breathtakingly beautiful. They were my mother, Sophia, and her older sister, Alexandra.

Movement on the monitor caught my eye as a lone male figure climbed the back staircase. I stepped back into the hall and pulled the bookcase door closed with a quiet click, then tugged a book off the upper shelves and opened it to read.

The words on the expensive paper swam out of focus as I turned all my senses toward the sound of the man reaching the top steps. I heard his hesitation when he saw me, but I pretended to be completely engrossed in the book I'd found. Which I might have been, if the book had been intelligible.

Black dress shoes with extra-long pointy toes that looked like wardrobe for a Goth vampire stopped in front of me, and I looked up with a gasp. The fake gasp turned real at the sight of Sterling Gray's narrowed eyes.

"Colette," he said, as though my sister's name were a full sentence.

"Sterling," I replied in the same tone.

"What are you doing up here?"

"Reading…" I turned the book over, ostensibly to show him the title, and then had to bite the surprise out of my own voice, "…*Beowulf*."

"In old English?" His tone sounded more stunned than suspicious.

"English major," I shrugged. Aaaaand, my boob popped out. "Damn it!" I clutched the shawl around myself furiously and managed to smack myself in the chest with *Beowulf*. "Oww!"

"Is everything okay here?" an elegant voice asked from the end of the hall. Heat flushed through my body, and I turned away from both men to shove the offending nipple back inside my shockingly inadequate dress.

"It's fine. I'm fine," I said to the bookshelf. I took a moment to replace *Beowulf* on the high shelf, and then had to grab at my shawl to keep it from slipping off my shoulder. "Damn it!" I whispered fiercely. So much for avoiding anyone's notice.

I heard a chuckle behind me, and I scowled. I had to play this cool for Colette to get her invitation back here, but I was almost certain Sterling Gray was laughing at me … her. I pasted a charming smile on my face, relaxed my death grip on the shawl, and turned to face Gray. My gaze flicked to the Disney Prince who was standing behind him, and his look of concern made some damn butterfly take flight from its perch on one of my ribs. I forced my gaze back to Sterling, and the butterfly froze in place and then dropped like a drunken frat boy.

"It's so odd how nervous I get around you, Sterling," I breathed. Those acting lessons were really paying off. Either that, or I'd suddenly become asthmatic. "It's like I'm sixteen again." I was laying it on with a trowel, and he was either an idiot or … yeah, no, he was an idiot.

"I'll take that as a compliment," Gray said with a slow smile that told me volumes about his feelings about nervous sixteen-year-old girls.

Over his shoulder I could see Darius's eyes narrow, and for one brief moment I had the impression he might actually dislike Sterling Gray too. But then he inclined his head very slightly and took a step back. "I'll just return downstairs."

He turned to go, and I had to tear my eyes away from broad shoulders that filled out his tuxedo jacket as though it had been sewn directly onto him.

19

Gray traced a line down my bare arm with his finger. It raised goosebumps on my skin that resembled the approximate texture of a recently plucked chicken. "What were you really doing up here, Colette?"

*Breaking into your panic room.* I almost said it out loud, and the part of my brain that reveled in verbal diarrhea *really* didn't like the metaphorical muzzle I clamped over it. I appeased it with a slightly less damning version of the truth. "I wanted to see your house, so I took myself on a tour. But books are my squirrels, so I stopped to look through yours, and here I am."

"Books are your ... squirrels?"

"You know, like I'm just going along, minding my own business, when ... 'SQUIRREL!' and bam! My attention is all about the books."

He was starting to get that *look for the exits* look so I changed tactics and kissed him.

Hi, my name is Anna Collins, and I make good choices.

Sometimes. Just not today.

It surprised him, so that was good. After a startled half-second, he slipped his tongue into my mouth and licked my teeth, and that was just gross. Who licks teeth? Granted, I wasn't a kissing expert, or really, even kissing proficient. Actually, despite a fairly decent list of one-night stands, I hadn't had all that much experience in really good kissing because I didn't usually kiss the same guy twice.

I pulled back, ostensibly to breathe, but really because I needed his tongue out of my mouth. A smile curved his lips, and in that moment I realized that Sterling Gray was actually pretty handsome. He was six-foot-something, gym-fit, with green eyes, well-styled brown hair, and a chiseled jaw. I had a thing for chiseled jaws, probably because a person couldn't have a weak chin with a chiseled jaw – it's structurally impossible. And nature abhors a structural impossibility, so, there you go.

"You're unbelievably sexy." His voice was low and growly. I didn't get called sexy. I might get 'pretty' on a good-hair day, or 'cool' when I stepped off a motorcycle in my leathers, and once I even got 'hot' from a guy standing below me as I scaled a rock wall. That one baffled me because those climbing harnesses did *nothing* for a person's rear view. But 'sexy' just wasn't in my repertoire, and if I was totally honest with myself, it kind of made his tongue a little less gross. Until he opened his mouth again.

"I wanted you the first time I saw you, Colette. I couldn't take my eyes off you."

Oh right. Colette was the sexy one. How could I forget?

"I have to put in an appearance at another event tonight," I said, trying to sound like I hadn't practiced the words, "and you're busy being the host here. But maybe, if you don't have other plans, I could come back for a nightcap?"

I had argued with Colette about the word 'nightcap.' I said it sounded like a Nick and Nora Charles movie from the 1940s, and after a look that clearly told me she thought I was a whackjob for my black-and-white movie reference, she said it was classy and sounded rich. It also indicated my wish to return the same night rather than at some later date. That was a point I could give her.

His smile didn't change, but he studied me as if I'd surprised him. I didn't like the scrutiny, because even though Colette and I are genetically identical, twenty-eight years of life and ten years spent mostly apart had changed a couple of things in our faces, so I turned and slid past him.

"It's okay, I know you're probably busy," I said as I started toward the back stairs.

He grabbed my arm a little too tightly, which he must have realized because he let his hand slide down to take my hand. "I'd love to see you tonight, Colette. Can you come back after midnight? Say, one o'clock?"

I darted a quick look at him, just to make sure he was serious. Colette had told me to walk away if he hesitated even a moment, and I was stunned to see she was right. He was one of those guys who only wanted things if he thought they were hard to get. Probably inherited the trait from his father who had our mother's stolen painting hanging in his panic room.

"I'll be noticed if I stand outside your front door at one o'clock in the morning." He might as well hang a flashing neon sign on my back that said *booty call*.

"Come through the kitchen door, by the garage. I'll open it for you."

I tried to keep the excitement out of my voice. He couldn't have been more perfect unless he'd handed me a key and the alarm code. "Are you sure?" I asked. "I mean I wouldn't want someone to think I was breaking in and accidentally shoot me." I was fishing.

He kept my hand in his and escorted me down the hall to the main staircase. "I pay my security team very well to keep me safe. An unlocked door isn't going to compromise that."

Hmm. That comment was vague enough to make me uneasy. "You have guards?"

"I have alarms and cameras. If I'm not in the kitchen when you come in tonight, you can find me on the third floor."

"What's on the third floor?" I asked innocently, though I knew the answer well enough from the floorplans.

Sterling Gray turned to face me and brought my hand up to his mouth to kiss my knuckles. "The master suite."

# [ 4 ]
## DARIUS

*"The best princesses are made of chaos and fairy dust, and they carry their own swords."*

- FROM THE T-SHIRT COLLECTION OF ANNA COLLINS

G ray came into the room looking satisfied and smug. His eyes found me, and he jerked his head sharply. "Is everything working properly?"

"It is. I've double-checked the locations of every alarm and camera in the house. The system is set to arm automatically at midnight and disarm at six a.m. unless you do a manual override. In that case you'll have to reset manually as well," I said as we walked.

"Set the system to manual before you leave tonight. I have a guest coming after everyone's gone."

Gray smirked, and I glanced at the back stairs. The young woman was named Colette Collins, according to Marcel. Gray arched an eyebrow at the direction of my gaze. "She was my architect's girl-friend. It didn't seem quite politic at the time, but now that the house is done, well ..." He let the thought dangle as though stealing a girl-friend was just another day for him.

23

And yet, I still didn't see it. The woman in question was far too ... unbridled for him. The word sounded strange, even to my own mind, but it was too easy to picture Sterling Gray as a man who insisted on reins. That thought led to analogies of stables and riding, and the strength of my reaction to the idea of them together was disturbing. This woman was irrepressible. She would not submit to Gray easily, and the thought of her doing so offended me.

"You'll need to reset the system from one of the panels yourself, then. The cameras will still record throughout the house, of course, but no alarms will sound." I sounded disinterested and professional to my own ears, but perhaps Gray had picked up the tone of my thoughts, because he snapped defensively.

"As long as the alarms you installed for the artwork frames work. You have nothing to worry about unless your system fails."

I bristled at the arrogance in his tone, the result of which was impeccable politeness on my part.

"I'll leave you to your evening, Mr. Gray, as you seem to have no further need of my company's services tonight."

I inclined my head very slightly and turned to walk away. Gray called after me in a voice I was sure he meant to be friendly. "Tell Quinn Sullivan my father will see him on the links next time he's in town."

I didn't respond, and my eyes searched the room for Ms. Collins automatically. She was nowhere in sight, though I supposed that if Gray wanted the security system turned off for her to return later, she could already be gone.

In fact, she stood just outside the front door waiting for her car when I'd finished with the alarm. She was visible to me through the leaded glass panes, and she appeared to shimmer under the lights. It was an appropriate description of her, and explained much more than her appearance.

"You're leaving so soon, Mr. Masoud?" the butler asked, as he retrieved my topcoat from the closet and handed it to me.

"It was nice to see you again, Marcel." I gave him a quick handshake and opened the door just as a dark sedan pulled into the circular driveway and the shimmery woman slid into the back seat.

She looked up at me through the window, and the surprise on her face seemed disproportionate to my sudden appearance. I smiled at her and raised my hand to wave, which may have startled me as much as it did her. She raised her eyebrows and then laughed as she gave me an exaggerated parade wave as the car drove away.

I chuckled to myself. "What a remarkably strange young woman."

"Remarkably lovely, I'd say," said Marcel from just behind me. He held the door for an older couple who were preoccupied on their cell phones and ignored both of us.

"What do you know about her?" I asked in a quiet voice as the couple swept past me to the valet.

"She seemed different tonight from the other times I've seen her, but maybe that was just because she came alone and may have been nervous. She's always kind and takes a moment to say hello, but I've never had much reason to speak to her otherwise."

"Gray said she dates his architect?" I said, and then immediately wanted to recall the words. I didn't actually want to know, because who Ms. Collins dated was absolutely none of my business.

"I suppose so, though I can't rightly say. She and Mr. MacGregor seemed friendly enough, but Ms. Collins was always a little bit removed. Maybe that's the difference. She was friendlier tonight. She looked me in the eye and thanked me when she said good night. There aren't many besides yourself who see me as more than the doorstop," Marcel said, with the slightest glance at the older couple now stepping into the back of a chauffeur-driven Mercedes.

I deliberately wiped the image of Ms. Collins out of my mind and threw Marcel a wave as I started toward the street where I'd left my old Land Cruiser parked under a streetlight. "Have a good night, my friend."

"You too, Mr. Masoud," he called after me. "I'll see you again soon."

"Very likely," I said under my breath as I walked, thinking about Sterling Gray and his penchant for prioritizing sex over a properly armed security system.

# [ 5 ]
## ANNA

*"Adrenaline is nature's way of telling you life's about to get pretty interesting."*

- ANNA COLLINS

The Disney prince had waved to me. He waved. And smiled.

The thought was a drumbeat in my head as I climbed the trellis the builders had so thoughtfully anchored to the side of the Gray mansion.

He waved. He smiled. At me.

Perseveration was most useful for mindless tasks like climbing and running. My problem was that I kept wincing after the 'at me' part, because he didn't wave and smile at *me*, the house-breaking, diarrhea-mouthed, engineer boot-wearing bounty hunter named Anna. He smiled and waved at pink dress, lip-slick wearing, girly-girl interior designer Colette.

Colette, who would be at the kitchen door in ten minutes.

Drumbeats and winces got me to the roof of the garage fairly easily; it was the jump from there to the tiny Juliet balcony off the second floor hallway that would require my rogue skills.

The character I'd made up for lunchtime D&D games when I was fourteen was a human rogue named Honor. At the time, I'd thought I was being clever and ironic, as fourteen-year-old invisible girls must be to be relevant when they have beautiful sisters, because Honor was a thief who roved with rogues and brigands and was therefore Honor among thieves.

I know, right?

Oddly, my character grew into her name. Her comrades could always count on her caper-planning skills, her moral code, and her fearlessness in the face of danger. She had taught them all a thieves cant so they could speak in code, and she seemed to excel at Robin Hood missions involving stealing from the rich to give to the poor. I wanted to be like Honor in real life, so I learned to climb and jump like she could – starting with the monkey bars, quickly moving to rock walls, and eventually free-climbing the 'easy' part of El Capitan on a trip to California after college. I'd stayed in climbing shape by scaling the back wall of any building I lived in, and from my current home I could do exactly three roof-jumps before I'd be stuck and have to climb back down the fire escapes of nearby buildings. Climbing was a useful skill for my bounty hunting work, and was the primary component of this breaking and entering plan.

Two minutes to go. I lined up my jump and then backed up the length of the pitched roof. The top was wider than a balance beam and put me high enough so that I'd reach the balcony rails on the top of my arc if I got enough speed.

Collette's taxi arrived and dropped her off out of my sight. I could hear her come around the back of the house though, and I checked my watch. Exactly one in the morning. Punctuality was one of the few identical things about us besides our genetic code, and I blew a kiss into the breeze for her.

I inhaled and let the drumbeat start again. *He waved. He smiled. At me.* I pumped my arms and pushed off hard at the end of the roof. *He waved. He smiled. At meeeeeeee.*

I flew the brief distance between buildings and grabbed at the Juliet balcony railing, gripping it with all the strength in my rock climbing fingers. My heartbeat hammered in my chest, and the drum in my head silenced as I listened for the sound of Colette's knock on the back door. There—

The murmur of quiet voices drifted up from below as my arms quivered with the tension of holding my body utterly still. The moment the door closed beneath me, I dragged myself over the railing onto the balcony.

I paused for the barest moment to catch my breath before I opened the glass-paned door that I had unlocked earlier, and then stepped inside the second floor hallway. I slid the locks home just as an electronic voice announced that the alarm system had been armed.

I sighed, knowing it had been too much to hope that Sterling would leave the house un-alarmed while Colette was there. It meant I would have to stay until she left.

There was a reason I didn't have long, heavy drapes in my studio. Two reasons, actually. First, they're fricking expensive, and the designer kind that perfectly matched a slipper chair or the headboard were the approximate cost of my first car. But more importantly, creatures could disappear behind them, and I had spent far too many sleepless nights hiding my neck from the vampires that lurked in my grandmother's curtains.

Happily, the Gray mansion had the perfectly designed floor-length heavy drapes that matched the antique gilt chairs on either side of the naked ballerina. I slipped behind one and twitched it closed around me. The hallway was lit by dim wall sconces, and I was wearing my stealthiest skin-tight, all-black house-breaker clothes, including a black balaclava to cover my face and hair that I counted on to make me anonymous in case the cameras actually were transmitting.

Voices drifted up the staircase as Sterling and my sister climbed, and I calmed my heartbeat to something I could eavesdrop over.

"I love what your decorator has done with the house, Sterling. She has excellent taste." Colette managed to climb stairs and purr at the same time.

I was reminded of the cat I'd met earlier, which must have

29

conjured him, because suddenly he was there, winding himself around my ankles with an even louder purr than Colette's.

*Oh no.*

"*I* have excellent taste. *She* has connections," Sterling answered with a degree of confidence that sounded smug to my ears.

The cat kept swirling around my ankles, making the curtain move alarmingly. Sterling and Colette had just reached the landing, and I sincerely hoped the naked ballerina would distract them from the ghost curtain.

Apparently she didn't dance down the hall for them, which sucked for them, and sucked for me, because Sterling's footsteps stopped.

"What the …?"

"*Reow*," I called out in my best imitation of feline distress. It was all I could do, and my muscles twitched in anticipation of the fight or flight I was about to engage in. Everyone froze – Sterling, my sister, and the cat.

Sterling took a cautious step toward my curtain, and I nudged the cat with my toe. It darted out with a hiss of pure feline annoyance.

"Aaahh!" he yelled, and I bit the inside of my cheek to keep from laughing out loud.

Colette didn't have my self-control, which was ironic in the extreme, and I almost threw something at her. She had the most contagious laughter of anyone I'd ever met; it was pure torture to anyone attempting stealth mode. Happily for me, it only took a few seconds for Sterling to join her. I was shocked to see that the man was actually laughing at himself.

"Come here, baby." Colette knelt down and cooed the cat into her arms. He purred with the approximate volume of an outboard motor, which was apparently the fate of all male creatures who ended up in my sister's arms.

She moved off down the hall in front of Sterling. "Don't tell me you're afraid of this beautiful—"

*Pussy*, my mind supplied.

"—cat," she finished with the barest pause, as though she knew exactly what I would not have been able to resist saying. Apparently Sterling had the same thought in his head, because I could hear the snicker in his voice as they walked away.

"I've never been able to resist … cats."

I rolled my eyes and sent my sister invisible hearts for distracting the guy with his own imagination. Also, for taking the cat with her.

When they had turned to go up to the third level, I pulled the first mini spotlight out of my pocket and slid it down the hall so it was approximately in front of the first camera. I hit the remote, and it flared to life. Then I eased myself out from behind the curtain and slunk along the opposite wall until I was in range of the second camera. I did the same thing with mini spotlight number two, then made my way down to the bookcase where I slid a third spotlight just across from it. When that one illuminated, I reached up, tugged on Moby's Dick, and was inside the room within seconds.

I said hello to Aunt Alexandra and my mom in their painting, but I started at the computer first. A standard video feed array showed a small window for every camera in and on the house. I studied the various feeds and isolated the ones that would have captured my entrance into the mansion. Cameras 14, 15, and 17 would have caught me, but the mini spotlights glared so fiercely that the shadows were nearly black in comparison. None of the other cameras were aimed in the right direction to view my catwalk on the garage roof, though several cameras had views of the exterior doors. I switched the feed, and camera number 24 was aimed directly at an image of my sister and Sterling Gray kissing in the master bedroom.

Ugh. I didn't want to watch. Colette had told me she would enjoy tonight. She thought Sterling was handsome, and even when she was dating Mac, she'd been intrigued by Sterling's pursuit of her. Mostly, though, she looked forward to treating him like a one-night stand, never picking up the phone if he called, and generally pretending they were barely acquainted if she ran into him at a party. She said it's what men like Sterling Gray did to women all the time, so she would be happy to give him a dose of his own medicine.

Keeping my eyes averted from the screen was approximately as easy as not saying the thing that made people wince, which for me was pretty much impossible. Colette wasn't as tall as Sterling, even in heels, but she was the one in charge of the kiss. Her hand trailed down his arm, then up his back, and his arm snaked around her and pulled her in close. She pushed him back with one hand, even as her other hand reached down and stroked him through his jeans.

Wow. My sister had moves.

And I felt like a dirty old man for spying on her.

On the monitor, my sister was still kissing Sterling, but they'd moved closer to the giant four-poster bed. I flipped back to the previous screen to look for any movement on the grounds. Everything was still except for the cat, which had made its way back down the stairs and was prowling the hall, throwing enormous cat-shaped shadows on the wall as it passed each of the mini spotlights. I was glad I'd closed the door to the panic room so the cat wouldn't accidently be locked inside when I left.

I turned my attention to my mother's painting. Its frame was heavy and made of gilt-painted carved wood, and was wired to the wall to prevent theft, so I left it alone. The painting itself was stretched over a thin wooden support frame, and it only took about three minutes with my very sharp pocket knife to carefully cut the canvas free, despite its surprising thickness. Once I had it loose, I rolled up Alexandra and Sophia and dropped them into the telescoping tube I'd pulled from the harness strapped to my back.

I had designed the harness for myself along the lines of the rig climbers wear, except it was for my back, shoulders, and waist. It was tight so it didn't get hooked on balcony rails or grabbed by people attempting to thwart my timely escapes. The tube for the painting fit neatly under the straps at my waist and shoulders and ran down the length of my spine. It gave me an old crone's lumpy back, but that only made the urge to cackle in a witch's voice slightly stronger than usual.

With the canvas safely on my back and my knife tucked in my pocket, I turned back to the monitor. Still no movement in the hall outside the panic room door, and nothing on the grounds that I could see. I braced myself for one last look at Colette and Sterling, just to make sure they wouldn't be roaming the halls anytime soon.

Whoa, nope. Sterling's naked butt glared at me from the screen, and I slammed my eyelids shut attempting to scrub the image from my brain.

"Ick. Blech. Ugh. Nope. No. All the noes," I muttered under my breath as I opened the panic room door and slipped out into the second floor hallway, where light-blind cameras now stood sentry over the naked ballerina's shadow dance. When I'd passed all three cameras I hit the remotes, and the hallway was plunged back into dimness. It took a minute for my eyes to adjust, then I scanned the floor for the lights. I was counting on their small size and discreet placement near the baseboards to render them invisible while I was still trapped inside the house. I could just barely see them from where I stood at the end of the hall. Good enough.

Sterling's cat waited for me at the door to the balcony and wound his way around my ankles twice before I slipped behind the long curtain and tucked it around myself. I crouched down to stroke his soft fur, scratch his ears, and calm my heartbeat with his rhythmic purring.

The hard part of my job was done. Now I just needed to wait for Sterling to turn off the alarm to let Colette, and me, out of the house.

Now that I knew where all the cameras were aimed, I planned my escape route accordingly. I didn't have to return to the garage roof, with its high potential for naked-eye visibility, and could instead drop down over the balcony railing and use the drain pipe to control my fall to the ground.

The cat nudged its way next to my hip and curled into a contented ball as I stroked its fur and tried not to think about how Colette had spent the past thirty minutes. She promised she would be fine, and I trusted her, but the thought of having sex with Sterling Gray held exactly point-five appeal on a hundred-point scale for me, and that was only because he had the good taste to build a secret bookcase door in his dad's house. Now his friend the Disney prince was up somewhere near the seventy-point range, with room to move up or down based on factors like hygiene, sense of humor, the sound of his chewing, favorite movie, and how well he kissed.

I sighed. Darius Masoud was not for kissing. At least not for kissing me. Whoever he kissed would not be the kind of person who needed an alibi for anything, much less a naked sister alibi.

I spent the next hour planning D&D campaigns for Honor and her thieves, and was startled when the electronic "Alarm, off" voice murmured from the hall. I dumped the sleeping cat off my lap, pulled myself up off the floor, and stepped out from behind the curtain to open the balcony door. I'd just closed it behind myself when I heard the alarm re-engage, and didn't even wait for the heart-pounding to still before I dropped down off the balcony, shimmied down the drain pipe, and sprinted away from the house. I bolted for the dark alley where I'd hidden my motorcycle behind a dumpster. The balaclava came off, my helmet went on, and a minute later I was an anonymous biker flying down the streets of Chicago.

# [ 6 ]
## DARIUS

*"Secrets are your greatest liability. Fear is your greatest weakness."*

– DARIUS MASOUD

C ouldn't have seen that coming.

I did try to withhold the smirk that had been threatening ever since we'd gotten the call from Gray about a theft at his father's mansion, but judging by the angry glare on Gray's face, I was only marginally successful.

"How could this have happened?" He turned from the front door and marched straight upstairs, leaving me to close the door.

"What time did your guest arrive, and what time did you reset the alarm?" I countered.

Gray turned to scowl at me. "Colette got here at one a.m., and I re-armed the system immediately after she was inside."

I tried to avoid the mental image of the beautiful blonde and her mischievous smile, but was unsuccessful. Her image winked at me as she stood at the bookcase door reading *Beowulf*. I shook my head to banish her.

"And did she stay the night?" I asked, with a morbid interest in the answer.

We reached the second floor landing, and he gave me a look as though I were a proper idiot for wondering. "Of course not," he snarled.

I'd had a lot of practice maintaining a neutral expression, which came in quite handy when dealing with Cipher Security's wealthy clients. "Well, let's review the feeds then, shall we?" I indicated that he should precede me to the panic room.

"I did that already, obviously. There's nothing." Nonetheless, Gray was already marching in that direction.

The bookcase door was closed, and I stopped Gray before he could pull the book to open it. I studied the shelves as he tapped his foot impatiently.

"Did you rearrange the books?" I asked.

"No." Annoyance seeped from his skin like a stench, and I had the sudden thought that Ms. Collins would likely have said something inappropriate to him about it. The idea of that made me smile.

Gray's scowl deepened. "Is something funny?"

I noted the change in position of several books, and realized that two of the rearrangements were next to the levered Melville. I studied them more closely. *Call of the Wild* and *The Jungle Book* had been placed next to *Moby Dick*.

"Clever," I murmured.

"What?"

"You haven't touched the arrangement of these books since the lever was installed?" I didn't think Gray had the imagination to place the anthropomorphized stories together, but the camera feeds should confirm my instinct.

"These books were bought and arranged by my designer. What purpose could possibly be served by moving them?"

Besides reading them? I would have been astonished if Sterling Gray had read anything since his days at Harvard but the stock market reports on his father's company.

I noted two other subtle changes to the book order and wondered at one of them. What could Octavia E. Butler and Mary Shelley possibly have in common … ah, besides feminism and ground-breaking gothic science fiction? I snorted to myself and donned a pair of gloves before reaching up to tug on *Moby Dick*.

I smirked like the adolescent boy I could still occasionally be, and the bookcase door swung noiselessly open. My first glance was to the monitor, where I was glad to see the various camera feeds still recording throughout the house. My job would have become considerably more difficult if the video surveillance system had been damaged in any way.

And yet why hadn't it been?

My gaze swung over to the elaborately carved wooden frame that now hung empty behind the sofa. I knew how heavy that frame was, as I'd been the one to install its security lock.

"What else was taken?" I asked as I entered the small room.

"It's not enough that this was?" Gray's tone was sharp and defensive, and I stored that impression away to consider later.

I allowed my eyes to flick to Gray's briefly before returning to my examination of the room. "I know we have the valuation docs at the office, but off the top of your head, what can you tell me about the missing painting?"

He huffed in exasperation. "My father acquired it from the artist, and he wanted it installed in the panic room for safekeeping."

"So the painting belongs to your father?" This hadn't been in the valuation file, but it made sense. Most of the Gray mansion's contemporary art and photography had been acquired and insured by Sterling Gray, but the painting of the two sisters was in a much more classical style and didn't particularly fit with the art in the public rooms.

"*Everything* belongs to my father, including your failed security system." Gray's anger was palpable. "Why are you so interested in the painting?" His movements were restless as he brushed imaginary dust from the desktop.

"I'd prefer that you touch as little as possible until the police have had a chance to dust for fingerprints."

"No police," Gray said sharply.

My expression remained casual and calm, even as instinct warned me that Gray's secrets could become problematic for Cipher Security.

"Insurance won't pay without a police report."

"The painting wasn't insured."

I allowed the surprise to show on my face. "It's valuable enough to keep in a panic room."

"My father saw no point in paying exorbitant insurance fees for something no one could steal." The restlessness was back, and it seemed all Gray could do to keep his fingers from tapping.

"And yet it has been stolen."

Gray held my gaze with a calm steeliness his twitching fingers belied. "No police."

"Cipher Security will not be held responsible for any monetary damages without a legal judgment."

Gray's eyes narrowed. "I don't need a legal judgment to hold Cipher responsible. The features editor at the *Tribune* is an old friend of my father's, and he owes Dad a favor."

My tone went flinty. "I suggest you take your threats directly to Quinn Sullivan, as I will not be passing them along without considerably unflattering editorial commentary."

Gray met my gaze for a long moment. "I don't make the mistake of underestimating the consequence of my father's wrath if that painting isn't recovered."

Interesting. It sounded almost as though Sterling Gray was warning me rather than delivering an ultimatum. "I'll need a few hours to go through the footage. Where can I find you if I have any other questions?"

He nodded. "I'll be in my office." Gray glanced at the empty frame on the wall, scowled, and then left the room.

I took a moment to do a visual sweep of the room. There was nothing obvious out of place, and as I didn't have a fingerprint kit or the resources to match any fingerprints that might be recovered, I sat at the computer and opened the storage files for the previous night.

There'd been no camera set up in the panic room; the senior Mr.

Gray had been adamant that there be one place in the house that was completely private. I enlarged the image from the camera that was aimed at the bookshelf door, and scrolled backward through the footage, beginning with my own arrival.

Sterling Gray entered the room at 8:17a.m. and came back out less than thirty seconds later with an expression of panic on his face. Again, interesting. He did not appear to be a man who panicked easily. I looked down to see Gray's cat, the same striped one that had wound its way around Ms. Collins' feet at the party, stroll into the panic room. I reached down to pet it as it rubbed against my legs. The light dimmed onscreen as I scrubbed back through the footage, and movement caught my eye at 2:33a.m. It was the cat, strolling in reverse to the window at the end of the hall. A few moments later, the hall sconces lit and Gray returned from downstairs alone, and a few moments before that, he and a woman with long, wavy blonde hair walked down the hall. I stopped the footage. 2:27a.m.

I rewound the tape and watched her walk. She wore the same hot pink dress she'd worn at the party, and it floated around her with each graceful step. She laughed at something Gray said as they walked past, and though the cameras had no sound, it seemed pretty and delicate, just like she was. It was as if being with Gray had lit a fire and burned all the awkwardness out of her, leaving behind pure grace and femininity.

I continued scrolling backward through an hour's worth of nothing when suddenly the footage went completely white. I hit the stop button and stared at the computer monitor.

There was an edge to the whiteout, and I could just see a shadow of ... something ... in it. I scrolled past the whiteout, and less than ten minutes later, the white screen disappeared, and the near black-ness of the hallway once again became discernable.

I stood so suddenly that I startled the cat, and it darted out of the panic room. I followed it out to the hall to find it cleaning itself, as though utterly unconcerned, right in the middle of the floor. Near the cat, up against the wall, was a small disk that almost completely blended in with the dark wood of the floorboards.

I bent to pick it up, and the cat unfurled itself to bump my leg for more petting. The object in my hand appeared to be a tiny, remote control-operated light. When I found two more along the wall heading toward the back staircase, I suddenly understood why the monitor had whited out.

"Very clever," I murmured to myself as I gathered the other mini spotlights from the floor. The cat strolled ahead of me down the hall to the French doors at the end by the stairs, behind the bronze statue of a ballet dancer. I followed it to discover if there were more spotlights down the staircase, but I found no others. The cat emerged from behind the heavy drape on the left side of the French doors to wind around my legs again for more attention, which I squatted down to give him as I studied the hall leading to the panic room.

Three lights across from three cameras. They could have been placed there at any time during the party, but a simple search of camera footage would reveal someone bending down to set them. I sent one of the lights sliding down the side of the wooden floor like it was on a shuffleboard. The light came to rest a few feet away from the third camera. I slid the next one with more force and it stopped directly across from the second camera. I studied the French doors behind me. I knew they were wired to the alarm, as I'd supervised it myself, but if the alarm hadn't been armed …

I gave the cat a last scratch and returned to the panic room to scrub backward through more footage. At 1:04a.m. Gray and Ms. Collins walked backward down the hall and out of frame. The landing just inside the French doors was out of sight of any camera, and I switched views to catch them in the stairwell. Damn. The landing was blind, which represented a weakness in my security system.

If, in fact, someone came into the house through the French doors, Cipher Security could be held responsible for the failure to capture an image of the thief.

First, though, I had to rule out the possibility that Colette Collins was the thief.

# [ 7 ]
## ANNA

*"I'm like the funhouse mirror reflection of my sister."*

- ANNA COLLINS

I felt like a thief every time I entered Colette's apartment through her bedroom window. But it was hardly sporting to walk in the front door when she only lived on the second floor, and climbing up the fire escapes kept my ninja skills sharp.

She was still sleeping when I flopped on her bed the next morning, and I grinned at her shriek of surprise.

"One-zero, Anna," I said cheerfully.

"I was up until three a.m. giving you an alibi, so two-one, Colette," my sister said, peering at me through sleepy eyes.

"Except I got Mom's painting, so we're two-two at least."

Colette sat up and rubbed her eyes. "Show me," she said, instantly alert.

I pulled the harness off my shoulders and opened the telescope tube. As kids, my sister and I had always opened presents together, so I'd held off looking at the painting until I was with her.

The canvas was thick, and I realized as I unrolled it that the backing was stuck to it. Colette shifted over, and I spread the painting of Mom and Aunt Alexandra out flat on the bed. The half-inch of canvas that I'd cut away from the edges to get it out of the frame hadn't affected the integrity of the image, as the room the young women were standing in faded to black around them.

Colette gasped quietly and touched the faces of our mother and her older sister with a delicate fingertip. "They were so beautiful."

"Mom still is, and the photos I've found of Aunt Alex show that she aged well too," I said solemnly.

Colette sounded wistful. "I wish I looked more like Mom."

"You and Mom have the same eyes – she just always looks like she's about to burst into song and start dancing around the room with teapots and kitchen implements."

Colette snickered, and I added a mental point to my score. I loved to make my sister laugh.

"Meanwhile, Aunt Alex looks like she knows where all the bodies are buried," I continued.

"Are you kidding? She's probably the one who buried them. Mom said Aunt Alex always treated rules more like guidelines, and sometimes she just flat out ignored them."

"So, like me," I said, as I studied the two young women in the painting.

She smiled at the comparison but didn't confirm or deny as she stroked the cut edge of the canvas. "You couldn't take the frame?"

I shook my head. "Wired to the wall." I studied my sister's face. Her lips looked a little swollen, and her jaw was slightly red. "Was everything ... okay? I mean, for you, last night." I stumbled over the words because it felt so hard to say them out loud. "He didn't hurt you or anything?"

"What? No." Colette flushed. "No."

And that, oddly, was all she had to say about that.

"Is that a flush, like *I don't want to talk about it*, or a blush, like *I can't tell you?*"

"I'm not talking about this with you right now, Sister."

We'd called each other Sister since we were little, just to confuse whoever couldn't tell us apart. At this point, I couldn't see anything *but* our differences, but I'd learned that most people were not very observant and saw whatever they expected to see. I was counting on it, in fact.

"You're okay though? Truly?" I studied my sister's face, and she met my eyes with the tiniest of smiles.

"Yeah, I'm good."

"You're good."

The smile on her face bloomed into something pretty and real. "I'm good."

She got off the bed and stripped off her tiny little camisole nightgown as she walked to the bathroom. My sister was the least self-conscious person I knew, and it was probably with good reason. Objectively speaking, she had a great body. Perfectly tanned all over in the way that only Saint Tropez or tanning beds can do, and curvy in a totally feminine way. "I'm going to shower. Make us some coffee, will you?"

"My hearts always turn out like penises though."

She turned to stare at me for exactly one second before she finally rolled her eyes. "Don't draw in the coffee foam, Sis. Coffee dicks are off-putting."

I grinned. "Not to mention unsanitary."

She laughed all the way to the bathroom. I could still hear laughter when the water went on.

"Four-two, Anna," I murmured happily.

I studied my mother and her sister for a long moment. Alex had died just over a year ago, but Colette and I had never met her. My mother and her sister had had a huge falling out when they were in their early twenties, and Alex had left Boston right after their fight. She'd moved to Chicago, our mother had moved to Rockport, Massachusetts, and the twin girls born to Sophia a few years later had never known their mother's older sister.

Aunt Alexandra had never had children of her own, and after she died it was a giant shock to all of us to learn that Colette and I were the main beneficiaries of her will.

That will was why we were in Chicago.

Alexandra Kiriakis had left her apartment to her firstborn niece, and Colette immediately moved into the badass brownstone in a part of the city neither of us could ever afford on our own. Colette had wanted me to live with her – the apartment had three bedrooms and it was huge – but Aunt Alex had left her art studio to her second-born niece, which was me. As a twin it was hard enough to find privacy, so I happily moved into the funky little downtown studio. It was much better for Colette and me that we didn't live together, and having my own studio to go home to was one of the keys to our sisterly harmony.

About a month after I moved into the studio, I found the letter from Alex.

*Dear Anna*, it began. *If you're as much like me as I think you are, you'll have found this letter pretty quickly.* It had been taped behind a painting, and my only excuse was that I'd been so in awe of the painting that I hadn't immediately looked behind it. Because really, who does? *I need you to do me a favor if you can. If you can't – or won't – I understand, but I think you're probably up to the challenge.*

Challenge accepted. I'd never met a dare I didn't take, or a bet I didn't win, and somehow, my Aunt Alex had known that about me. Her letter went on to tell me about a painting that had been stolen from her, and how important it was that my mother get that painting back. It was a painting of Alex and Sophia that she called *The Sisters*. It was the last art piece they'd worked on together and it had been stolen years before. A man named Markham Gray had it and refused to return it, so the only thing Alex could think of was that it had to be stolen back from him.

*I've tried to get it back from Markham for thirty years, and it's just one more way that I've failed my sister. Please, if you can, take it from him and give it to Sophia. Perhaps then she'll understand why I did what I did.*

"I'm thinking about how to frame the sisters. How much canvas did you have to cut when you took it?" Colette asked as she walked out of the bathroom. She pulled the hair tie out of her hair and shook it down in a curtain of blonde curls around her shoulders.

"Not much. Probably half an inch all the way around."

"I'll have to make a custom frame before we give it to Mom," she said as she slipped a dress over matching pink lace bra and panties.

I shook my head at her lingerie finery. "I'm lucky if I can even *find* a bra, much less one that matches my underwear."

She shook her head at me with a sigh. "You're so weird. Do you think we should go with gilded wood or plain?"

"It was in a heavy gilt frame in Gray's panic room, and they looked like princesses locked in a tower. They should celebrate being let free with all the finery we can dress them in."

Colette nodded absently as she studied the painting. Then she looked me in the eyes. "You did good, Sister."

"Thanks. You too."

I watched her choose a nail polish color to match her bra, which matched her panties, which would only be visible without the dress. I couldn't imagine who would even notice that they matched. "I'm not good at being you, Sister. I kind of suck at it, actually," I said.

"Well, considering that I can't rock climb, ride a motorcycle, scuba dive, or jump out of planes, I figure we're pretty even," she said as she dropped the nail polish in the pocket of her dress, then tucked the heavy canvas of Alexandra and Sophia into a large portfolio and slipped it under her bed.

I thought of the boob-tastrophies in her pink dress and shuddered in horror. "Nah, you win. Ten-six, Colette."

# [ 8 ]
## DARIUS

*"When the winds of change blow, some people build walls, others build windmills."*

- CHINESE PROVERB

"Colette Collins is a twenty-six-year-old interior designer. How does she afford that address?" my colleague at Cipher Security, Shane, said through the sound system in my car.

"You should see it in person. People give left testicles and first-born children just to get on the waiting list for a place like this." I'd parked across the street from the graceful old brownstone and was sipping cold coffee as I debated my next move.

The computer keyboard clacked through the speaker. "The apartment is part of a family trust from the mother's side," she said.

"Those are the kind of trusts that usually require break-ins at attorney's offices to dig into." I winced at the prospect as I took another sip.

"She's not a suspect though, right?"

The irrefutable evidence of Colette Collins' innocence had been replaying in my mind since I saw the footage of her having sex with Sterling Gray.

Once I'd determined it was, in fact, Ms. Collins' perfect naked ass that Gray had in his hands, I'd shifted my gaze to the timecode and kept it there until they'd dressed and left the room. At no time did he leave her alone, nor did she even excuse herself to use the bathroom. In fact, there was never a time during Ms. Collins' visit to the mansion that she was out of sight of Gray or a camera. She came, she came, as it were, and then she went. Apparently in that order.

"She was with Gray the whole time she was in the house." Was it the coffee that was so bitter, or my suddenly foul mood?

"Well, if you need any B&E, I know a guy," Shane said. I could hear the grin in her voice, and then the sound of a kiss.

"Hey Gabriel," I said, because no one else would be kissing Shane.

"Masoud. Everything okay?"

"Stolen painting from a system I designed. Just trying to tie up some loose ends."

"Good luck," he said.

"Let us know if we can help," Shane added brightly.

I hung up, and "Bohemian Rhapsody" continued playing through the car speaker. My phone was playing all its music on random shuffle, and I just let it play. The only thing I couldn't abide was Christmas music at any time other than between Thanksgiving and New Year's Eve; otherwise, the randomness just felt like a soundtrack to my life.

If I was completely honest with myself, and I generally was, I had found the shimmery blonde intriguing – a strange and wonderful party bulb in a room of designer recessed lighting. She was lovely to look at, but so was every other blonde Gray had ever chosen. It was her utter disregard for convention – a recklessness in her conversation that I could imagine spilled over into her everyday life – which had captivated me.

I had thought her unconventional, but sleeping with Gray had been a conventional choice.

So I'd put the spark of interest I felt into a box and tucked it into a dark corner of the mental closet in which I compartmentalized my life. Except that when I saw her round the corner from the alley that connected to the back of her building, that box tipped over and her strange light came spilling out.

I was out of my car and across the street to intercept her before I'd made up my mind to move.

I dimly registered her outfit – a white T-shirt under a motorcycle jacket, jeans with a rip at one knee that looked like it was from wear, not fashion, and low engineer boots. On another woman it might have been fashionably rebellious, but these looked like her everyday clothes. This was who she really was.

"Colette?" I said as I neared her. She was lost in thought and didn't seem to hear me. "Miss Collins?" I tried again.

She looked up suddenly and stopped dead in her tracks. Her expression did something I've never seen a human face do – every emotion on the spectrum from fear to pleasure bloomed on her face at once, and the moment was somehow the longest single second I'd ever experienced.

"Hello," she said a little breathlessly.

"Hello." My answering smile was reflexive, and I could feel an odd giddiness bubble up at the delight on her face. But then her eyebrows wrinkled in a frown.

"Why are you here?"

"Why are you?" I said quickly.

"My—" She cocked her head sideways and studied me. "You're here for me."

"Why do you say that?" My parents were journalists, and our dinner table conversation had been an education in information gathering techniques.

"Because you know my last name, and you know this address." She started walking again, and I realized she was heading toward the L train.

"I have questions about last night," I said, as I fell into step beside her. "Can I give you a ride somewhere?"

She stopped and stared at me. "You have a horse?"

"What?" I stared back, a little incredulous. "No."

"You don't?" Her expression fell. "I love horses. Bicycles are harder with two people, and I don't think you meant for me to ride you like a cowgirl." She almost seemed to be talking to herself, and my sudden burst of shocked laughter seemed to snap her back to our conversation.

"My car is parked just there." I pointed at the Land Cruiser across the street.

"Then you should have said drive. You don't ride a car. You ride a horse, or a bicycle, or a bull. Well, I don't ride bulls, they're too big and mad, and rodeo clowns scare me almost as much as sewer clowns do."

I didn't even try to hide the grin on my face. My interrogation skills may have been excellent, but her answer-avoidance ones were off the charts. I surrendered. "Sewer clowns are definitely worse."

She nodded, as though this required agreement. "What kind of questions do you want to ask? I mean," she continued before I could answer, "are they specific questions that you've already thought of, or are they more general, like about the weather in Dawson City, or the price of gold, or what exactly are woodchucks? Are they marmots, or ground squirrels, or groundhogs? And why would they call a groundhog a groundhog when he's no relation at all to a pig?"

"Are you done?" I finally asked.

She narrowed her eyes at me. "Probably not. How much more distracting can I be?"

I pointedly avoided looking at her curves. "I won't be distracted," I lied, since I'd been nothing but distracted by her since I'd called her name.

She sighed, as though every conversational twist and turn had been a deliberate attempt to confuse me. "Of course not. Well, then, where are we going?" she asked, as though our meeting had a quality of unwelcome inevitability.

"I assume you're on your way to work?" I said, as we crossed the street toward my truck.

She opened her mouth, then closed it, then finally spoke. "No one's clamoring for me to find them today."

Most people had their designers on speed dial, or at least the people I knew who had designers. Though to look at Colette Collins in her jeans and boots, with a messenger bag slung over her chest and some sort of harness on her shoulders, she didn't appear to be about to visit design clients.

I opened the passenger door of my Land Cruiser, and she unslung her bag, and hauled herself in. "Nice truck," she said, with an impressed nod at the exterior.

I was not susceptible to women in the way they often wished I were. Perhaps it was because the women I encountered in Chicago were so aware of how I spoke and how I looked that it felt as though I'd been assessed for my non-existent fortune in Middle Eastern oil reserves before a proper conversation was ever had.

Some might say I read too much into others' reactions to me. Maybe. Maybe not. I had learned, however, to build three extra hours into every airplane travel day so the inevitable questions by TSA didn't cause me to miss my flight, and I carried my passport with me as my daily identification in the event either my direct manner of speaking, my 1990s truck or my brown skin warranted a closer look.

Somehow, the fact that this woman was even less inclined to pretension and social graces than I, was far stranger than anyone I'd ever met, and admired the Land Cruiser rather than sneered at its obvious age made my mouth open of its own accord, and then words fell out that had no business being said.

"Do you want to see my boat?"

# [ 9 ]
## ANNA

*"Owning a boat is basically standing in a cold shower, tearing up hundreds and watching them go down the drain."*

- MAX COLLINS

"You have a boat?" I might have squeaked. Yes, it was entirely possible that I had squeaked like an excited little mouse about to get batted around by a sadistic cat.

"I do." He looked pleased at my reaction, so I narrowed my eyes at him.

"Sail or power?"

He sighed. "I'm not significant enough to have a sailboat, sadly."

"Define significant," I snapped back to cover my giddiness at meeting a Disney prince with a boat.

He got in the driver's seat and turned to me before he started the classic body Land Cruiser, about which I had serious car envy. "Motor boats require no particular skill to operate," he said wryly.

"Owning any boat is like standing in a cold shower tearing up hundred-dollar bills, my dad always said. That's pretty significant."

He started the truck and pulled away from the curb to cover a smirk, but I still saw it. "So, you'll join me?" His phone took a second to sync up to a bluetooth speaker and then something that sounded like a soundtrack came on. It was haunting and lovely, and I just barely resisted changing topics completely.

"Can we take the boat out?" I seriously tried not to bounce in my seat like a five-year-old who had to pee, but I'm pretty sure I failed.

He chuckled. "Yes, we can take it out."

My self-preservation instinct had clearly taken a major backseat to the giant one I had for adventure. "Okay, good. Now first, what is this music, and second define significant."

He drove smoothly with one hand on the top of the steering wheel. "This is my favorite song from the soundtrack of *Aashiqui 2*." He stole a quick glance at me to see if I knew the movie, and I shook my head. "It's a Bollywood romance with more than a passing resemblance to *A Star is Born.*"

"*A Star is Born* isn't a romance," I said firmly. "It ends badly."

He nodded. "Fair enough. It's a romantic musical, then."

"Wait, you agree?" I stared at him.

He smiled slightly as he made the turn into the Diversey Harbor parking lot. "I generally find that picking fights about things for which I don't have strong opinions makes little sense. I tend to save my bullets for things that matter."

"Hmm. You've answered my first question, but added a third," *with the kind of grammar that makes your education sound expensive,* I thought. The music had shifted to a punky cover of "Sweet Dreams" *(Are Made of This),* and I held up my fingers. "So number two is still define significant, and number three is, what matters?"

"Those are fairly existential questions, aren't they?" Darius Masoud navigated his truck into a parking spot in the nearly empty lot and turned it off.

"Are Disney princes incapable of existential thought?" I was having way too much fun with this conversation to attempt to filter more than was absolutely necessary, preferring to save my own self-control bullets for things like not blowing my alibi.

He looked startled for exactly one second, then smirked. "I

suppose it depends on the Disney prince. I mean, Aladdin and Beast might have a slightly better shot at existential thought than Prince Charming, for example, considering that he's the man who thought finding a woman by her shoe size was a reasonable course of action."

I laughed as I grabbed my stuff before exiting the truck. "You do realize that being able to discuss Disney princes with any degree of fluency is grounds for man-card removal."

He shrugged. "An acceptable risk when my membership is already tenuous at best."

"Because you're not a man?" I asked with a grin.

"Define man," he said with an answering smirk, as he unlocked a gate and held it open for me to precede him down the dock.

My heart did a little happy dance in my chest. It was a rare person who could play Disney prince with good grammar with me and not run away screaming. "You first. What makes a person significant, and what matters?"

We had arrived at a slip where a gorgeous 1950s wooden yacht – probably about thirty-five feet long, with a gleaming deck that looked freshly varnished – was moored. "Never mind," I said as he hopped on the deck and held out his hand to help me onboard. "It may or may not matter, but I officially have significant boat envy."

He chuckled as I took his hand. I admit it was just for the excuse to touch him, and his fingers were crazy warm when they wrapped around mine. Sparks shot out from our palms like mini fireworks and tendrils of dragon's tongue wrapped around our wrists, binding us together.

Until he let go. I flexed my hand to dispel the leftover sparks, and I saw him wipe his palm on his jeans. I hoped it was residual sparks for him too, and not a hand-slime reaction. Hand-slime was a chemical reaction produced by contact between two people who had no business touching, usually because one of them was a disaster. Like me.

I prowled around the deck to cover my nerves, then dropped down into the cabin. Below deck was a comfortable space with a small galley kitchen, a built-in table with bench seats, and a forward hold with a tiny toilet room and a fairly large triangle-shaped bed. The bed was designed to fill every inch of the bow of the boat, with built-in shelves on either side that were overflowing with battered paperbacks.

I was aware he was watching me silently as I scanned the titles quickly – everything from non-fiction adventure stories to historical romance. I didn't see a lot of sci-fi or fantasy, which actually surprised me more than the historical romance did. "See anything you like?" He sounded amused, and I suddenly realized I'd plopped myself on the man's bed to look at his books.

I looked back to catch his eyes, and just barely stopped the words *now I do* before they tumbled out. "Have you read all of these?" I asked instead.

"These are my re-readers. Most of my library is on my phone," he said in a way that made all the breath leave my body. Or maybe it wasn't the saying of the words, it was the words themselves. A man who read actual books, and then read them again. It was almost as sexy as … well, nothing, because nothing was sexier than a man who read.

*Except a man who read naked. Out loud. With chocolate.*

"Come up," he said, "and let's take her out while the water's still calm."

I jumped up and almost cracked him on the chin in my hurry to escape the mental image that had begun to form. "Oooh, sorry. Can I cast off from the dock?"

He laughed and stepped back to let me out of his bedroom. "The mooring lines are all yours."

Colette and I had sailed a lot with our uncle in Boston when we were younger, and I was always in charge of untying the boat and casting the lines in to coil on the deck. I loved pushing it out of the slip and then timing my jump onto the deck for the last possible moment before it got too far from the dock.

Darius went to work pulling slip covers off the wheel and priming the engine, while I leapt onto the dock and began coiling lines to toss onboard. It really was a beautiful boat, and the name,

*Ashti*, was painted in Arabic-style calligraphy. The engine rumbled like a contented cat, and I walked the cruiser out of its slip and jumped aboard as if I'd always done it. Darius looked approving.

"You've handled boats before."

"One of my uncles had a sailboat, and I was always the first mate." I bit down on the second part of that sentence – *as opposed to my sister, who felt it was her duty to stand on the bowsprit like a beautiful masthead.*

"My parents got this boat when we moved here from Iran. I bought it from them a few years ago, and now I live on it." Darius stood like the captain of his world at the wheel, and I envied the wind as it ruffled his thick brown hair. Wait, what? I didn't have thoughts like that. Not when I had things to hide and people to hide them from. "So, what'd you want to talk about?" I asked, because I was determined to slip on the verbal diarrhea that was sure to come out of my mouth.

He navigated past the breakwater and out onto Lake Michigan. The day was sunny and bright, and the breeze on the lake was brisk. I finished coiling the last of the mooring lines and perched on the roof of the cabin to watch Darius while he steered the boat.

He sighed, which I took as a bad sign. "I have to ask you about Sterling Gray."

I twitched involuntarily, and I realized it might have looked like I wrinkled my nose. Maybe because I actually did. "What about him?" I tried for casual, but to my own ears I sounded too bright. Kind of pastel, actually. I hated pastels.

"A painting was stolen from his panic room last night, and I saw you discover the door." He sounded tired, like this wasn't a conversation he wanted to have. Good. Neither did I.

"Really?" I asked. Sometimes less was more.

"Was the painting really stolen, or did I really see you?" His sighing tone was gone.

I held his gaze and shrugged. It was a technique I used to great effect with the bounties who demanded to know what they'd done wrong. People who didn't like the spaces between questions and answers filled them with all kinds of incriminating words. I didn't mind the spaces, because I usually just filled them with corgi puppies and their butts.

One corner of his mouth quirked up, and I almost asked him if he saw a corgi butt too. But he didn't. "I work for Cipher Security, and the Gray mansion security system was my design."

"Bummer."

It probably sounded snarky, but it actually was a bummer. In the course of planning a crime, the thieves generally don't consider the consequences to the designer of the security system. I mean, it makes sense that the guy's professional reputation was on the line, so he was maybe going to look into what happened. I didn't like the thought that I'd caused Darius Masoud a professional discourtesy.

Next, his left eyebrow quirked up. "Indeed. I'm sure you didn't imagine that your discovery of the panic room behind the bookcase, or footage of your late night visit to the Gray mansion, would be observed."

*Actually, I counted on it*, my mind fairly yelled while I shaped my mouth into saying something less incriminating. "Hidden rooms behind bookcases are like catnip to me. I can never resist – especially when there's a clever book pull." My eyes narrowed. "The entry system was your design?"

He smirked. "Sterling didn't see the genius of using *Moby Dick*."

"He wouldn't," I said, trying very hard not to elaborate on my feelings about Sterling Gray.

Darius wore a proper smile. "Your re-arrangement was brilliant, by the way. I don't usually think of Octavia Butler as a feminist."

"*What we don't see, we assume can't be*," I quoted, and he quirked his head at me. "You're awfully quirky, aren't you?" I said, because he quirked like a champion quirker.

"I would say the same about you. Not many people of my acquaintance can quote dead science fiction authors," he said, with what I hoped was an admiring glance my way.

"*Beware; for I am fearless, and therefore powerful.*" I gave him my own half-quirk smile. I could do this all day.

He burst into laughter, and a butterfly broke away from the rest and began fluttering around in my chest. I tried to push it back down with my hand, but the little bastard ignored me.

"Everything okay?" the fricking Disney prince asked with a concerned look on his face.

"You laugh and the sweaty butterflies go crazy. Knock it off."

He pressed his lips together while his damn eyes kept shining, as though a torrent of laughter was going to stream out of him at any moment.

"Besides," I continued, "you don't have any sci-fi books on your shelves. How do you know enough to recognize quotes?"

"My sci-fi books sleep under the covers with me," he said without blinking.

"Really?" I definitely squeaked this time.

He laughed. "No. My little brother came through like a locust and stole them all."

"I would totally sleep with my favorite books, except I read on an iPad, and it keeps conking me in the head when I fall asleep holding it."

Darius didn't miss a beat at that, and we spent the next hour talking about books. All kinds of books. But as one does when talking about books, we weren't just talking about the words on the pages. Little bits of ourselves kept escaping into the conversation – like his obsession with historical novels and the real truths that inspired them, and mine with travel stories and the secret places no tourist would think to visit.

He told me he was born in Tehran, and spoke no English when his parents moved to the U.K. when he was seven, and then to the U.S. a year later. He had listened to the first four Harry Potter audiobooks back to back, so it was Jim Dale's fault that he occasionally still pronounced words with a British accent.

"*Harry-eeee,*" I said in a deep voice, trying to sound like the narrator's Hermione impression.

Darius rolled his eyes. "The one flaw in Dale's performance, and

I can't seem to access the Stephen Fry narration, even when I'm in England. I try every time I travel."

"You do?" The idea of this sophisticated, urbane man trying to track down a particular recording of Harry Potter made another butterfly lift off my sternum.

This led to a discussion about the merits of young adult literature, the Vampirism in Lit class he took in college, and the rules of time travel. The sweaty butterflies were taking flight with alarming regularity, until finally, when he took out his phone to make a list of my fantasy book recommendations, the last two launched themselves, and a flush of heat washed over me like a flashover fire. It was unbearable.

I hopped down off the roof of the cabin, dropped my jacket on the floor, then pulled my shirt off over my head.

"Ah, what are you … is everything okay?" Darius's expression was so odd that it took a second for me to evaluate what he was seeing. Me, standing in the cockpit of his boat, wearing jeans, boots, and a yoga bra, holding the T-shirt I'd just ripped off my body.

"Hmm. Probably requires more explanation than you're going to get," I said, as I kicked off my boots and unbuttoned my jeans.

His eyes were riveted, and if I hadn't been so suffused with the need to get out of my clothes, I might have paid a bit more attention to what was in his gaze.

I left my jeans behind on the deck of the boat and launched myself off it into the freezing cold lake.

# [ 10 ]
## DARIUS

*"Foreplay happens all day. The rest is just laughter and naked dancing."*

- FROM THE T-SHIRT COLLECTION OF ANNA COLLINS

"Sweaty Butterflies," she said, as she came up gasping for air.

It must have been catching, because the sight of this woman's glorious body right before she plunged into the frigid lake took my breath away in a way that had nothing to do with the chill in the air. I cut the engine and let the boat drift as I watched her swim with powerful strokes to catch up.

Who was this woman who spoke in non sequiturs like they were an intelligible language, and was somehow both oddly innocent and utterly brazen? She had just exposed an unbelievably erotic amount of herself to a virtual stranger, and yet it felt as though it was as natural to her as shrugging out of a jacket might be.

She reached the ladder at the back of the boat and hauled herself up without hesitation. The smile on her face was so joyful, I just managed to curb an instinct to hug her by grabbing a towel from beneath a bench cushion.

"That was perfect," she laughed through chattering teeth as she took the towel. "Totally shut them down."

I chuckled. "Sent mine right into flight."

She stopped drying herself to stare at me. "You have sweaty butterflies too?"

"Apparently they're contagious."

"Oh," she whispered, and the sound traveled straight to my chest and settled in my heart. She dropped the towel, and her eyes held mine for a long moment, far longer than was comfortable for a gaze between near strangers.

"Um, Darius?" She spoke so tentatively that it was almost painful.

"Yes." Whatever she was about to ask, the answer was yes.

"If you don't kiss me right now, I'm going back into the lake to drown the butterflies."

I pulled her to me and kissed her before I'd even finished saying the word *yes* in my mind. And then words fled, and my senses took over *everything*.

The surface of her skin was cold from the lake, but the spot where my hands held her arms was oddly searing. I slid my palms around to her bare back and pulled her closer. The wet fabric of her bra soaked the front of my shirt, and her pebbled nipples sent a bolt of electricity straight through me. I tasted honey on her lips, and I moaned against her mouth when her thigh slipped between my legs and I realized she was pressing herself against me. It didn't seem possible that I could get any harder, but feeling her use my body for her own pleasure was unendurably sexy.

I slid one hand down over her perfect ass, round and strong with muscle, and pulled her closer. With the other I tugged the strap of her bra off her shoulder and followed the wet fabric with my mouth as I exposed her breast. She arched into me, simultaneously pushing against my leg and leaning back to give me access to her nipple. I licked it gently, tasting salt and heat and something vaguely coconut, until she moaned.

"Harder," she gasped, so I drew her into my mouth and pulled hard. She ground herself against my thigh, and I suddenly needed to feel her weight on top of me.

But then she stepped back from me, and I saw uncertainty in her eyes. One breast was bared, and that nipple was a deep rose color from the force of my mouth. Her breath came fast, and her words sounded shaky.

"I'm not very good at not saying the things that run through my head, so if what I'm about to say is too much, I understand."

She pulled the bra off over her head, and the triangles of pale skin created by a bikini top automatically drew my gaze. Her small, high breasts were perfect, and I licked my lips, wishing I could taste her again.

"When I kiss you, blood rushes everywhere in my body and makes it all heavy and too hot, and all I can think about is that I don't know nearly as much as I want to about how you taste and feel," she looked pointedly at the erection pushing forward in my jeans, "and I do want to." She dragged her gaze up to meet mine, and my heart beat hard in my chest. "What do you think about that?"

"I don't seem to be capable of thought right now," I said. A slight frown creased her forehead until I added, "I just want you."

"Oh," she said brightly. "Good."

Then she hooked her fingers in her panties and slid them down curved hips until they dropped to the deck. She stepped out of them toward me and reached for the buttons on my shirt. "Now you."

I forced myself to hold still while she made quick work of the buttons. Then she smoothed her hands over my chest as she pushed the shirt off my shoulders, bringing back the searing heat I'd felt before when our skin touched. My eyes never left hers as hers flitted between my face, my chest, and my abdomen.

"Touch me please," I practically groaned.

She surprised me when she leaned in and smelled the skin on my neck, just under my jaw. "Mmm. You smell exactly right." Then she leaned up to my earlobe and took it gently between her teeth. A bolt of pure lust shot straight through me, and I gripped her hips to steady myself. Her skin was so soft I could have spent hours tracing every inch of her body, but my own body had a very different agenda, and when her hand cupped me over my jeans, I captured her mouth with my own, moved her hand, and made fast work of the zipper to get them off.

Though we were an hour up the coast from downtown Chicago, there was still enough occasional boating traffic to warrant discretion, so I took her by the hand and led her down into the cabin. I stopped at the bottom of the steps to let my eyes adjust to the dim light, and she smacked my ass and ran past me into my bedroom.

"First one to the bed gets to be on top."

I laughed and grabbed her just before she could leap – yes, she was planning to leap – onto my bed. She shrieked and wriggled to get away, but was giggling too hard to be very effective. Until she turned in my arms, kissed me full on the mouth, and then whispered in my ear, "Let me win."

And just like that, I let go, and she leapt.

## [ 11 ]
### ANNA

*"I licked it, so now it's mine."*

- ANNA COLLINS

Darius Masoud was a beautiful man. He looked like a bronze statue, sculpted with perfect proportions to include those v-lines that were the Pied Piper of male body parts. *Follow me this way*, they said, so when he crawled up my body from the foot of the bed, I hooked his leg and flipped him over onto his back so that I could follow them – straight down.

He looked shocked for exactly one second, and my brain froze. *Uh-oh, I did it again.* But then he grabbed my hand to get my attention, and the expression on his face shifted into something mischievous.

"Show me what you just did."

*Yes!*

So I did. And in case there was any question about the sexiness of naked wrestling, let the record show those moves are best done without a stitch on. We were laughing so hard by the time he mastered the leg-hook that I said out loud, "This is already the best sex I've ever had."

He seemed stunned as he looked up at me. His dark chocolate eyes studied my face, and then he reached up to trace the path his eyes traveled – across a cheekbone, down to my lips, then my chin, along my jaw, and down to my collarbones. A trail of fire burned wherever his gaze touched me, and his fingers were the wind that fanned the flames.

A whole new crop of butterflies had taken wing inside my chest, and as I bent to press it against him, I took full advantage of the access it gave me to his beautiful mouth. His hands trailed their fire lightly over my back and down my sides, while his lips danced a tango with mine, giving … taking … teasing … caressing, until I ceased to be a body unto myself and became only points of contact between us.

And suddenly the points of contact were too many, and I wanted – no, I needed them to be just one. I pulled my face back and looked into the pools of heat in his eyes.

"Now's a good time to find a condom," I said, trying for conversational. My voice sounded alarmingly sultry to my own ears, and I cleared my throat. "Just in case."

His mouth quirked up on one side again. "In case?"

"You know, in case we need some way to catch rainwater, or the boat springs a leak, or … something."

He tried not to laugh, and the urge to tickle him to distract him from the sheer nonsense coming out of my mouth was so strong I had to sit on my hands.

"Mmm, do that again," he said.

I realized I was still straddling him. "Find a condom."

"Inside one of the Bareknuckle Bastards books. *Brazen and the Beast*, I think," he said in total seriousness.

I knew the book. I'd read the book. And I laughed out loud as I reached for the one he meant. "Using it as a bookmark?"

He smirked at my expression when I opened the book to find a hollowed out middle with six foil packets inside. "Best way to keep my brother from stealing my supply. He doesn't read romance."

"But you cut up a Sarah MacLean book."

"I have it on my kindle," he said, as if that made up for the vandalism of a book I'd loved. It did though, kind of, especially since I was currently sitting on the man without a bit of clothing between us and he'd just admitted to buying Regency romance in ebook and paperback formats.

He plucked one foil-wrapped package from its hiding spot in the book, and then held it up. "Now what?" There was a mischievous grin lurking in his expression.

"I'm sure you'll think of something," I said as I casually leaned over him to put the book back on the shelf.

He thought of many somethings, the first of which involved his mouth capturing a nipple that flew too close to it. His tongue and the pressure of his suction sent electrical currents straight down my body, and I ground myself against him.

"Mmm, you'd better put that condom on in case you accidently slip inside me." Those words sounded far too confident to actually have come from my mouth, so I figured he read my mind when he opened the package without losing his place on my breast.

He was apparently not someone to go up against in a game of blind man's bluff, because he had no problem navigating the condom or himself with his eyes closed. He continued to savor my nipple as my hands moved his aside and guided him into me.

My brain ceased talking to me as my body adjusted to the fit of him, and then the music started. A song from the *Twilight* movie, "A Thousand Years," played on a loop in my mind as we moved together, and the lyrics said what I felt. I'd waited a thousand years to love like this, or maybe just a lifetime to actually make love. What had started as pure butterfly-induced lust was now consuming all the air in my lungs and turning the bright flames into blue fire that danced in my veins and that filled me with heat.

He watched me with his smoky-quartz eyes, and every one of my senses focused on the most intense point of contact between us. Our eyes. All the other senses – the deliciousness of building pressure, the scent of our bodies, and wood polish, and the lake, the sound of his breathing, growing deeper with every rock of our hips, the taste of his lips still on my tongue – they found focus in the gaze that was locked on mine. His eyes held a kind of wonder that I felt all the way down to the center of my being. I sensed a connection that went far beyond the place our bodies joined, and I could see the tendrils of soul that reached out through his skin toward mine. When I came with him, a gasp of surprise went through us both. My own bits of soul had found his and recognized them as *known*.

I collapsed down onto him, and the music stilled in my brain, and the words stayed silent while I felt our heartbeats calm through our skin. His hand traced lazy circles on my back, and the first and last thought I was conscious of having was that his skin smelled like the bark of a cinnamon tree.

# [ 12 ]
## DARIUS

*"Sometimes it's not your accomplishments that define you, it's your scars."*

— REZA MASOUD

I couldn't stop staring.

I crouched at the top of the stairs and looked below deck to where she still lay, utterly asleep and perfectly bare-assed on my bed.

She was a stomach sleeper; one leg was bent to the side in a pose that made her look like a sprinter about to take off. She hadn't moved when I'd slid out of bed and started up the engine, and didn't even twitch when I'd docked the boat in its slip and tied off. We'd been gone from the city for three hours, and somehow everything had changed. Who was this woman, and how had she gotten past the guards at the door?

I had been operating on pure instinct where she was concerned since the moment I laid eyes on her, and that disconcerted me. Instinct was fallible, dangerous, and untrustworthy in my experience, and yet it had led me to this remarkable woman. I couldn't have planned for her even if I'd been able to conceive of her existence.

She was the complete opposite of me in every way, and somehow she fit as though every one of her odd angles and strange curves connected perfectly to my straight lines and sharp edges.

I let my gaze wander one last time up her athletic legs, over her perfect ass with its tan lines that spoke of skin no one else got to see, to the small of her back and up her spine to the tightly-muscled shoulders of a woman with strength. She was so utterly mysterious to me, and yet she seemed to say exactly what she thought without care for the consequence. I was fascinated by her, and just three hours earlier I'd had no interest or time to be fascinated by anyone.

Impulsively, I took out my phone and shot a picture, just to preserve the beauty of the moment, then promptly felt like a creep. I didn't erase the photo, but I did move it to the 'hidden' file on my phone where no one else could stumble upon it by accident.

And then I thought about hidden images ... and hidden cameras. This incredible woman who had derailed my day so completely had been the co-star in surveillance camera footage during the commission of a crime. Never mind that the footage exonerated her *of* the crime – the fact that she had, just twelve hours before, been in Sterling Gray's bed was ... troublesome, and not something I particularly wanted to examine at the moment. To be perfectly fair though, it wasn't the fact of her having had sex with someone else twelve hours before that unsettled me. She could have climbed out of someone else's bed directly into mine and I wouldn't have been less mesmerized by our encounter. But there had been a crime committed, and she was indirectly involved in the circumstances around it, and I would have to do my job despite whatever this was that I was feeling.

I wasn't quiet when I dug out paper and a pen and left a note on the table, but when she didn't stir, I let her sleep. There were things we still needed to discuss, but they weren't appropriate topics to bring up to the naked woman in one's bed. My email had suddenly populated on our return to cell coverage indicating I had to make an appearance in the office, but I hoped she would accept my invitation to dinner.

I left the marina humming the tune to an old Abba song covered by Blancmange in the 80s, because "The Day Before You Came" suddenly felt like the soundtrack to my life – a life that had become very strange indeed.

When I got into my truck I thought I caught a hint of her wild-flower scent, and the image of her eyes, lit by something primitive and alive when she came, drove from my head the unsettling thoughts of this case and what she meant to it ... and to me. Fortunately, traffic was light through downtown, and I made it to the Cipher building without difficulty. Stan was behind the desk in the lobby, and he held up three slips of paper.

"Sterling Gray was pretty insistent that you get his messages, and he knows enough to call the lobby desk instead of just relying on email."

"It's quite efficient of him to pack so much arrogance, entitle-ment, and privilege into one person," I said with a frown as I took the slips from my colleague. "I'm sorry you had to be the recipient of his ire." I liked Stan. He had a ready grin and an easy way about him that big men confident in their power often had. "Is Dan or Quinn in?" I asked, ready to adjust my plan of action according to which owner of Cipher Security I spoke to.

"Quinn went home early," he said, and at my raised eyebrow, added, "Janie called to ask him where his electrical wiring toolkit and volt-meter were."

I laughed as I pictured the flare of panic in the eyes of a man whose cool was legendary about everything that wasn't his wife.

"Dan's upstairs?"

"Check the boardroom on the third floor. He's been working with Shane and Gabriel to tie up the last of the ADDATA case fallout, and they like the Nespresso machine in there."

"You want me to bring you one?" I asked as I headed for the elevators.

"Nah. I have more than a cup a day and I get the jitters," Stan said.

I turned and stared at the security agent who topped me by more than five inches. "I could hook up to a caffeine IV and have nary a tremor, and you can't take more than one cup?"

Stan shrugged. "Can't drink either. My mom always says the ones who shouldn't can't, and we ignore it at our peril."

"Your mother sounds like a wise woman," I said, delighted beyond words at the idea that Stan quoted his mother.

I rode the elevator up to the third floor and contemplated my approach to the Sterling Gray situation with Dan O'Malley. Dan was a field operative who had partnered with Quinn Sullivan, the big banking corporate man, to start the private security firm. Cipher was moving away from close protection except for special clients, and I'd been brought on specifically for those hand-picked personal clients. The home security systems I designed were part of the layers of protection Cipher offered them, and the fact that one of my systems had been breached did not sit well with me.

I knocked once for courtesy before opening the glass door to the conference room. Shane had been working with us for less than a year, but she already felt like an integral part of the team. She and Gabriel lived together and usually worked from their apartment, so it was a pleasant surprise to see them both in the office.

"Hey Darius, how's the boat?" Shane asked, with a welcoming smile. She was a striking woman; tall, athletic, and graceful in the way long-distance runners can be. I couldn't help comparing her to the woman currently fast asleep on the boat in question. One was tall, the other, average height. One a brunette with long straight hair, the other a blonde with a wild, curly mane. One was lean and lithe, the other had the kind of curvy, fit build that suggested capability, strength, and endurance. Yet despite every difference, they had the same eyes. Not the color or shape, but the life in them. They fairly crackled with energy and intelligence, and it was their most striking feature.

"Still floating," I said with a smile that I hoped didn't reveal the thought I had about the naked woman on it.

Shane grinned, "Better than the alternative." But Gabriel studied me with a raised eyebrow for a moment, and I had the disconcerting impression that he could see the secret behind my smile.

So I met his eyes with a brief nod, then looked at Dan. "Do you have a minute to talk about Sterling Gray?"

My boss looked up from the file he'd been studying and met my gaze. Dan O'Malley had the appearance most people would identify as 'street.' The top of a tattoo was visible above his collar, and I assumed there were several more underneath the well-tailored suit. He was the type of man who made women feel either attraction or fear at first glance, and his Boston accent gave him an added edge. I'd met his wife though, and she was the most feminine, buttoned-up beautiful waif I'd ever seen. I could almost imagine that she fastened every button not because she was necessarily so modest, but rather to masque something slightly wild and magical.

I suddenly had the thought that if Colette were here, she might have said something about fairies or woodland sprites, and I barely resisted the accompanying rueful smile.

"You look like you know something you're not saying, or you're planning to beat the bishop in the closet after this. What's up, man?" Dan gave me a nod that would have seemed curt except for the smirk that went with it.

"Beat the—" Shane started, but then she scoffed. "Really, Dan? That's all you've got? How about jackin' the beanstalk, or yanking the doodle dandy."

All three of us gawked at her like boys encountering naked breasts for the first time.

"Is it wrong that I want to learn what else you know such vivid slang for?" Gabriel asked in an awed voice.

"What do you call it when a woman…" Dan waved his hand at her to fill in the blank, and Shane smirked at him for not saying it out loud.

"Executes a manual override?" she finished.

"Come on! From *Cryptonomicon*? You must be joking!" Gabriel laughed. He was talking about a sci-fi book I'd never read, and it added another point to my respect for him.

"About *menage à moi*, I don't joke," she said, as if that ended it. And it did.

Dan laughed and shook his head. "You win this round, Shane P.I. Well done."

Shane had the grace not to look smug as she settled back in her seat and took a sip of her coffee. Dan returned his attention to me.

"So, the rich bastard spending Daddy's fortune for him. How'd the party go last night?" His tone was back to all business.

"The party was fine – unremarkable in its pretension. The problem is that a painting was stolen from the panic room sometime last night."

As I expected, the mood in the room shifted, and all three sets of eyes turned to me.

"A system failure?" Gabriel asked.

I shook my head. "A very clever work-around. The thief used mini spotlights to blind the cameras, and then became virtually invisible in the shadows. Access to the panic room was the same used by the homeowner, and the painting was cut from the frame, rendering the alarm moot. So technically, there was no failure on our part, considering we gave the client exactly what he asked for, but he's threatening to turn the press against us unless we can recover the painting."

Dan's expression went from thoughtful to severe. "What do the cops say?"

"He won't bring them in," I said. "I told him he couldn't file a claim without a police report, and he said the painting isn't insured."

"Bag of dicks," Dan snarled, and I wondered if it was a curse or a title. "Means it's already dirty, so he'll be a mud-slinging pig in shit. I assume you've already been there?"

"This morning. There's video of a party guest discovering the panic room door."

"Bring him in," Dan said with a scowl.

"It's a her, and I'm seeing her tonight," I said, hoping for several reasons that it was true.

"I can change my plans if you want to take a woman with you," Shane said.

"I'll call you if I need back-up, but I should be good. I actually talked to her at the party last night." *And had amazing sex with her on the lake today*, I didn't say.

"Right, well, we should run the video from last night past the kid. Maybe he can spot something the low res system missed. You got it on you?" Dan asked, gesturing to me to follow him out of the conference room.

"Don't keep Jorge late," Shane called before the door closed. "He's taking Oscar for a run when he gets home." Oscar was her giant dog, and the 'kid' was her neighbor, Jorge Gonzales, an eighteen-year-old MIT student who had interned in our tech department over the summer and ended up creating a whole new video surveillance system for us. Dan and Quinn hired him every time he was home on break.

"Yeah, I have a copy. Gray has already called three times in his unsubtle attempt to light a fire," I said as Dan opened the door to the stairs.

The basement of the building was noticeably cooler and housed the bank of computers that operated as Cipher Security's nerve center. I didn't have the details on our cybersecurity, but I knew it was better than the Pentagon's.

Jorge was sitting at a table that held three monitors, all of which appeared to show one contiguous image. Next to him was a glass wall that glowed with a faint green light, and the room beyond appeared to hold the Cipher mainframe. The kid was of the tall, skinny, loping variety, but I didn't doubt that the lope could turn into a prowl as the situation warranted. He wore glasses, which were new since the last time I saw him, and "Schrödinger's Cat was a Quantum Cheshire" spelled out the grin without a cat on the front of his T-shirt.

He looked up with a smile and stood to shake our hands. "Hey guys. Welcome to Swordfish."

I winced. "You did not name this computer after the movie."

He grinned. "Yep. So technologically implausible you had no choice but to sit back and enjoy the ride. And Halle Berry."

I shook my head with a laugh. "You're too young to have dug that thing out of the discount bins."

Jorge's expression turned serious, as if I was missing a very significant point. "Halle. Berry." His gaze bored into mine until I held up a hand in surrender.

Jorge's grin burst out of him like a smile emoji. "What can I do for you guys?"

I handed him the thumb drives from my pocket. "A painting was stolen last night from a system I designed. I've scrubbed through the footage on the original system, but I'm hoping you can pick up any details I might have missed. This one is from the time of the actual theft," I said, pointing to one of the drives.

He popped it into his machine and ran through a couple of screens until he'd loaded the file. "Do you have a timecode?"

"Start at one a.m." Dan and I flanked Jorge to watch his monitor, which was a much higher resolution screen than the one I'd worked on that morning. "Focus on the second floor hallway first."

Jorge pulled up the multi-cam screen to monitor nine views at once, six of which were on the second floor hall. We watched as Sterling and Colette walked through, and I was unpleasantly aware that my fists tightened at the laughter in her expression when she looked at him. Less than two minutes after they'd passed, the first screen went white.

Dan flinched. "What was that?"

Jorge leaned in to study the next screen right before it, too, went white. "There," he pointed to the third hall camera, "watch the floor near the wall." We could just make out a bit of movement as a mini spotlight slid into place right before the third screen went white. "Clever."

"You need heat sensors," Dan said, turning to me.

"My original proposal was for thermal. The client said no."

"You got that in writing?" Dan's accent was pure Boston street.

"Emails. They're archived."

He grunted something that sounded like approval, while Jorge ignored us and concentrated on the multi-view panel. "What was stolen?" he asked.

"A painting. From the panic room." Nothing moved on any of the six remaining screens.

"No camera?" Dan asked.

"Client wanted one eyeball-free zone in his house," I said with disapproval.

"Not the master bedroom?" Jorge sounded incredulous.

"Flip to camera twenty-four," I said, the disgust in my tone evident even to me.

He hit a couple of keys, and the screen changed to a single, full-screen view of the master bedroom where Sterling Gray and Colette Collins were in the process of stripping off each other's clothes.

"Well okay then, guess it wasn't the girl who threw the spotlights," Dan said as he peered closer. "This who you're going to talk to tonight?"

"She's the one." I looked away from the screen. The image of Gray kissing her made me want to punch him.

"Nice ass," Dan said thoughtfully, as though describing a garden statue.

I looked reflexively and was indeed faced with the very nice rear view of a very naked Colette. She was the aggressor in this particular part of their dance as she walked Gray backwards to the bed and pushed him onto it. Her back was to the camera, and she was all blonde curls and one long, uninterrupted expanse of tanned skin.

Wait … no. It was wrong.

"Freeze that frame," I said, my heart suddenly racing.

Jorge did and Dan smirked. "Never figured you for a voyeur, Masoud."

I stared hard at the screen. "Can you magnify the image?"

"Sure," Jorge said. "What do you want me to focus on?"

"He's clearly an ass man," laughed Dan.

"Really?" Jorge hit some more keys, and the image of a beautiful, heart-shaped ass filled the screen. "Halle Berry. I'm just sayin'."

"Kid, breast men are just less-evolved ass men. You've got time," Dan assured him.

I interrupted their banter. "Are there tan lines on her skin?"

Dan leaned in and studied the skin I already knew was perfectly even-toned. "Nope. Your girl does a tanning bed. You can see the marks here," he pointed to slightly red patches on her shoulder blades, "and here," he said pointing to her hips.

"So there's no way that this skin is going to develop tan lines overnight," I said with an instant sense of relief, and a growing feeling of dread.

Dan studied me. "What are you saying, man?"

"Screenshot that and send it to me?" I asked Jorge.

The kid was still smirking. "Sure."

I turned to Dan and met his gaze squarely. "I need to check something out, but I'm on this."

Dan hesitated only a fraction of a second before nodding. "Do you want a partner?"

I shook my head. "I may need some research support from the office."

"I'm down," said Jorge.

"I appreciate it," I said. I looked over at his computer screen to see the frozen image of Colette's perfectly tanned backside, and I suddenly needed to get out of the building. I needed to walk, to breathe, possibly throw something, and definitely, inevitably, have a serious talk with one bare-bootied, bikini-lined blonde girl about the fact that at one point the night before, *she'd had no tan lines.*

# [ 13 ]
## ANNA

*"Never, under any circumstances, take a sleeping pill and a laxative at the same time."*

– ANNA COLLINS

I jolted awake with a deeply pressing need to use a toilet and absolutely no idea where I was. Pure instinct dragged me off the bed and into the room … closet … cubby that held a toilet. It wasn't until I was seated and in the process of emptying my bowels that I blinked properly and realized I was on a boat.

I was on Darius's boat.

And I was naked.

And pooping.

On Darius's boat.

"Ahhhh!" I gasp-screamed out loud, then slapped both hands over my mouth in case he heard me and wondered why I was in his bathroom screaming. I also, ridiculously, attempted to stop pooping, only to learn that it can't be done.

*No, no, no, no, no!*

So, instead of pointless self-recrimination about pooping in a boat toilet that had to be pumped out to be emptied, I considered my situation. Clearly, I'd been exhausted from a night of painting-theft, because I was not, by nature, a napper. Whether it was a lack of sleep or an excess of orgasm that did it, I'd effectively gone down for the count.

I shushed my brain so I could listen to the sounds of the boat. I could hear water sloshing as though against a dock, and the distant sounds of traffic, which meant I was probably back in the marina. Harder listening resulted in no further information – like whether Darius was still on board. I hoped he wasn't. Bad enough that I'd fallen asleep stark naked on his bed, but to be found in his toilet was far too much information for a guy I hadn't even had a first date with.

Which made what we'd done earlier a what? A dalliance?

Clearly I'd been reading too many historical romance novels.

I was gratified to find water in the tap for hand-washing, and then I resigned myself to flushing the toilet, which I did. And that was how I discovered there was *no water pressure.*

No water pressure in the toilet. No way to flush the poop down.

Crap.

Literally.

"Crap!"

The way I saw it, I had three choices. Either fill a bucket with water and pour it into the toilet bowl in an attempt to force it down, but risk creating a poop floater for Darius to find, or leave it in the toilet as it was, which was essentially the same thing minus the float. Or, I mentally sighed because I knew what the right answer was, I could take it with me.

First, I needed my clothes, and the last place I'd seen them was on the deck, which, if the boat was parked in the marina, meant illegal naked activity. I poked my head out of the head, and smirked at my own feeble joke. The cabin was empty of human life forms, for which I was profoundly grateful. I felt like a cartoon burglar, creeping toward the cockpit of the boat, wondering if I could actually slither on my stomach up the steps to retrieve my clothes without any human eyeballs spotting my shiny white butt.

And then I saw the note, placed on top of my neatly folded clothes, sitting on the table. Bless the man for his forethought and consideration. I quickly got dressed as I read the note, which was an invitation to join him for dinner that night. I might have accidentally kissed the note for delivering such a lovely invitation before I set about rummaging through the man's galley for something with which to transport my unpleasant cargo.

It was too much to hope for that he had a dog poop bag onboard somewhere, so I settled on a Ziploc baggie and then grabbed a pair of wooden chopsticks. Tongs would have been nice, but I wasn't sure I was up to the task of disinfecting them afterward.

Getting the poop into the bag was not easily done, and wasn't even the most horrible thing I'd ever done, which was a story for another time. I was quick and efficient with the chopsticks, as one was when one traveled as much as I did, and then dropped them into the Ziploc with the poop and sealed the whole thing up with a nod of appreciation for the engineering of a well-made plastic product.

Three minutes later I was sauntering down the dock like I wasn't carrying a bag of poop, mentally planning what I was going to wear to meet Darius for dinner.

# [ 14 ]
## ANNA

It hit me in the shower.

Actually, it ran me over like a delivery truck full of stolen TVs. I'd had sex with a man who— my brain screeched to a halt. I had made love. Full stop. I'd had sex, a fair amount of sex given my age and lack of relationship of any real duration. When I went diving, or mountain climbing, or bungee jumping, it was fairly normal to run into a group of guys who were doing the same thing, then find one of them cute enough to hook up with during the after-math adrenaline rush that inevitably hit when one survived doing a thing that sometimes killed people.

But those were hook-ups – the kind of swipe-right sex people find through dating apps that is only slightly more or less satisfying than a good vibrator, depending on things like his hygiene and how much I'd been talking (i.e., how glazed his eyes were). But this hadn't been swipe-right sex. Darius and I had connected *because* we'd been talking. Somehow, I hadn't sent him running for the hills the first time my brain had disconnected from my mouth, or even the next, or the time after that.

And now I had a problem, because I was the thief who had broken through Darius's security system. And I sucked at lying. Actually, I SUCKED at lying.

I knew his scent – there was no way I'd be able to keep lying to him. One doesn't lie to people one can identify by scent. And his skin smelled so good. It was softer than any other man's skin I'd ever known, and smelled like a combination of nutmeg, musk, and vanilla. I was getting all warm again just thinking about it. Yeah, lying was pretty much out of the question.

Which meant I had two choices: I could either tell him the truth, or I could stop seeing him.

I sat down on the floor of my shower and curled up under the spray. The water was hot, and tattooed my skin with dark, tribal patterns that felt heavy and significant, when what I really wanted was dancing butterflies with tiny wings to trip daintily all over me. I indulged my self-pity until I couldn't stand to be in my own skin another minute.

Then I stood up, cranked off the hot water, and let the icy spray wash away the tattoos that had been beaten into my skin with ink and thorns. I was almost surprised to look in the mirror and discover that my only actual tattoo was the small fish hook I wore on the edge of my left hand below my thumb. Colette had a matching one on her right hand, and when we twined our fingers together, they made the shape of a heart. One heart for two people. Colette had always joked that I should wear it for both of us. I probably wouldn't break it, she said, because of my tendency to bounce.

I wasn't feeling very Tigger-like at the moment, and I stared at myself in the mirror for a long time. I was wrapped in the blue Turkish towel that I used instead of anything fluffy because it packed down to nothing and could double as a scarf in cold climates. My hair had already begun forming the springy curls that were its default, and would be a tangled mess if I didn't run my fingers through it before it dried. I liked the squinting-in-the-sun lines at the corners of my eyes that I hoped would grow into proper laugh lines when I got older, but I didn't like the look of uncertainty that I saw reflected back at me.

Our mother was a beautiful woman who laughed easily, could talk to anyone about anything, and seemed to attract women and men to her like bees to honey. When she'd turned fifty, she told us that she loved to flirt – it made her feel alive to pay a compliment or drop a teasing line and watch another person's eyes light up with interest. And she'd loved to be flirted with – to feel attractive and interesting and desirable, whether or not she had any intention to act on the attraction.

She was also fifty when she learned the sister she hadn't spoken to in nearly thirty years had died of a brain aneurysm. I was there when Aunt Alex's trust attorneys had given our mother the letter that made her finally break down in tears. I didn't read Alex's words to her sister, but the lawyer had a letter for me and Colette too.

Alexandra told us how sorry she was that she had never met us, and that she hoped we were better sisters to each other than she had been to our mother. *No one else will ever know how it was to grow up in your family, only your sister will,* she'd written to us. *Losing Sophia was the worst thing that ever happened to me, and there isn't a day that goes by that I don't wish I'd made different choices. Colette, you are the firstborn like me, so I give you my home. I've treasured the independence it has given me, and I have made a haven inside its walls. I hope you might one day feel the same sense of completeness and safety there too. And Anna, what little I know of your travels and of the adventures you've had leads me to believe we might be more alike than not. I'm leaving you my art studio to work in or live in as you see fit. It's a strange and wonderful place, and I love its unusual angles and colorful surprises. I hope that you, too, delight in its oddities, find adventure in its secrets, and I wish you the peace of acceptance there.*

That was six months ago. We were twenty-seven years old, holding the keys to an apartment and an art studio in a city neither of us had ever before visited, and that same day we'd gone out to get the fish hooks tattooed on our wrists.

I needed to talk to Colette.

I threw on jeans and a T-shirt that declared in black-on-black writing, "Feminist as f**k," pulled a hooded sweater over my head, stuck my wallet and my phone in my back pockets, lip balm went in my front pocket, and then at the last minute, I dabbed a little bit of amber oil on my wrists on the non-existent chance I ran into Darius again. I knew that whatever this randomness was between us would end, but I could admit that I wanted him to be sorry about it, because I would be.

I paused by the fireplace, as I always did, to admire the tile with the heart carved in it. Colette and I had toured the studio right after I'd gotten the keys - and it was the one tile that we'd both remarked on. The shape of the heart was what had inspired the fish hooks, and since I'd moved into the building, I'd found several other tiles scattered throughout with the same design.

My unit was part of an arts complex called the Carl Street Studios built by Edgar Miller and Sol Kogen. It was one of thirteen condos converted from a Victorian home and coach house in 1927. The various artists who'd lived and worked there had embellished the building with mosaic and stained glass windows, Art Deco tiles, carved doors, frescoes, and carved and painted ceilings. My aunt had used the space as an art studio, but over the twenty-plus years she'd owned it, she had gradually turned it into a second home. She had modernized it without changing it, and if I hadn't known there were no such things as grounded electricity and instant hot water heaters in the 1920s, I would never have been able to tell it had been altered at all.

I dialed Colette's number on my way out of the building. She picked up on the first ring.

"Hey, do you have a minute?" I asked.

"Yeah, I was just going to call you. Come over."

"I'll be there in ten," I said, then I clicked off my cell and slid it back into my pocket. It was actually an eight-minute walk between our places, but I kept two in reserve for climbing up the fire escape to her bedroom window.

I scanned the street for Darius's Land Cruiser, half hopeful, half dreading the sight of it. I pulled my hood up and slouched into a guy's walk, which was a trick I regularly used to blend into the shadows, even though the cars on the street were all the usual BMWs and Audis. The West Burton Place district was one of the first arts districts in Chicago, and had evolved into a vibrant gay scene, which very often came with double income, no kids. Colette's neighborhood was close enough to mine to walk to, but swanky and leafy, while mine was the kind of place where shadows had dance parties on the walls to the snippets of piano tunes wafting from open windows, while cats serenaded the stars with glittering voices.

I turned down the alley. "Hey, Harry," I said to my favorite orange-striped tomcat. He looked up from his tongue bath with a silent "hey" as I hopped up on the dumpster and jumped for the lowest rung of the fire escape ladder, which was rusted stuck at three-quarter extension. Honor, my D&D rogue, would have flipped up, hooked her legs on the bottom rung, then swung up to grab the higher rungs in a move worthy of a circus acrobat. I satisfied myself with a simple hand-over-hand haul until I was high enough to use my legs. Even if Colette hadn't left the window unlatched, I had a way in. But she was expecting me, so the window was wide open.

"Hey, Sister," I said as I dropped into her bedroom. She was sitting on her bed surrounded by fabric swatches trying different pairings in the evening light.

"What does this make you think of?" she asked, holding up a gold-colored swatch of velvet next to something mossy green.

"An Irish moss giant. If they nap long enough in the sun, they start to grow daffodils," I answered.

"Of course they do," she sighed.

I shrugged. "You asked."

"Where were you today? You're all pink-cheeked." She studied my face.

"On the lake. I went boating."

She raised an eyebrow. "With who?"

"A guy I met." I'd gone there to talk about Darius, so I wasn't sure why I was being cagey.

Her lips quirked up. "He's what, a commercial diver, or maybe crew on a racing boat?"

I shook my head. "He designed the security system at Gray's mansion."

The smile that had been forming on her mouth disappeared. "Cipher Security did Gray's system," she said sharply.

"Yeah, well, I guess he works for Cipher." I studied the fabric swatches on her bed, then started rearranging them so I didn't have to meet her eyes.

"The job is done, Anna. Why were you on a boat with the Cipher guy?"

I paired a rich wine silk with a green the color of stuffed grape leaves, then added the deep silver brown of gnarled vines. "He asked me to."

"And what else did he ask you?" Colette's voice held the barely contained impatience she sometimes had when I went down rabbit holes of imagination.

"He asked me about Sterling."

She exhaled. "So he saw the footage."

I winced. I'd seen the footage too, and the idea of Darius Masoud thinking that I'd been with Sterling Gray made me crampy.

"It's what we expected." Colette sounded cautiously optimistic.

"It's not what I expected," I said dismally.

"Why not?"

"I didn't expect to have sex with the security guy." The words fell out of my mouth like toads, slippery and loud. They tasted sour because I didn't want them to be toads. The words should have been cinnamon-flavored, like Mexican chocolate, but I didn't get to savor them like they deserved to be – like I wanted to. So, toads.

Colette stared at me. "You had—"

"Yes!" I cut her off because the toads were making me nauseous. "I know it was a bad idea, okay, but, well, it also wasn't."

"A bad idea?" she asked tentatively.

"A bad anything," I sighed.

"Oh."

I looked up from the swatch vineyard I'd arranged on the bed to see my sister studying me.

"I'm sorry," she said finally.

I nodded, dejected. "Yeah."

"What are you going to do? That's pretty by the way. It reminds me of Italy or France." Colette indicated my grapevines.

"This would be Italy." I added a burnt orange swatch. "And this makes it France." A pale blue went onto the pile. She studied it thoughtfully.

"Maybe you got Mom and Alexandra's artistic genes," she said with an edge of something in her voice. I didn't dig into it because I didn't have the tolerance for much more pain at the moment, and things with edges were usually sharp. I just shrugged.

"Speaking of Mom and Alex, I have something to show you." Colette hopped off the bed and pulled the portfolio out from under it. "While I was sizing The Sisters for their frame, the backing separated from behind the canvas. Except it wasn't backing." She pulled a painting out of the portfolio. "It was this."

I stared at the older woman in a black satin dress, seated against a black background, looking back at me. Her expression was pinched and unhappy, as though she blamed me for uncovering her secrets, and I felt judged by her for it. She also looked familiar.

"Who is she?" I asked, looking away from the judgy gaze and back to Colette.

"Madame Auguste Manet," she said flatly.

"Manet, as in Manet the French Impressionist?"

Colette nodded unhappily. "His mother."

"What was she doing hiding behind The Sisters? Shouldn't she be in a museum somewhere?" I couldn't help looking back at Madame Auguste. I could just picture her creeping across the wall and slithering behind young Alex and Sophia, hoping they wouldn't notice the shadow she cast.

"Apparently, the original is in Boston at the Isabella Stewart Gardner museum." Colette's voice was weirdly flat.

"Didn't Mom and Aunt Alex intern there when they were in art school?"

"Yes." The word came out choked.

"Why do you sound so strange?"

Colette met my eyes. Hers looked slightly panicked. "Because I'm not sure this is a copy."

I stared at her as the nauseating little toads in my stomach grew to the size of Komodo dragons. "Why would you say that?"

"In design school they teach you to spot the fakes. This isn't obviously fake." She sounded supremely unhappy.

"But it was behind our mom's painting," I said, already cringing because I knew what came next.

"Wired with an alarm to the panic room wall in a multi-million-dollar mansion."

Shit. "Did Alex know it was there, or did Gray just use our family's painting to hide this one?" I asked, as the Komodo dragon started swinging its tale and knocking dread into my lungs

"That's the ten-million-dollar question, isn't it?" she said.

I exhaled sharply, my mind spinning with the attempt to see this from every angle. The obvious first step was that Colette's twin had to disappear for a while, so there could be no connection between my sister and the missing painting. "I have a contract in Boston that I've been putting off. I'll go see what I can find out about Madame Auguste while I'm there."

She nodded. "Yeah, okay. It's probably good for you to get out of town long enough for Mr. Cipher Security to forget about you anyway."

Even though it's what I intended to do, I didn't like that she made it about Darius and me. I wanted her to say something like *you're unforgettable*, or *you should totally keep him*. Not *yeah, don't let the door hit you on the way out*.

The buzzer for the front door to the building sounded down the hall, and Colette got up off the bed. "That's my client. Do you mind if I show her your color scheme for her living room?"

I started for the window, but turned to look back at the color swatches on the bed. "Don't let her add any purple to that room. Bacchans would wreck the vines with their drunken orgies."

She rolled her eyes dramatically, but her mouth was a thin line as she left the room.

# [ 15 ]
## DARIUS

*"It's only obvious in retrospect, and then it's the only thing you can see."*

The friendly smile on Colette's face fell off the moment she opened the door and saw me.

"Who are you?" she asked with confusion.

I almost laughed out loud, and if it had been the least bit funny, I would have. Instead, I studied the woman in front of me.

"It's only when people don't expect twins that you look alike," I said, noting the slighter build, the salon cut on the mane of blonde curls, and the expertly applied make-up.

Her eyes widened almost imperceptibly, while her expression remained politely curious. "I'm sorry, do I know you?"

I smiled then, though I felt bitterness at the edges. "You should, or rather, you would if you weren't a twin." I held out my hand to shake. "I'm Darius Masoud, of Cipher Security."

Her gaze seemed to sharpen, and I thought she might have heard of me. From her sister, or from Sterling Gray?

I heard a sound on the steps behind me, and Colette, or whatever her name was, looked relieved as a woman in her mid-forties approached. "I'm so sorry I'm late, Colette," the woman said in a tone of voice that wasn't at all sorry. "The traffic downtown is just awful."

Colette answered with the solicitous bustle of someone grateful for the interruption. "It's no trouble at all, Michelle, but let's get right to business so you don't get stuck in the theater traffic too."

Michelle shot me an assessing glance as she stepped past me on the landing, but Colette didn't even meet my gaze until the woman was inside the apartment.

"It was interesting to meet you, Mr. Masoud," she finally said as she closed the door. I heard the lock turn, and I smiled grimly.

"Interesting to meet you, too, Colette." *This* was Colette Collins. Colette owned this apartment, and it was an elegant, expensive address. The woman who had answered the door had the make-up, the hair, and the lithe sleekness of someone who put effort and means into looking the part of the successful designer. She was exactly the type of woman I'd expect to attract Sterling Gray. The woman with whom I'd spent such a memorable day on the lake was strong rather than sleek, hadn't been wearing make-up, and styled her hair as though she didn't own a comb. Not at all Gray's type, which should have been a relief.

Unfortunately, she was, apparently, a thief.

# [ 16 ]
## ANNA

*"Dear Life, when I said 'Can my day get any worse' it was a rhetorical question not a challenge."*

- FROM THE T-SHIRT COLLECTION OF ANNA COLLINS

He knew I was a thief.

He knew I had a twin, and that I'd used her as my alibi.

Crap, crap, crap!

I had just opened the window to slip out of Colette's room when I heard the voice of my Disney prince. *No, he's not mine*, I mentally corrected with a surprisingly painful pinch. Not if I wanted to remain at liberty.

He knew Colette's address, and he knew her name. How long until he found me? Actually, with Cipher Security at his back, he could already have my name and address and have people at my studio waiting for me.

Crap!

I sat on the bed and forced myself to calm down and think. Okay, I'd just decided to go to Boston, so that was what I needed to do, immediately. Cipher wasn't the cops, so they wouldn't necessarily have the airports watched – that took too many resources. I had my messenger bag with me, which had my wallet, keys, a cell phone charger, and a clean T-shirt – because a person never knew when spaghetti bolognese was going to jump off their plate. I was wearing my favorite jeans, engineer boots, and the leather, fleece-lined bike jacket I'd splurged on, so I just needed socks, underwear, a couple more shirts, and something to wear while I did laundry.

My heart was hammering in my chest as I raided Colette's dresser drawers. Socks – I took three pair. Underwear – no, I'd buy new ones. I grabbed an extra bra for when the one I was wearing got stinky, plus two T-shirts I'd given her for Christmas that didn't look like they'd ever been worn. To be fair, they were my style, not hers, but I remained hopeful that I could convert her to my subversive ways. She had more yoga pants than I had statement shirts, which probably said something less "down with the patriarchy" and more "up with all parts prone to sagging." I took a pair of those, plus a hand-knit sweater our mother had made when we were sixteen. Mine had been worn to rags years before, while Colette's was still pristine. I tied the sweater around my waist, rolled the rest of the clothes into tight little sausage rolls that fit in my bag, and then looked around Colette's room for anything else I might need.

I couldn't hear Darius's voice anymore, though Colette was still talking to someone. If he decided to push his way in …

I slid Madame Auguste back inside the portfolio, zipped it closed, and threaded the handles through the strap of my messenger bag. I didn't know where *The Sisters* painting was, but I wouldn't leave Madame where she could point her finger at my sister and yell, "She did it!"

I was down the fire escape ladder and three alleys away when the panic finally loosened its grip on my rational brain. I'd had the vague plan of getting to the airport and buying a ticket to Boston, but the logistics of it had been elusive during my mad dash and dodge through the alleys away from Colette's building. I'd just slowed down to an unremarkable, head-down, eyes-zipping-everywhere-for-signs-of-Darius's-truck stroll when my cell phone vibrated in my pocket.

I almost panicked again for one brief second until I remembered that he didn't have my number. Then I looked at the screen and the panic sat back down.

"What's up, Spark?" I said, relieved to see the number of the Dungeon Master on my screen.

"You're late," he said without preamble.

"I'm not coming today."

"Yes you are. I wrote a campaign specifically for Honor. She has to be here. It's a moral imperative." I had met Sparky online through a Dungeons and Dragons game finder site and had joined his weekly game as soon as I moved to Chicago.

"Honor doesn't do moral imperatives," I said as I considered my best options for getting to the airport.

"Honor is all about moral imperatives, and you know it," he said impatiently. "Okay, here's the real reason you need to come."

I smirked. Sparky was like that kid who couldn't keep a secret if his life depended on it. He was just too excited about everything not to share it with his friends, and I considered myself pretty lucky to be a peripheral one, even if it was just because of Honor.

"I'm trying to lure a friend of mine into the game, and she and Honor have that whole kick-ass heroine thing going on, so I wanted them to meet," he said.

I scowled. "You want your friend to meet my imaginary character because *they* have a lot in common? Thanks, Spark. You really know how to make a girl feel seen." I didn't know why I let his words hurt even a little bit. I mean, it's why I created Honor in the first place – to be the girl I wished I could be.

"Come on, you know I didn't mean it like that. Honor is your avatar, which means she's kind of an extension of you. I just think Shane would be more likely to join our game if she knew you played too."

"I'm on my way to Boston to do a job," I said, despite being slightly intrigued at the idea of meeting someone like Honor in real life.

"When do you leave?"

I checked my watch. "I don't know. Depends on when I can get to the airport."

"You don't have a ticket?" I could hear his computer keyboard clacking in the background. "Southwest leaves Midway at 6:45 and 9:10. You won't make the 6:45, but I'll take you in time for the 9:10 if you come here now."

I looked around, trying not to imagine Darius driving around the neighborhood searching the streets for me, or parked outside my studio with a warrant for my arrest.

Sparky almost whined. "Come on, Anna. Taylor and Ashley are on their way over with bacon-wrapped little smokies, and if you don't leave now, you won't make it in time to get any."

"Ok, that's just mean," I growled. Actually, my stomach growled. In another life, I might have had dinner with a Disney prince tonight, but instead I was running away from home.

I sighed. "Fine," I said, realizing I meant it. If I couldn't have dinner with a prince, I'd have D&D and bacon-wrapped smokies. Ashley drizzled them with brown sugar, making them pretty much just bacon candy. She also had a cupcake-baking habit, and I was always happy to help her dispose of the evidence. So, besides bacon and D&D, going to Sparky's gave me a place to lay low where Cipher wouldn't find me.

I hung up my phone and shoved it in my back pocket, then caught a bus to Sparky's neighborhood. Fifteen minutes later I could smell the bacon in the freight elevator.

"Get your hands off my smokies, William!" I called out as I hoisted the freight door of the elevator and stepped into his loft. Ashley had just lifted the foil off the platter she'd brought, and I could tell Sparky already had three or four stuffed into his mouth.

"Back away slowly, Spark," I said in my most menacing voice, as I tried not to laugh at the expression of *busted* on his face.

Bill "Sparky" Spracher was about my age, 6'2", and looked a

little bit like Chris Pratt on a really good day (his, not Chris Pratt's). He was a crazy-smart bio-mechanical engineer, and his loft always looked to me like a cross between Caractacus Potts' workshop in *Chitty Chitty Bang Bang* and the warehouse for the company that did special effects for *Tron*.

Sparky grinned and put his hands up theatrically as he swallowed the bacon smokies in his mouth. "I was just testing them to make sure they lived up to your standards, Anna-banana."

"I haven't had dinner, and you're in danger of losing fingers," I growled at him before turning to Ashley with an admiring visual sweep of her outfit. "I wish I could do girly like you do, Ash. That's a fantastic dress."

Ashley was gorgeous, and the fairy lights in her eyes sparkled with every smile. The skirt of her knee-length, 1950s-style dress flared in a perfect bell as she gave a twirl. "I made strawberry cupcakes for dessert and frosted them to match it," she said, flashing a fairy-lit smile at me.

"Ashley?" I said as I popped a bacon-wrapped smokie in my mouth. "Martha Stewart called and said she wants her talent back."

"Well, she can't have it. I'll need it when I take over her empire."

I hi-fived her, grabbed another bacon smokie, and dropped my bag and the portfolio in a corner next to a mannequin dressed like Wonder Woman, whose weird fashion hands had been replaced with robotic ones. I was proud that I only jumped a little bit when the hand at her hip moved.

"Um, Sparky? Why is the hand opening and closing like it wants to punch me?"

He looked up from the plate of Ashley's cupcakes he was holding and licked pink frosting off his finger. "Diana's testing five-finger joint durability. Be glad it's not the day for middle digit isolation." He shuddered theatrically. "It's pretty tough to come back from being flipped off by Wonder Woman."

I got myself a sparkling water from the mini fridge. "Taylor? Ashley? There's lemonade, bubbly water, and fruity iced tea in here if you want any."

Ashley's husband, Taylor, was a sports reporter for a Chicago suburb's local newspaper, and he looked and talked the part of an athlete. He was 6'4" and a sports superfan, but I had witnessed him hit his head on the corners of walls, and stumble over the dust bunnies on the floor enough times that I could see the signs of the kid who grew too fast to learn proper coordination. He was also the biggest gentleman I knew, and he adored his wife, so he came to get her lemonade himself.

"Have any good cases lately, Anna?" Taylor's tone was always cheerful, even when our D&D games got intense and his character took damage from Arkhan the Cruel or a White Dragon Wyrmling.

"I ran a bail-jumper down the main street of a town outside Lansing a few weeks ago. He was crazy fast, and I ended up having to grab some kid's bicycle off his lawn to catch him. The kid's mother yelled at me for ten minutes until I gave the kid five bucks for the bike rental."

He smirked and clinked the neck of his lemonade to the neck of my water bottle. "Well done."

"What about you? Any good interviews lately?"

"I met Bill Russell the other day. He signed a ball for me," Taylor said happily.

Ashley came over to join us and slipped under her husband's arm. "Taylor's sports memorabilia collection gets much more attention than my signed book collection does."

"*Nothing* is more important than your signed book collection." Taylor looked at his wife with such tenderness that I almost "awww'd" out loud.

"Okay, guys, ick. Too many," Sparky called from the gaming table where he was placing bowls with chips and dip.

The freight elevator groaned into place, and the metal gate was lifted by a woman who stepped into the loft like she owned the place. She had the kind of classic beauty that would have fit right in with models from the 1970s, but she was way more interesting than her looks. She was tall, so maybe it was the confidence that height added, but I finally recognized it when she smiled at Sparky.

She was magnetic.

"Shane! You came!" Sparky had a bubbly happiness in his voice that sounded like pop rocks in soda.

"Are you kidding? I was never cool enough to play D&D in elementary school. I had to see what I've been missing," she said, in a voice that sounded like it should be served on the rocks.

I decided then and there that I wanted to be her when I grew up.

Ashley went straight up to her and shook her hand. "I'm Ashley, and this is my husband Taylor, and if you're hungry, you need to horde some food before Bill and Anna eat it all."

"Bill and—" Shane looked at me, seemed to study me, and then a slow smile crossed her face. "Sorry, I always forget that Sparky has a name."

"Shane, meet Anna Collins, bounty hunter," Sparky said brightly. He handed Shane a glass of red wine, then turned to me. "Shane's a P.I."

"I thought bounty hunting was illegal in Illinois," Shane said to me as Sparky ushered us all to the gaming table he'd set up on a cleared-off workbench in his loft.

"It is. But I've been collecting licenses from most of the Midwest and eastern U.S. since I graduated from college, and being able to cross state lines has gotten me enough work that I can live pretty much anywhere."

"She's heading to Boston tonight to catch bad guys," Sparky said as he straddled a chair between me and Shane. She gave us a speculating look for a moment until Taylor piped in with his customary enthusiasm.

"I was just there to have lunch with my friend at *The Globe*. Five bucks says it snows while you're there." Ashley rolled her eyes at Taylor's bet. His "five bucks" statements were legendary, and I was pretty sure he owed me about thirty-five dollars at this point.

"You don't carry a gun when you're bounty hunting, do you?" Ashley asked as she passed the last of the bacon smokies around the table.

I shook my head. "Too hard to transport, and I wouldn't want to accidentally shoot someone just because they made me chase them. Martial arts and handcuffs are usually enough."

"Yeah, I'm not a firearms person either," Shane interjected. "And Sparky keeps finding new and inventive ways to stick blades in my legs."

"Um, really?" I asked, staring between my friend and this fabulous woman.

Shane laughed at the expression on my face. "He designs my prosthetics, and has decided I'm his crash test dummy for whatever MacGyver leg he dreams up in his large and twisted brain. Speaking of legs, Spark, can I get another one of the Amp'd Gear sleeves? I haven't had a hot spot or a blister since I started wearing the one you gave me."

"Yeah, sure. Those guys have designed a foot you can wear with flip-flops, by the way."

"Yes, please," she said with a grin before turning to me and Ashley. "I don't miss the leg as much as I miss the *shoes*." She said it with a sigh, and Ashley nodded as if to say, *the struggle is real*.

Two hours later, we were all comrades in arms, and after hugs all around, we disbanded until the next adventure. Taylor and Ashley left first, hand in hand, which was probably the same way they'd arrived. Shane's eyes moved from me, not moving from the chair into which I'd slunk down in exhaustion, to Sparky, who was putting bottles and cans into the recycling bin. She stood up with a smile and held out her hand.

"It was really nice to meet you, Anna. Sparky was right, you are pretty kick-ass."

I laughed. "He said the same thing about you." I closed my eyes and sighed, then hoisted myself out of the chair and picked up the portfolio and my bag. "Ready, Spark?"

"I need to grab my coat. Can we give you a ride anywhere?" he said to Shane as he called the elevator for her. I sank back into the chair.

Shane gave Sparky a hug and whispered something in his ear. The surprise on his face as she closed the elevator gate made me wonder what she'd said. When she had descended out of listening range, Sparky burst into laughter.

"What's funny?" I grumbled from my exhausted stupor.

"Shane thinks we're together," he said, still chuckling. "She said we make a great couple."

I wrinkled my nose. "No we don't. I'm too weird for you, and you're too ..." I waved my hand in an up-and-down assessment, from his pink Croc-wearing feet to the tips of his messy Calvin-and-Hobbes hair, "...many for me," I finished vaguely.

"Right?" he agreed.

"Hey! You don't have to agree with me. You could pretend to pine a little for the love that will never be," I groused.

"I suck at pining," he said cheerfully. "When Shane hooked up with Gabriel I pined for like, three minutes, and those are three minutes I'll never get back. Life's too short to pine."

I sighed dramatically. "She's tall, she's beautiful, and of course she has a boyfriend. He's probably as pretty as she is, and they do yoga together in slow motion on the beach as her hair flips in the wind and he worships—"

"Dude." Sparky's word screeched a halt to the soundtrack that was swelling in my imagination. "They're not slow-motion people. They're in-motion people. They're like, badass private security agents who take down corrupt dickheads and have the feds on speed dial."

"I thought you said she's a P.I.," I said, with a growing sense of uncomfortable prickles on my skin.

"She is," Sparky said, "but she got hired by Cipher Security when she and Gabriel worked a case together."

"She works for Cipher?" I whispered.

He shot me a strange look. "Yeah."

The mental image of a Disney prince that I'd locked behind the door of possibility suddenly burst into the room of my imagination, and the memory of him wasn't just in my head, it was in all my senses too. The scent of spices in his hair, the taste of his skin, the sound of laughter in his voice, and the feeling of his fingers trailing down my arms and tracing the path of the chills he inspired – it all washed over me in a tidal wave of sense memory and blended right in with the danger I could be in from yet another Cipher agent, who knew I was leaving town, and who may or may not be able to connect me to my sister.

I groaned. "Let's go."

Sparky still looked worried, but he pulled on his coat as we waited for the elevator. "You sure you're okay, Anna-banana?"

I pulled a smile out of the acting lessons closet and put it on with what I hoped looked like sincerity. "I'm cool. How about you? Do you think you'll survive our break-up okay?"

He grinned at that. "Oh yeah, I'm already plotting how to spin that to my advantage the next time I meet someone with potential."

"Nobody wants to hear about the heartbreaks, Spark," I said as we got in the freight elevator.

"True. But when you come out on the other side of heartbreak, you're a survivor. And if you can have a sense of humor about it, you're like one of those Kintsugi teacups, with pretty gold lines where you patched yourself up," he said, beaming.

I shook my head in wonder. "You wear pink Crocs and you know Japanese pottery techniques. You're so cool."

He snorted. "You have no idea."

The grin on my face faded as soon as I stepped out into the night. The handsome Disney prince still sat in my imagination, but he had a frown on his face as he looked at me from the shadows.

# [ 17 ]
## DARIUS

*"Tell a lie once and all your truths become questionable."*

- DARIUS MASOUD

I frowned at the half-inch of canvas left on the wooden stretcher behind the elaborate gilt frame in Gray's panic room. The painting of the two women had been cut cleanly with a very sharp blade, but the edge of a second canvas, painted black, was clearly visible behind it.

Sterling Gray watched me examine the stretcher with crossed arms and an impatient glare. "I don't know what you think you can learn from something the thief left behind."

I studied him. He was impatient and annoyed. "Mr. Gray, I need to know whatever you can tell me about this painting."

He narrowed his eyes. "I have told you what I know. It's my father's, and he's had it as long as I can remember. My mother hated it, so he kept it in a safe until she died, and now it's here, where he was supposed to be able to finally enjoy it."

I searched the edge of the canvas that remained on the stretcher. "Who are the women? Who is the artist?"

The rigid tension in Gray's shoulders loosened slightly with his sigh. "How the hell should I know? There were two signatures on the bottom – Alexandra something and S."

"Two signatures?" I looked up sharply from my study of the edge of remaining canvas. "Approximately where were they on the painting?"

Gray pointed to the lower left side of the empty stretcher. "Alexandra something was here, under the woman on the left – the usual place for an artist's signature, and the letter S was sort of carved into the paint in the lower right corner, under the other woman."

I'd seen the painting of course, when I wired the frame to the wall, but I hadn't studied it. The style had been European, from a century or two ago, and I'd had the impression of youth and beauty in the women. "Are you saying there were two artists?"

Gray shrugged. "There might have been. I always assumed the women in it were sisters – they looked enough alike – so maybe they painted it? Who knows?"

Sisters who looked alike.

Twins.

Identical twins. Thieves?

"Why does your father place so much value on this painting?" I asked, the blood beginning to pound in my veins.

"I don't know. He said it was worth a fortune, but I don't know why." Sterling scrubbed his hands through his hair in an uncharacteristically tense move. "I just know that the painting was supposed to hang in this room, and after me, Cipher will be the next target of Markham Gray's ire."

"Talk to me about Markham Gray." I sat down in the chair across from Dan O'Malley and Quinn Sullivan, the owners of Cipher Security. We were meeting in the third floor conference room at my request.

"Boston establishment," said Dan.

"His corporations own everything from major commercial real estate to banks, and his ventures don't tend to get scrutiny by agencies of oversight," added Quinn. I'd been surprised that he was in the office when I'd called Dan to meet, and even more surprised that he joined us. Quinn Sullivan had the direct line to several heads of government departments programmed into his cell phone, and his own oversight tended to be of the multi-national corporation variety.

"In other words, he's got some people in his pockets," Dan said.

"You're working on the theft of the painting from Gray's house, correct?" Quinn got up to make himself a coffee.

"I am, and I have questions that will need to be addressed by Markham Gray personally."

Quinn nodded. "I can facilitate a meeting."

I considered the men sitting across from me. I'd worked with Dan directly on an operation and considered him to be straightforward and unreservedly honest. I'd had far less personal experience with Quinn.

"There's a chance Gray won't like my questions," I said carefully.

"The fact that his kid won't bring in the cops is a fucking road sign to that," said Dan with a snort.

"Gray's contract with us is substantial," Quinn began.

I tensed and prepared to push back from the table. "Right, then."

"Darius," Quinn's tone brought my eyes up to meet his, and our gazes held for a long moment. "Gray's pockets may be deep and full of the kinds of people who clean up after his messes, but I'm not afraid of his dirt, nor of you digging in it."

The spinning wheel of my thoughts finally settled on one. "I don't trust easily. Too often, in my experience, people do what's easy rather than what's right. Placating Gray makes sense from a business standpoint, but if he has something to hide, I stand on ethics rather than ease."

Quinn narrowed his eyes and watched me for a long moment. "You left Iran when you were young."

I deliberately kept my expression impassive. Of course Quinn

Sullivan had a file on me. His business was security. He had a file on everyone.

"You and your parents fled your country, first to England, then later to the U.S. in the wake of their investigation into the Chain Murders, after a newspaper editor was shot in the head."

"Hajjarian had spearheaded his paper's own investigation. My parents had shared information they had with one of his reporters." I forced my muscles to relax.

Quinn turned to Dan to answer the question that hadn't been asked. "The Chain Murders of Iran were a series of murders and disappearances of poets, writers, journalists, translators, political activists, and other intellectuals who had been critical of the Islamic Republic system in the late eighties and nineties. It is believed the murders were carried out by internal Iranian government operatives."

Dan's eyebrows rose as he nodded, and Quinn's clear gaze returned to me. "I am in the business of security, which not only focuses on safety, but also on the business of knowing things, finding facts, and uncovering deceptions. I cannot imagine the fear your parents experienced to make them leave a country which they obviously loved enough to want to tell the truth about. Nor can I imagine what a seven-year-old boy and his little brother experienced of their parents' terror. What I do know is that a person doesn't come through experiences like that unscathed."

He stood up from the table and buttoned his suit jacket. "I'll set up a call with Markham Gray, and I'll send over the file we have on Gray Enterprises.

"And if I find something?" I asked as I stood to leave the room.

"Come to us and we'll figure out what should be done together," he said as he gestured that I should precede him through the door. "You were ready to push back from the table when I mentioned the size of the Gray account," Quinn said, using his casual tone to mask the laser focus of his observation skills.

I stopped and turned to look at Quinn, who stood several inches taller than me and practically radiated strength. "As you said, my parents' lives were threatened in an attempt to hide the truth. And in my experience, people with something to hide are the most dangerous."

"And in my experience," Quinn said with the smallest quirk of his mouth, "it's the people with something to hide who most often hire us."

I offered up a wry smile that I didn't feel. "Touché."

Quinn's tone was serious. "There is no attorney/client privilege in the security business. If, in the course of our relationship with a client, it becomes evident that there is criminal activity going on, our integrity, and the integrity of our other clients demands swift and immediate action." His gaze was that of an alpha, completely secure in his power and dominance.

My eyes held his a moment longer than necessary before I said simply, "Thank you."

He nodded and then left the room.

Dan went over to the sideboard and prepared a cup of coffee. "Quinn's the only guy I know who lives with his fucking gloves off," he said quietly.

"I'm not sure I know what that means," I said, suddenly tired of all things that weren't spelled out.

"You know the saying 'the gloves come off,' when a guy's ready to throw down for real?"

I nodded. "A boxing term. Keeping gloves on means no one gets seriously hurt."

"There's also a tradition up north that no matter how cold it gets, you take your gloves off to shake hands. So living with his gloves off means he's not hiding anything, or hiding behind anything. He lives his fucking life out loud, even when he's not saying a word."

Dan's coffee had finished brewing, and he knocked it back in one blazing hot slug. Then he shuddered, slapped me on the shoulder, and steered me out of the room. "Come on. Let's go see what kind of dirt we can dig up on the senior Mr. Gray."

# [ 18 ]
## ANNA

Sub rosa work sucked. The coffee was always cold, the food was either fast or packaged, and because the food was such crap, the car inevitably smelled of farts.

I mean seriously. Cheese puffs farts were the *worst*.

At least it was a rental, so the stink saturation wouldn't be my problem for long. Although at the rate my stakeout of Donnie "Junior" McConnell was going, my clothes were going to need a wash soon enough.

Junior's apartment was on the fourth floor of a 1950s style cement-block building, with all the charm of a Soviet era gulag. The front gate was heavy and locked automatically, and every tenant I'd seen go in or out had to dart through it to avoid being crushed in the mandibles of iron that kept the place bounty hunter-free. I was pretty sure that all the criminals were on the inside, and even the postal carrier looked terrified of being caught in the jaws of death.

Public records had given me Junior's parole officer, and he'd given me Junior's brother's address. The brother's imagination as to why a woman would want Junior was clearly limited to sex, so he happily gave me the address where he paid Junior's electric bill, and here I was.

I considered what I knew about Junior. He was forty-eight years old, born and raised in South Boston. He got popped for the first time on a weapons charge on his seventeenth birthday, and he'd been in and out of prison since then. He'd never married, though some people might consider him good-looking in an alcoholic child star way, and when he wasn't doing time, he worked in a muffler shop that fronted one of the branches of the Irish mob.

He was also a barfly. So, I just had to find a bar within stumbling distance, and I'd get my guy.

The dive bar was a block away from Junior's building, and the faded sign out front proclaimed Guinness Beer as the drink of choice in the no-name establishment. I was not a particular fan of Guinness – anything that mixed with Jägermeister was suspect at best. I had learned to sip whiskey when in dive bars where a person was lucky to find wine at all. It was a matter of self-defense when dive bar wine so often resulted in purple teeth. This place looked like a prime whiskey-drinking establishment, so I hitched up my tough girl attitude and strode in the door.

The bartender looked at the door when I walked in, and my first thought was that I couldn't tell whether her deep wrinkles were from scowling or smiling. "You're new," she spat – literally spat on the floor – right before she slid a beer down the bar to an even more wrinkled man sitting at the end. Her voice wasn't just gravelly, it sounded like the rock tumbler I'd had as a kid that took three weeks of constant grinding to turn out five semi-shiny pebbles. I was so fascinated by her I had to shake myself out of staring to take another step inside.

I was in a no-name dive bar deep in Southie, looking to extract a guy twice my size from a place where he likely had allies.

It was a neighborhood bar filled with an assortment of regulars – a table of young people, a couple of hipsters, a few guys who stopped by after work at the plant or the office, and Junior, lounging at his table, nursing a glass of something amber-colored without ice.

The bartender looked at me expectantly, and her rock tumbler voice sounded almost kind. "The happy hour wine is rotgut, but the whiskey is my brother's blend, and it's worth it."

I wondered if it had given her that fantastic voice. "A whiskey then, please, and one for my friend." I tossed my head in Junior's direction, and the bartender's eyebrows rose in surprise.

"That one drinks alone."

I shrugged and put a twenty on the bar next to the glasses she poured. "Then we won't be disturbed."

I took the two glasses without waiting for change and placed them on Junior's table. Then I spun a chair around backwards and sat down across from Junior. I slid one glass to him and raised my own. "Sláinte," I said, and took a sip. It was good, and surprisingly smooth. I raised my glass to the bartender and caught her eye. "It's good," I mouthed. She harrumphed and moved down the bar to help another customer, and my attention returned to Junior.

He watched me through narrowed eyes. "What do you want?"

"Your brother thought we should meet," I said with a smile.

His eyebrow raised. "Why would Henry think that?"

"Maybe *Eric* thought we'd have things to talk about." Using his brother's correct name seemed to make Junior let his guard down slightly. He sat back and slugged the last of his own drink.

"What things?"

"Connecticut things," I said, and took another sip. I watched him steadily; he'd definitely flinched at my words, and his guard was back up at full strength. I sighed and pushed my drink across the table to him. He was going to run, and I didn't want to get splashed when he shoved the table out of the way.

"So, Junior, how does a guy like you dip his toes into the embezzlement pool? That's pretty white collar for a Southie." I deliberately let my accent slide south.

His elbows tensed, and I debated a right dive or a left dive. Then

113

his fingers flexed. I stood up smoothly and pushed the back of my chair into the table to stop it from slamming into me.

He bolted for the door, but I grabbed his coat as he went past me. "Damn it, Junior," I snarled as he shrugged out of the nylon coat and pulled a chair behind him to block me. I vaulted the chair and accidentally sent a full beer flying from the hand of a guy who stood up to stop us.

"Hey!" he yelled indignantly.

"Sorry. I'll get your next one," I called over my shoulder as I sprinted out the door after Junior. He was only about ten paces ahead of me, but whatever whiskey he'd consumed was fueling his rocket engines. Flames had erupted from the heels of his running shoes, and that's what drew my eye to the fact that they were actual running shoes. They weren't actual flames, of course, but when he put on a burst of speed, they flared bright orange. Running shoes. Really? Junior was a runner? How very inconvenient of him.

His lead increased to fifteen paces, and I mentally revised my plan. I was younger and not powered by rocket fuel panic, but his legs were longer and he seemed to be one of those strange humans who enjoyed running for its own sake. He could probably hold out a lot longer than I was willing to put into this pursuit.

I once took care of a friend's young male Australian shepherd, and that lovely, pain-in-the-butt dog herded me all around my apartment. He cut me off and pushed against my legs until I had to either plow into him or veer around him. It was a remarkably effective way for a much smaller creature to dominate a bigger one, and when I saw some guys bouncing a basketball on the sidewalk at the intersection, I had my inspiration.

"STOP! THIEF!" I yelled, in my most terrified girl voice.

The guys looked over at the little blonde sprinting after the big guy, and I saw the moment on their faces when indecision shifted to purpose. Junior did too, because he muttered something unrepeatable under his breath as he changed direction to sprint away from the young guys, who suddenly joined the chase.

Young male herding skills are not to be underestimated.

The direction change sent Junior toward his own apartment building, and I counted on his homing instinct to send him into the safety of it. There was a second when he hesitated, and I sent a silent whisper up to the æther that he choose unwisely. At that moment the door to his building opened and an old woman stepped out. It was the deciding factor. Junior darted across the street and dragged the cell block door of his apartment building behind him. It slammed shut, and the woman stared at the door as if she could see the sound waves still rippling from the force of the blast. The basketball guys turned and shrugged their shoulders at me and walked away. I gave them a quick wave and then sprinted down the alley to the back of the building. During my stakeout in the fartbox I'd killed time by counting windows, so I had a better than fair idea of which apartment was Junior's. I was on top of the dumpster and up the rusty ladder fast enough to see Junior explode into the apartment and throw a hefty deadbolt on the door he pulled closed behind him. Then he bent nearly double, hands on his knees, and heaved gasping breaths.

I saw all of this from outside the window, and then I heard his muttered curses as his eyes darted around the crappy little apartment. I recognized the signs of a cornered animal, and I'd seen enough of them to be wary. Junior had about fifty pounds on me, plus a hefty dose of desperation, but I had the element of surprise and a pocket full of zip ties. It would do.

He didn't move away from the door for a solid five minutes while he considered his options. Someone must have walked down the hall, because there was a moment when he tensed and then looked toward the window like he was debating jumping through it, and I had to fight the instinct to duck back. The windows were dingy enough that he would have had to be looking for me to realize the shadow at the edge was human-shaped. As long as I didn't move, he wouldn't see me. Eventually, the absence of sirens or door pounding, or maybe just the need to pee sent Junior into the tiny bathroom out of the sight of the window. Of course he didn't close the door, but the sound of urine hitting porcelain was hopefully enough to cover the slightly bumpy slide of the sash window. I paused outside the window for just long enough to hear that he was still peeing – seriously, how much whiskey had the guy consumed? A moment later I was inside and pressed against the wall next to the open bathroom door.

And still, Junior peed, while I contemplated the American habit of calling it a bathroom, despite the fact that most such rooms didn't have a bathtub. Or worse, a restroom, where *no one* in the history of resting would ever choose to rest. Europeans called the room a toilet, which made far more sense to me, but even that concept was strange when considered from the point of a view of a dog, like Boris the Aussie, who always followed me in and inevitably gave me the side-eye when I peed into a bowl *inside* the house.

Finally, the flush. I readied, and a moment later, Junior emerged, still zipping his pants.

Ick.

Sigh.

I threw my shoulder into him, which sent him off balance into the wall. He put his arms out to fend off the attack, and I grabbed the one closest to me, turned, and flipped him over my shoulder. He landed with a thud and a grunt that signaled the breath leaving his lungs. So, while he gasped air back into them, I rolled him and zip-tied his hands and feet so he was trussed like the marinated turkey he was.

Then I rolled him back over and hauled him into a sitting position so his back was against the wall. His eyes opened wide to see me, and I rolled my own at the shock in them.

"Who'd you expect?" I snorted in disgust as I stood up and went in to wash my hands. I dried them on my jeans rather than risk the towel that hung from a hook on the wall. "Also, gross. You didn't wash your hands after you used the toilet."

I returned to glare down at him. "Donal McConnell, you are under arrest for being an idiot."

"You can't arrest me," he snarled.

I sighed. "I just did."

"Show me your badge." He was trying to intimidate me, which

was pretty funny considering he bore a remarkable resemblance to Thanksgiving dinner.

I smiled. "How about I show you my bail piece instead," I said, referring to the paperwork that showed that he was a fugitive, and which gave me almost more rights over him than a cop had, since I didn't need a warrant to be in his apartment.

"I want to call my lawyer," he huffed, not yet giving in to the inevitable defeat.

I squatted in front of him just out of spitting range and studied the subject of my pursuit. "That's the thing, Junior. When you signed that little piece of paper at the bail bondsman's, you gave up your Constitutional rights. You don't get to speak to your lawyer until you're back in police custody. In Connecticut."

The bluster in his voice shifted to something like a whimper. "Come on. I just need to make a call."

I stood up in one fluid movement, a direct contrast, I suddenly recalled, to the way I'd stood up in my sister's hot pink silk dress. And with that flash of memory, I felt a sudden, aching emptiness where a Disney prince had once stood right in front of me.

Memory Darius smiled at me before I blinked him out of existence, and my throat constricted with the tears I would never cry about his absence.

I shook my head. "Sorry, bud. You're worth too much to me to risk with calls to guys named Guido or Mac."

Junior shook his head. "Nothing like that, I promise."

"You do realize exactly what your promises are worth, right?" I said, beginning to get exasperated with him. "You signed a piece of paper that said you wouldn't run, and then you ran. And that piece of paper is why I'm here."

"I needed to see my mom," he said petulantly.

I sighed. "Well, now she can visit you in jail."

"What if I traded information? I'll give you something the Boston P.D. wants, and you let me go," he said quietly.

"Not a chance." I hauled Junior up by his armpits and then immediately wanted to go wash my hands again.

"Call them. Ask them if they want a name for the Gardner heist." Junior was starting to beg, and it sent ants skittering up my spine.

"Nope."

"C'mon, Blondie, give me a break. Just let me make a call."

I patted down Junior's pockets, removing his wallet and a pen knife, both of which I stuffed in my own pockets.

"Reach in my front pocket and you'll get a surprise," he said in a smarmy voice.

I spun him to face me and he almost toppled over. Granted, I may have zip-tied his ankles a little bit too tightly for proper balance, but that was a tactical decision based on relative size. "Be honest, Junior. Has an invitation like that ever worked? Has a woman, when propositioned with a front pocket surprise, ever reached in and said 'oooh, Junior, give me some of that surprise'? Because I've got to tell you, on a scale of mildly disturbing to properly revolting, a pocket surprise in your pants is about as appealing as biting into a hot dog and finding a vein."

He winced, and I gave myself three points.

"Let's go," I said, spinning him toward the door so I could cut the zip tie at his feet.

"Seriously. The Gardner heist. They're going to want what I know, and you could be the one to give it to them if you play your cards right."

I opened the apartment door and pushed Junior through it ahead of me. "Or I could take you in, collect my bounty, and then you're someone else's problem."

I could feel his scowl through my hand on his arm, and I stepped back from him so I didn't accidentally catch his bad mood. I was in a fine mood – cheerful, even. Junior didn't speak again until I shoved him into the back seat of the fartbox and got in behind the wheel.

"Take me to the Boston P.D. then." He sounded near tears, and I looked up sharply into the rear-view mirror.

"Why?"

"I'll make my own deal with them. You'll still get your bounty if I'm in custody."

I studied him in the mirror. "Why put yourself at the mercy of B.P.D.?"

He stared back for a long moment, and I had the thought that there was a wrestling match going on in his head. "My little sister tried to commit suicide last month. She hates me and wants nothing to do with me, but my mom's having a hard time with it, and I'm the only one who can get her to talk about it."

I closed my eyes against the plea in his voice. "Crap," I muttered under my breath. "I'm not letting you go," I said, when I finally started the car.

"Fine. Just don't take me out of state yet. Mom needs to stay here with Darcy, and I don't want to leave her alone."

I started driving. "What's the Gardner heist?" I said after ten minutes of silence.

The only noise that came from the back seat was the sound of Junior's snores.

# [ 19 ]
## ANNA

*"Always know where the exits are."*

- ANNA COLLINS

The Boston Police Department was remarkably eager to take Junior off my hands when he mentioned the Gardner heist. It took me exactly two minutes on my smart phone in the parking lot at police headquarters to figure out that he was talking about the Isabella Stewart Gardner Museum where the *Madame Auguste Manet* painting hung. In 1990, thirteen paintings and the eagle-shaped finial from a Napoleonic flag were stolen from the Gardner Museum by two men dressed as police officers, and the museum was offering a ten-million-dollar reward for information leading to the recovery of all thirteen pieces in good condition.

Suddenly I wondered what, exactly, Junior could know about missing artwork worth ten million dollars, and why this museum had come to my attention twice in the past twenty-four hours.

The museum was just across from the College of Art and Design, where our mother and aunt had gone to school, and it was a five-minute drive from police headquarters. I checked my watch and real-

ized I'd probably need to book a hotel room for the night anyway –
I'd crashed the night before in a way-too-pricey airport hotel and had
already checked out – so another hour more or less wasn't going to
change the fact that I had no plans.

I parked near the museum, paid my admission, walked through
the new wing and into the old, and then stepped out into the most
glorious central courtyard garden I'd ever seen in my life. Four
stories of building surrounded me on all sides, with a mix of Gothic,
Byzantine, and Venetian style arched windows and openings rising
with the walls. It took my breath away, and I hopped over the rope
and sat cross-legged in the middle of a mosaic-tiled patio in the
center of the courtyard to absorb it. The tiles were cold in the frigid
early spring air, and the sun had gone down, so most of the Thursday
evening patrons had gone inside to wander the rooms full of art. The
courtyard was lit by discreet lamps, and the archways added their
golden glow to the walls. I lay back on the tile floor to gaze up at the
arched glass-tiled conservatory roof overhead and imagined the stars
giggling behind cloud hands as they looked down at the crazy girl on
the floor staring up at them.

I pictured Honor climbing up from the courtyard floor, using
window ledges and railings to pick her way up to the fourth floor. I
visually mapped the path she would take and realized it actually
could be done without ropes, though not likely without being
arrested.

"Planning to rob the place?"

The deep voice was hard, and it shot a jolt of pure electricity
into me. I tilted my head back to see the upside down face of Darius
Masoud. No part of him was smiling, and several parts, including
crossed arms and tense shoulders, were very definitely
disapproving.

"Just seeing how it could be done," I said as casually as a person
could with a thousand-mile-an-hour heartbeat and the instinct to flee.

One of his eyebrows went up as he studied me, and then he
shocked me when he sat down and stretched out on his back on the
tiles. "Show me," he said in a tone that was more command than

request. I turned my face to see stern lines around his mouth, and I tried not to remember how soft his lips were.

Then I looked back at the building rising around us and raised a finger to trace Honor's path up. "From the staircase rail, up to the lower ledge, across to the Juliet balcony, up the column to the railing, then across to that column, up again, use the decorative stonework as hand and footholds, and then finally in at the fourth floor."

He nodded. "It would take skill."

"It could be done," I said, suppressing the itch to try it.

"Is that why you're here?" His tone was cold, and I didn't like the sharp edges in it. They hurt.

"I'm not a thief."

He looked sharply at me. "Aren't you?"

I sat up to escape the barbs in his gaze and wrapped my arms around my legs to defend against the chill that sent a tremor through me.

There was ice in his voice. "The lights to blind the cameras was a clever touch, I admit, but I'm not certain I admire your use of your identical twin as an alibi quite so much."

I got to my feet and turned to help him up, but he ignored my outstretched hand, so I hopped the rope and stepped back into the corridor.

He followed me and spoke in a low tone that could have seemed intimate to someone who didn't understand the context. "I saw you naked. I know you have tan lines. There are no tan lines on the woman who was, shall I say, *with* Sterling Gray while his father's painting was being stolen."

I flinched at more than just the words. Tan lines. I thought about my sister's perfectly even tan. I wouldn't be able to hide my tan lines if they arrested me tomorrow. My God, I could be sharing a cell with Junior tonight if Darius had already called the cops. At least maybe then I could find out what he knew about the Gardner heist.

I stopped suddenly and turned to face Darius. "What are you doing here?"

"What are *you* doing here?" he countered.

"I was in the neighborhood," I said.

"That's why I'm here," he answered in the same tone of voice.

I stared at him. "You followed me?"

His expression was totally neutral. "It wasn't hard."

"How," I demanded.

He almost rolled his eyes, the jerk. "Shane recognized you the minute she saw you, or rather, she recognized your sister and realized – like I already had – that you're twins."

"Identical in every way except all the ways we're not," I muttered to myself.

I strolled down the corridor, mostly to get away from his angry intensity, but also because I was curious. Why had Darius Masoud followed me? Was he here to take me in for the Gray mansion break-in? He didn't have any real evidence unless he had the painting, and technically, there was no proof that I'd even been at Gray's mansion. Colette Collins had been the name on the invitation, the man at the door had greeted Colette Collins, and Colette Collins had slept with Sterling Gray that night.

The only thing the Disney prince had was a mental snapshot of my tan lines and some speculation.

"Why *are* you here, Ms. Collins?"

I froze for a moment, then stuck my right hand out to shake his. "My name is Anna. I'm sorry I didn't introduce myself properly."

"You lied," he said, and there was an edge to his voice.

"Not to you," I countered, with some in mine too.

"Then tell me why you're here, in this museum, at this moment." He ground the words out between clenched teeth, and I was surprised at how much I wanted the fight.

And that made me smile sweetly – the kind of expression that generally guaranteed a lost temper in the opposition. It had worked like a charm on my sister growing up and generally made bail jumpers do crazy things like throw punches, which put them off balance and made for an easy over-the-shoulder flip. So, I pulled out the sweet smile and total honesty. "I just brought a bail jumper into the Boston P.D. He tried to trade his freedom for information about the Gardner heist. I did a little pocket research and then came straight over from police headquarters to see if I could figure out what he could possibly have known. Mysteries are kind of my thing."

His head exploded in a most delightful, Disney prince-ish way. First his eyes opened wide, then they narrowed as he tried to gauge my level of truthfulness, and then they crinkled at the corners as he … laughed?

"Shane said you were a bounty hunter, and it fits you so much better than interior designer did."

I crossed my arms in front of me and glared at him. The laughter annoyed me, and I wasn't sure why, because I was used to guys not taking me seriously, especially about my job.

I tried to pick through all possible retorts to that statement and none of them really said what I was feeling. Probably because I had no idea what I was feeling – annoyed and defensive for sure, but also a little fluttery that I'd made him laugh and that he thought about me at all.

So, instead of speaking, I stalked off down the corridor again, and turned into the first room I saw.

The walls of the room were covered in watery blue fabric, and paintings hung in odd groupings and at strange heights all around the space. The paintings seemed to be as jumbled in their themes as their arrangements were, until I began to look more closely.

I stopped in front of one wall. Darius came up behind me and stood at my shoulder, so I talked to him instead of talking to myself like I usually did. "An Egyptian bust, a goat, and some people on the beach," I said, indicating the three paintings hung one beneath the other, "by different artists. Why? What are they looking at?"

The subjects of all three paintings were looking to my right, out of frame – it was the only thing they all had in common. So then I looked right as well, and a small portrait of a young boy caught my eye. I walked over to it and studied the image.

"Why this boy?" I asked. "What was special about him?"

An attractive young woman with corkscrew curls and shiny eyes came over to stand next to us. "He's called *The Little Groom.*

Isabella Stewart Gardner bought him from a doorman in Italy. I think he reminded her of her son who died of pneumonia when he was two."

I looked back at the right-facing paintings, then at the boy. "Yes! They're definitely looking at him, and they want us to look too." I met the young woman's eyes. "There are stories here, aren't there?"

The woman, whose badge said her name was Crystal, grinned happily. "They're everywhere. A group of landscapes with a single portrait of a person looking at them tells the visitor they should stop and pay attention – there's something interesting to see here. The statue of the elf, missing his legs, has a perfect view of the outside so he can imagine himself dancing there. And almost none of the columns in the loggias actually match each other, but somehow they look like gorgeously dressed guests standing around a ballroom waiting for the music to begin."

The grin on my face must have been huge, because Crystal began walking me around the room talking about this painting and that fragment of fabric, this book and that drawing, until we arrived at a console table, above which hung a small empty frame with a large empty wall above it. Darius, who had been following us without saying a word, came up beside me.

"What went here?" I asked Crystal.

"The Manet painting that was stolen in 1990 – *Chez Tortoni*. The museum has left the empty frames in place so you can see how large, or in this case, small they were," she said, in a voice that sounded like the tinkling of a chandelier.

"No, not that. The space above it. Something else should be there," I said, looking for any signs of discoloration on the fabric.

"That's where the other Manet usually hangs," Crystal said. "*Madame Auguste Manet* is on the fourth floor for a private party tonight."

I swallowed hard and Darius looked at me oddly, maybe because I suddenly looked like I wanted to throw up.

"Can we see her?" he asked.

Crystal looked startled. "Madame Manet? Ah, no, I'm sorry, not unless you have an invitation. The fourth floor is off limits to museum visitors. There's a print of her in the gift shop if you'd like."

Darius hadn't taken his eyes off me until he finally nodded and answered Crystal. "Yes, thanks. We'll stop in there. What's on the fourth floor?"

"It was the apartment where Isabella Gardner lived, and now it's where the museum director and her staff have their offices. But I don't get to go up there very often – the interns from MassArt don't get staff privileges."

"Massachusetts College of Art and Design?" I asked, happy for the change of subject.

She perked up. "Yeah, a lot of us do internships here. It's pretty great to have this place right around the corner from school."

"My mom and aunt went to MassArt. What's your major?" I was afraid that my desperation to keep the subject away from Madame Auguste was painted around me like an aura.

"I'm studying dance," she said with a smile. "And before you ask, yes, there's totally a connection between the old master paintings and dance."

"Right? I mean some of the old potato farmers are a bit heavy-footed when they step out of their frames, and the wooden clogs of the Dutch ladies get loud on wood floors, but the little girls holding puppies always leap out of their portraits like they have wings on their feet, and I've seen whole ballets performed to Romany music by some of the Degas dancers." I had grown up with my mother's art books, and the paintings in them were like kindling to a girl with my imagination.

"Exactly!" she said excitedly. "No one else here has ever heard the clogs upstairs, but that's all I ever hear in the Dutch Room." Suddenly her walkie-talkie squawked, and a voice murmured from her hip. "Sorry, I have to answer this."

She moved away toward the door and left us alone.

Darius continued to study me, and in the reflected light of the blue silk walls, his skin looked shimmery. "What is it about the missing Manet that makes you so nervous?"

He didn't look at the empty wall behind him, but I knew it's what he meant. I shrugged. "I'm not nervous," I said, totally nervous – practically shaking with it.

His eyes narrowed. "What aren't you telling me? Perhaps doing a little recon for your own heist?"

I stared at him. "You think I'd steal from the Isabella Stewart Gardner Museum?"

Darius raised one eyebrow and wore an expression that said, *Maybe.*

I threw my hands up in the air and huffed out an exasperated breath. "Oh, come on!" I said a little too loudly. Two ladies who lunch glared at me, and Crystal looked up from her walkie-talkie conversation in surprise. I grabbed Darius's hand and pulled him out of the Blue Room, not stopping until we were back outside in the deserted courtyard.

Then I stopped and turned to face him, hands on my hips and a scowl on my face. "You called me a thief, and yet you have no proof that I stole anything. My sister happened to be with Sterling Gray when his painting was stolen, a fact you've apparently verified from her lack of tan lines. So she has an alibi, and – interestingly, so does he." I let righteous indignation fill my voice with snark before I continued. "And other than that, the only thing you have on me is that I may not actually be quite as indiscriminate in my sexual encounters as you must have thought I was."

His jaw clenched as he considered me for a long moment. "I met you at Gray's party."

"Did you?"

"You said your name was Colette."

I blinked slowly. "I don't introduce myself with my sister's name."

"You lied to me." His voice was angry and sharp, and I realized this was a big sticking point for him. "Outside your ... her apartment. I called you Colette."

"I didn't correct you when you called me by my sister's name. Do you know how often that happens to me? Do you realize how petulant and fussy it sounds to my own ears every time I correct someone who mistakes me for her? I've learned to roll with it in self-defense."

He looked baffled by my b.s. for exactly one second and then he shook his head. "Enough, Anna. I may not be able to prove that you and your sister stole Gray's painting, but you and I met that night at the party. That was you in the hot pink dress, looking like something that rose from a field of wildflowers, smelling of spring, and speaking inanities that lit up the room with pure, ridiculous joy. That was you, not your sister, and it was you I encountered outside her apartment building. It was you who went out on the boat with me, and it was very definitely you I made love with on the lake."

I felt like all the air had been sucked out of the courtyard – as though a glass pane in the roof had opened, broken the pressure seal, and all the oxygen had rushed out in a whoosh, taking the breath from my lungs with it.

Darius spun around and strode several feet away from where I stood on surprisingly unsteady legs. He sat on a bench, his elbows on his knees, as he studied the mosaic tile pattern of the floor. I watched him from a safe distance for a long moment, then finally found enough air to exhale before making my way to the bench. I sat beside him and looked at his hands where they cupped the sides of his head. They were strong hands with old scars and the callouses of a person who handled ropes. I knew the touch of those hands on my skin, and I reached out to trace the line of his index finger. He flinched, but I didn't pull away until I'd traced all the veins in the back of his hand.

He finally sat back and met my eyes. "What's the deal with the Manet?"

I flinched and tried to stop the words I knew were coming. With a filter, I could have lied to him or even just stayed silent. But if I'd ever had one, it was broken, and being with him had scattered the pieces. "I … found one."

# [ 20 ]
## ANNA

*"The only bad taco is the one you didn't get to eat."*

- ANNA COLLINS

He stared at me. "You *found* one? What does that even mean? You found a print of *Madam Auguste Manet*?"

"Not a print," I whispered. "It didn't come from here, though." I'd almost said that I didn't steal it, but he was close enough that I could smell his shampoo, and his scent filled my memory with truth serum. Not being able to lie to him was a serious problem.

"A copy of a Manet. You found a copy."

I stood up and away from him in hopes of finding little bits of my broken filter and using them to cover the naked parts of me. "People copy the old masters all the time. My mom's an artist, and she spent her whole youth training in the old master art techniques." It was a diversionary tactic that could never work with someone like Darius Masoud. I knew it, he knew it, and yet he let the diversion hang in the air as a docent emerged into the loggia to tell some other guests that the museum would be closing in ten minutes.

He stood and met my eyes. "And you're here to look into the

Gardner heist?" It almost sounded like he was trying to convince himself of something.

That question was easier, and I didn't even have to evade any part of it when I answered. "Honestly – I did ten minutes of online research after Junior tried to use it to get me to let him go, and I couldn't *not* come here to see for myself."

I cast a longing glance down the corridor as we made our way toward the exit along with the other stragglers. "I'll be back tomorrow to poke around the Dutch Room and the Short Gallery, in case you're still following me then."

Hope and fear had a fierce little battle in my chest as the words left me, and the expression on his face turned thoughtful.

He followed me to the coat check, and it wasn't until the guy behind the counter came back with my things that I remembered I'd checked both my messenger bag *and* the portfolio.

Darius eyed the portfolio but said nothing about it as he held the door for me and we stepped out into the cool night air. The Fens beckoned to the north, and I had the momentary impulse to disappear among the trees, but then he finally spoke.

"Do you paint?"

The question startled me until I saw his eyes stray to the portfolio slung on my messenger bag. I still couldn't lie to him, and I was too tired to try to evade the question. "I never learned how. I was too busy climbing and running and jumping and generally acting like a wild thing. I like colors though, and patterns. I like putting colors together in ways that tell me a story."

He cast another look at the portfolio, and we walked in silence for a minute.

"Is Colette actually an interior designer?" he finally asked.

"Yeah, she does a lot of apartments for people who want to look fancy and rich," I said.

His mouth quirked in the smallest smirk, and it felt like a reprieve to see his expression shift away from its usual thoughtfulness. "Not the actual fancy and rich people, just the ones who want to look that way?"

I grinned. "Exactly." We began walking down the street, away from The Fens, and it felt a little like making a choice. Darius's stride was casual and matched mine easily.

"How does one choose bounty hunting as a career?" I could hear the vaguely European accent of his youth in the carefully worded question.

"One generally doesn't choose to become a bail fugitive recovery expert, one falls into it, or almost falls." I looked at the scars on my hands for a moment before pointing one out to Darius. "I got this from a rock face in California when a piece of the boulder I was hanging from broke off and I had to grab at a scrubby manzanita brush to keep from splatting. There was a guy on the ground with another climbing group, and he said he needed someone with my skills for a job he had coming up in San Francisco. I'd graduated from college and was just doing odd jobs to finance my travel habit, so I said yes. Turned out he was a bail bondsman, and the bounty who'd skipped on him had holed up in a brick warehouse he'd fortified like a prison. He wanted me to climb the outside of the building and then open the front door from the inside. It was an easy way to make a couple of hundred bucks, and now it's an easy way to travel and see the country."

He scoffed. "I imagine you see some pretty unsavory parts of the country in your work."

I shrugged. "Some. But I can always find someplace green and something interesting to see. It's not all fugitives and criminals."

He glanced at me, then at the portfolio, and back at me before he came to some sort of decision. "I'd intended to take you to dinner the last time we saw each other. May I do so now?"

I hesitated. My reasons for not seeing Darius were still valid – there was no way I could lie to the man, and telling the truth put much more at stake than just my own freedom. He continued before I could say no. "I won't ask about Gray's painting, I promise. I just want to get to know you a little better."

His eyes had lost all the flinty edges they'd flashed at me earlier, and I felt myself wishing I could sink into his gaze.

"Depends," I said as I tried desperately to cling to whatever self-preservation instincts I had left.

"On?"

"Whether the restaurant you choose happens to be shaped like a taco truck."

He burst out laughing, and the damn butterflies winged into flight.

"Are you parked someplace secure?" Darius asked as we waited at the light.

"Sure. It's a crappy rental. Why?"

"Because I'm staying just here," he said as he pointed to an apartment building on the next block, "and it's a good place from which to plot our tour of the museum tomorrow."

*Our* tour? I was in sooooo much trouble.

"That's convenient. It's not really a taco truck area though, is it?"

He smiled. "You let me worry about hunting down the tacos."

We actually found an excellent taco truck parked outside the lot where my rental car was, so we grabbed the tacos to go and went to Darius's apartment.

"You got this place for a week?" I said as I looked around the fairly spacious one-bedroom, modern-style apartment. "Why?"

"I thought you didn't want to discuss the Gray theft," he said as he held up a bottle of red wine. "Would you like a glass?"

I glanced at the bottle and nodded. "Sure, but what does Gray have to do with Boston?"

"Markham Gray is from Boston, and much of his fortune was made here."

"So?" I dropped my bag and the portfolio on a chair and parked myself on a barstool at the counter as Darius pulled the cork on the bottle.

"I have some questions I'd like to ask Mr. Gray about the origins of the painting that was stolen from his panic room." His eyes remained on me as he poured two glasses of red wine.

My heart hammered in my chest, and I felt sure he could see my pulse beating in my throat. Or maybe he was one of those shapeshifter princes whose animal senses let them hear the blood rushing through someone's veins. Would he be a dragon prince, or maybe something lupine or feline? He was definitely a predator of some variety – the question was, what kind of creature was I? Predator? Prey? Non-binary? Other?

I suddenly realized he was still watching me, waiting for me to take the wine glass from his outstretched hand. "Where did you just go?" he asked me quietly.

"I wondered what kind of animal you shapeshift into," I said with forced cheerfulness, in hopes that a smiley tone would cover for the still-pounding heart.

"What kind of— what? No," he seemed to shake himself. "Never mind."

Whew. I raised my glass to him. "Cheers," I said, taking a sip.

He drank from his own glass, and I thought I heard him murmur, "Jaguar."

That did it. The fact that he could play with the sheer nonsense I came up with was the battering ram that took down the last piece of self-defense I had. I exhaled, winced at myself for what I was about to do, and then said the words that had been pushing their way forward since we'd left the museum.

"Want to see something cool?"

# [ 21 ]
## DARIUS

*"The handwriting on the wall might be a forgery."*

— REZA MASOUD

I studied the painting of Madame Auguste Manet that lay on the kitchen table in front of me. Anna stood back, holding the now-empty portfolio.

"Come and tell me what you see here," I said, indicating the painted canvas. I wasn't accusing her and deliberately kept my tone of voice mild.

She stood beside me, and I pretended not to notice how close she was. Then my gaze returned to the painting.

It was beautiful. Not the subject, because no matter how well-painted Madame Auguste was, she would never be a lovely woman, but the art itself. Manet had caught the tension around her mouth, the fine hairs of a dark mustache on her upper lip, and the disapproving lift of her right brow. She was slender and looked small, even slouchy, in her chair, and the fat sausage rolls of her hair didn't look like they'd have been in fashion even then. And yet, the black satin of her mourning gown gleamed against the black wall, and the gold of her rings shone with only slightly less fire than the light in her eyes.

"The brush strokes are long and loose, and her skin tone has the flat light of a photograph," she said. "My mother calls this style early modernism. Everything about it seems impossible." The last words left her in a whisper.

"What does?" I watched her eyes as she looked up into mine. There were flecks of gold in the irises that seemed to glitter in the light.

She shook her head.

"What's impossible?" I persisted.

She exhaled. "It's impossible that this painting could look so much like a Manet. I mean, obviously it's in his style, but *Madame Auguste* was bought in 1920 and has been hanging in the Gardner collection since then."

"Not so impossible, really, if you consider digital photography," I said thoughtfully. "Theoretically, someone could paint this from a photograph."

She looked sharply at me. "So, it must be a copy."

"You tell me," I said simply.

"I can't. I don't know." She blew out a frustrated breath and then picked up her wine glass. She stepped back from me and took a sip.

"What *do* you know?" I asked casually.

"I found it," she finally said, studying the red wine in her glass. It seemed to pain her to say the words, and then they tumbled out as if she had no control over them. "It was hidden behind another painting on the same stretcher."

There it was ... and yet wasn't. She seemed unable to hide the truth from me, and yet it wasn't the whole truth. It was too much to ignore, and not enough to condemn, and every word she uttered stabbed me with the certainty that this was somehow a part of the theft at the Gray mansion. I studied her for a long time. "What else do you know about it?"

This time she met my eyes directly. "The edges of it were left behind on the stretcher – about half an inch, I'd guess. It was stuck to the back of the other painting."

My heart sank and lifted at the same time. There'd been another set of edges behind the painting that had been stolen from Gray, but this was just one more piece of circumstantial – not damning – evidence that she was *giving* me. Giving freely rather than having it wrestled or tricked from her. And despite my warring thoughts, all I could see were eyes the color of the sky on a stormy day, with flecks of light that shone through dark gray clouds. I wished I could see into her brain, to know her thoughts, to understand her, but I couldn't seem to find my way past her eyes.

"I find hidden paintings pretty intriguing, don't you?" I finally said.

"As it happens, I do." She breathed deeply, as if she'd been holding her breath before that moment.

"I'm inclined to see if the Manet is back in public view tomorrow and perhaps study the two paintings side by side," I said, still in the casual tone of voice I'd adopted to cover all the questions I wasn't asking.

"We could go tonight."

"No," I said sharply, "we can't."

She smiled slowly as she took another sip of wine. "You're no fun."

My gaze narrowed. "You were joking?"

Her smile got bigger. "Maybe." She shrugged. "Probably."

She finished her glass of wine and stepped around me to tuck the painting back inside its portfolio. Then she slung her messenger bag back across her chest and turned to face me.

"Thank you for the tacos and the wine. I'm going to go find a place to sleep now, and I'll meet you back at the Gardner when it opens. Cool?"

Apparently, she could read faces, because I hadn't realized I'd been so transparent until she nodded as I walked her to the door.

"Good choice. Not trusting me to show up would have been a bad move, and definitely would have pushed all my 'you're not the boss of me' buttons. Also, you're still pissed because you feel like I lied to you, and I get that. So, have another glass of wine. I'm going to stop off at the taco truck for more *carne asada*, because I haven't hit my taco limit yet. Come to think of it, I don't think there is a taco limit – at least not an enforceable one."

I smiled at that, but it was a fleeting thing. I didn't trust her, and that bothered me. The part of me that wanted to invite her to stay was silenced by the part that wondered if it was because I was attracted to her or because I didn't trust her not to run. Neither was acceptable under the circumstances, and she seemed to know it.

"Anyway," she said brightly, "have a good night, Darius. Dream about things that make you smile."

When I closed the door behind her, I had no idea what those things could be.

I poured myself another glass of wine and sat down at the table where the painting of Madame Auguste Manet had been. I could still catch hints of Anna's scent in the air. It was disturbing, disconcerting, and utterly distracting – just like her. My concentration had been shot since I spotted her in the museum courtyard, and I couldn't seem to focus on more than one thing in any given moment: the tone of her voice, the riot of curls and the way the light shone in her eyes. I was in danger of becoming a poet's nightmare of bad verse and trite metaphors, and through it all I was still so *angry*.

Angry at having been lied to, angry that she was a thief, and angry that I was so fucking attracted to a liar and a thief.

My cell phone rang, and I was surprised to see the Cipher office number onscreen.

"Masoud," I said as I answered.

"Darius, it's Shane. You're on a speaker with Jorge, and we're down in his Swordfish lair at Cipher."

"It's almost midnight. You should be home with your man and that ridiculous beast who vaguely resembles a dog," I said, happy for the distraction from the noise in my head.

"I know, right?" Jorge said with a grin evident in his voice. "But he's not really my man, and this task-master won't let me leave until she tells you what I've been digging up."

The sound of a playful punch carried through the speaker phone. "Hey!" Jorge complained.

"Shut it, genius," Shane said impatiently, and then apparently to me she added, "We've been digging for information on your twins."

*My* twins. No, they weren't mine, *she* was. Except she wasn't. She was a suspect in the burglary of a home protected by one of my security systems. That was all.

I realized Jorge was talking, and I had to focus on his words to hear them. "...hard to find the public record connection between Anna and Colette Collins. It was tough to even link them together as sisters, much less as twins. They were born in a little coastal town in Massachusetts that still has all their birth records on microfiche, and they haven't lived in the same city for a decade."

"Were you able to use the tracking device I slipped in her bag?" Shane asked.

"I waited until she was on the move again before we called," added Jorge.

I settled back in my chair. Shane had been a private investigator before she came to work for Cipher, and Jorge was her genius neighbor whom I'd met when he was just eighteen. They worked together with a shorthand that was similar to how Shane worked with Gabriel, and I realized I was a little jealous of their easy relationship.

"Darius?" Shane asked.

"Sorry. She was at the Isabella Stewart Gardner Museum to investigate the thirty-year-old heist."

"What? She said she was going out of town for a bounty," Shane said.

"Apparently the guy had some information on the Gardner heist that he wanted to trade for his freedom. She turned him in to Boston P.D., then went to the museum to learn more. I found her there, and when the museum closed, we came back here."

The apartment was one that Cipher Security kept available for its agents who traveled to Boston for work. Dan O'Malley was from

Boston, and Cipher still had several clients in the city. The fact that the apartment was a block from the museum was a happy accident for my purposes.

I traced the etching in my wine glass. "There may be some connection between the painting stolen from the Gray mansion and one hanging in the Gardner Museum."

"What kind of connection? That painting wasn't of any particular value that we know of, was it?" I could hear Jorge's computer keys clattering in the background as Shane spoke.

"I don't have proof of anything substantial, and my suspicion is purely a gut level thing, but the vehemence of Sterling Gray's refusal to call in the police feels like there may be something else to the story of the painting, its provenance, or what it may have been hiding."

"And you developed this theory after your evening with the sister of your thief?"

"Actually, I'm afraid the sister *is* the thief, but I can't prove it." Suddenly, I remembered a bit of conversation from earlier. "Jorge, can you dig into the twins' family? Apparently their mother went to MassArt, which is right around the corner from the Gardner."

"All roads lead to Boston, huh?" Shane said.

"Something like that," I answered.

"I'll get you whatever I can find on the family," Jorge said over the clatter of his computer keyboard.

"I asked Quinn to have Alex look into the client, Markham Gray. Maybe you could do that too?" I said.

Shane answered. "Apparently the senior Gray is heading to Boston from Europe as we speak. Quinn's trying to set up a meeting for you, and Dan may go there to help facilitate."

"That would be good. I appreciate Quinn and Dan taking my request seriously."

Shane snorted. "We all know what happens when we start investigating the clients, don't we?"

I smirked, remembering the case that brought her into Cipher. She'd been investigating one of our clients for infidelity, and it turned out he was guilty of much more than just cheating on his wife. "Quinn has governments on his client list now. It's in his best interests to cut out any criminal element that might be hiding in the shadows," I said.

"There are no shadows deep enough to hide from me," Jorge said in the background. He already sounded distracted by whatever he was searching up on his computer.

"Let me know if you need any other help, Darius," Shane said quietly. "Gabriel and I just finished a case, so we have some time."

"Thanks, I appreciate it." I didn't usually work with a partner because in my specialty, it was just me, the electricians, and the engineers. Investigation was something new to me. "Shane?"

"Hmm?"

"What did you think of Anna when you met her?"

Something in the question or maybe my tone must have inspired the smile I heard in Shane's answering voice. "I liked her. She's smart and funny and weird enough to be friends with Sparky. He wanted us to meet because he thought we'd have a lot in common."

"Was he right?" I asked, thinking about the strength, grace, athleticism, and fierce intelligence of my colleague.

"Yeah, I think he was."

# [ 22 ]
## DARIUS

*"Game shows are designed to make us feel better about the random,*
*useless facts that are all we have left of our education."*

- FROM THE T-SHIRT COLLECTION OF ANNA COLLINS

Anna handed me a cup of black coffee when I met her in the courtyard of the Gardner the next day. "You didn't have any cream or sugar on your boat, so I took a chance and left it black."

I had the sudden flash of her naked body sprawled in satisfied sleep on my bed, and I was disturbingly glad to think that she had taken the time to know things about me.

"Your powers of deduction are strong."

She grinned. "Comes with the job."

I soaked in her smile as though it had rays of sunlight in it, and I allowed myself to relax in the knowledge that Anna had kept her word. She'd met me, as planned, and she seemed to have lost some of the wariness she'd worn around me, almost as though she'd surrendered it. Her smile gave me permission to relax some of the tension I'd been carrying around her too.

She carried the portfolio on a strap over her shoulder, and I wondered if she had checked her messenger bag or left it wherever she'd slept last night, which made me wonder where she'd slept, which made me wonder if she slept naked. I changed the subject of my thoughts with a question to her. "Speaking of your work, what happened with the case that brought you to Boston?"

She shrugged. "I stopped by police headquarters this morning where a very nice officer named Kennedy, who takes his coffee with cream, four sugars, and almond flavored syrup by the way, assures me I'll get credit for his arrest. Boston P.D. is cutting a deal with the Connecticut D.A. They wouldn't let me see Junior, so I still don't know what he told them about the heist, but I have a call in to a friend of a friend at *The Globe* to fill in the blanks from my internet research."

"Newspaper friends and very nice officers are useful in your line of work, I'd imagine. And coffee is a standard bribe?"

Her smile seemed genuine. "Coffee, whiskey, donuts … it's not too hard to figure out the little ways to grease the wheels."

I rubbed the back of my neck to get rid of the prickle of unease the words inspired. I had always been uncomfortable with the culture of favors because I'd grown up hearing about all the ways it could be abused.

Anna's head canted to the side. "That bothers you." She nodded as if it fit some version of me she'd decided on.

"I've seen the worst sides of small favors."

"In the security business, or someplace else?" We'd sat down on a bench to drink our coffee, and I considered her question for a long moment before answering.

"My parents were journalists in Iran. They and some of their friends belonged to the Iranian Writer's Association, which was openly critical of the Iranian authorities. Because of the IWA's fight against censorship, it was banned shortly after the Islamic Revolution of 1979, but members managed to get around the ban by meeting for dinner at each other's homes. Our home was always full of writers, poets, and journalists, and it seemed as though every conversation involved discussions of exposing the rampant practice in Iranian society of offering favors and bribes to government officials who had one hand out and the other on their gun. In 1996, a bus of IWA writers was nearly driven off a cliff – twice – and two years later, a series of brutal murders of IWA members became known as the Chain Murders. An investigation revealed there were similar deaths stretching back ten years, and all the deaths appeared to be linked directly to ministers inside the government."

I finally looked up from the paper cup in my hands to see Anna's eyes, wide with shock, watching me.

"So, my parents left Iran when I was seven and my brother was three. They left because they could no longer tell the truth and expect to survive it."

I finished my coffee and stood to throw the cup away. Anna had huddled herself on the bench with her feet up and both arms wrapped around her knees. She looked up at me with still-wide eyes.

"I'm sorry for what they experienced," she said quietly.

I shrugged in an attempt to appear unaffected by the fact that I had just told a virtual stranger more about my family than I'd shared with anyone in years.

"I'm sorry that they had to leave their home to keep you safe."

"Me too," I said. "Not that I remember much about living in Iran, but I do realize how much they gave up. Intellectuals, no matter how privileged their former lives were, are just immigrants in another country."

Those were exactly the conversations I didn't have out loud, which was why my voice sounded too bright in my ears when I said, "Not a comfortable subject, in my experience. Let's go inside, shall we?" I held a hand out to her to help her rise from the bench. It was unnecessary and overkill, but it made me feel better to touch her for a moment as she stood.

"To the Blue Room?" she asked as she dropped her coffee cup into the bin.

"It's either that or we have to talk our way onto the fourth floor," I said, less jokingly than I was comfortable with.

She waved her hand airily. "I have a plan for that."

"I don't want to know," I said with genuine feeling.

Her smile was wide, and I enjoyed seeing it far too much. "Good. Because I'm not going to tell you."

We were walking down the West Cloister toward the Blue Room when Anna suddenly stopped in front of a planter full of daffodils. "Do you think any of the worms are left over from the dead guy who used to sleep in this?"

I stared at her for a shocked moment. "Well, that's a remarkably disturbing thought," I said when I realized that the planter was in fact a repurposed sarcophagus.

"I think it would be exceptionally cool to meet a worm descended from one who had eaten Socrates." There was a glint in her eyes that didn't bode well for decorum.

"Don't say it," I warned as we passed a man whose expression was the picture of pomposity.

She grinned mischievously. "Who else could reasonably say they'd gotten inside his head?"

I couldn't help the laughter, and the ridiculousness of it made me feel lighter. But Anna wasn't done. She added, "Which begs all the questions about zombie worms, and whether we are who and what we eat, and if so, shouldn't there be hemlock growing in there?"

"Hemlock?" I asked, helpless against the laughter.

"It's how they killed Socrates."

"Why do you know that?"

She smirked. "Why don't you?"

"What else do you know that I don't?" I demanded, trying and failing to control the smirk on my own face. She seemed to accept my challenge though, because she stopped and considered me for a moment before answering.

"Three percent of the ice in Antarctic glaciers is made up of penguin pee."

She delivered the fact with a completely straight face, and I bit the inside of my cheek to keep the smile at bay. "I didn't know that."

"The reason Queen Elizabeth I had such elaborate scrollwork

under her signature was to fill the page so no one could add anything else to the document she signed."

This time my eyebrows arched in surprise. "Seriously?"

She grinned. "One more and you buy me an ice cream?"

"Sure, if you think you can stump me." In fact, it fascinated me that she knew such random and obscure bits of information, and I found myself revising my expectations about Anna Collins.

"Okay, who is the biggest tire manufacturer in the world?" Anna bounced on the balls of her feet, and her excitement lifted something heavy from my chest.

"Hmm, Goodyear? They have the blimp after all."

"Nope." Her grin was huge, and I couldn't help the answering smile. "It's LEGO. They make fifty percent more tires than Bridgestone or Goodyear." She held out her hand to shake mine. "I like really good gelato, or anything chocolate, just so you know."

I gestured for her to precede me into the Blue Room as I asked, "Internet or books?"

"Both," she smiled happily. "I especially love everything in *Atlas Obscura*. I plan my trips around the random stuff they write about."

"You like to travel?"

"I love to travel. I've never actually lived any place longer than six months because I get itchy and want to explore." She stopped suddenly and stared at the wall where Madame Auguste now hung. "Oh!"

My gaze followed hers as I tried to ignore the hollowness her words had provoked. How long had she lived in Chicago? And how soon would it be time for her to move on?

I followed her to the painting Manet had made of his mother and studied Anna for a few stolen moments while she studied the painting.

She looked free, as though she were only slightly domesticated. Her hair was riotous, her skin was bare of make-up except for some smudges of old mascara that served to make her eyes look smoky rather than unwashed, and her uniform of jeans, boots, a T-shirt, and a man's jacket was perversely feminine.

"So, do you have any other cases to do here?" I asked, so that I didn't ask about when she planned to leave Chicago.

She shook her head as she studied Madame Auguste. "Nothing on the books. I'll put the word out that I'm on the East Coast and find out if any of my regulars have work for me here. Are you seeing this?" Her voice had a breathless quality that finally turned my attention to the painting in front of us.

*Madame Auguste Manet* was hung high on the wall in an ornate gold frame, which made the painting all the more imposing. It was difficult to discern the details in her face, but the skin of her hands and the details of the cuffs of her dress seemed identical to the painting that Anna carried in the portfolio on her shoulder.

"It's beautiful," she breathed as she studied the delicate black lace peeking out from beneath an inky sleeve. The long strokes just visible in the black on black paint blended with enough white to mimic the sheen of silk.

She turned to me with wide eyes and whispered, "We have to see them side by side."

My eyes darted around the Blue Room, empty now but for a bored docent near the door. Anna's gaze followed mine, and she thought for a moment, then handed me the portfolio and strode off toward the man. "Excuse me," she called, in an apologetic tone. Her voice dropped to something conspiratorial, and when they bent their heads together to speak, I quickly removed Anna's painting from its case.

I held it up to compare the two paintings. Anna's had clearly been cut from its frame, but the image was the same size as the Manet on the wall above me.

"There, the brush strokes are the same," Anna whispered at my shoulder. Her return to the Manet corner of the Blue Room had been completely silent, and I looked over my shoulder, expecting the docent to be glaring at us.

"He's gone to get maintenance to plunge the toilet. We have about three minutes. Hold it close and I'll photograph what I can."

Her voice was quiet and yet totally confident, and her phone was already in her hand aimed at the Manet on the wall.

Two minutes later, we strolled out of the Blue Room and ducked behind a pillar as the confused docent hurried back into the now empty room.

I knew there were cameras in the Blue Room, but I also knew they weren't manned, and therefore, unless something went missing, the recordings wouldn't be reviewed by human eyes. With Anna's painting stowed safely back in the portfolio that hung over my shoulder, we strolled back out to the museum café and grabbed a table in the corner of the big, wide-open room.

Anna sat down and pulled out her phone to scroll through the photos she'd taken of the two paintings. She enlarged each one and studied them for several minutes before she handed the phone to me.

"They're identical," she said.

"There are lots of ways they could be different." I wasn't exactly sure what I was arguing for, because the certainty about my purpose here had begun to slip since I'd seen Anna again.

"You're right. Canvas, types of pigment, age, x-rays to show progression ..."

She reacted to the surprise that must have been on my face. "My mom's an artist, remember? She actually restores paintings for a living. That kind of stuff tends to seep into dinner conversations, you know?"

This woman continued to surprise me. I felt as though I wore a perpetually startled look whenever I was with her. "Your mother restores art? Would she be able to tell when your Manet was painted?"

Anna scowled. "It's not my Manet. I told you, I found it."

I stood up before I said something I'd regret. "I know it's not gelato, but will ice cream from a café do?"

She gave me a side-eyed glance. "If you want bites of ice cream sandwich, you get your own, because I'm not sharing."

I shrugged, barely suppressing the grin her petulant-five-year-old expression inspired. "I'm getting a 50/50 bar. I don't want your ice cream sandwich anyway."

Her side-eye turned speculative. "What's that?"

"Really? You mean there's something I know that you don't?"

She rolled her eyes and pulled out her phone. "Not for long."

"Okay fine. It's a vanilla ice cream bar with an orange popsicle coating outside. You can get the same effect, only better, if you mix frozen concentrate orange juice into a bowl of vanilla ice cream."

Anna wrinkled her nose, then seemed to reconsider. "Sweet and sour. Yeah, I get it. Kind of like you." She flashed me a giant grin and I chuckled all the way through the line to buy our ice cream.

# [ 23 ]
## ANNA

*"Being a reporter is as much a diagnosis as a job description."*

- ANNA QUINDLEN

Questioning the museum docents about the Manet seemed pointless in light of the fact that nothing with Madame Auguste was amiss, and they definitely didn't want to talk about the heist. They all just seemed to answer with rehearsed phrases about focusing on all the amazing art still in the building, even though the empty frames on the walls practically begged for heist questions. I wanted to talk to Crystal, the lovely young MassArt student, but she wouldn't be in until after two p.m., so I checked the portfolio into the museum coat check, then returned a call to my D&D friend Taylor's contact at *The Boston Globe*. That was how Darius and I came to be seated across from a guy nicknamed Double D, whose byline was Dave DeAngelis, and who had been writing for *The Globe* since 1988.

We were at a small table in the back of a bar that could have been the set of any mob movie from any period of American history in the past hundred years. D, which is how he'd introduced himself, had a pint of some very dark beer in front of him. Darius had ordered a lager, and I had a glass of some Italian red wine that didn't look like it would leave me with a purple tongue. We sat in the nearly empty bar listening to D lay out the timeline of the Gardner Museum heist.

"First, you should know that Isabella Stewart Gardner left an endowment for the museum when she died, the terms of which stipulated that nothing could be changed. The board of directors took that to heart and didn't install the upgraded security that other museums were doing at the time. They also couldn't afford to insure any of the artwork in the museum. Besides infrared motion detectors and four cameras outside around the perimeter of the building, the only security at night was provided by a twenty-three-year-old guard named Rick and a twenty-five-year-old guard named Randy who were paid just slightly more than minimum wage."

D had a great voice, and I wondered if he had ever done any radio news. I didn't think he'd done TV because he didn't have that news anchor face. His face was more guy-in-a-dark-bar-talking-about-thieves. I looked over at Darius and was oddly pleased to realize he was as intrigued by D's story as I was.

D took a big swallow of beer and gave us equal attention as he continued his tale. "The thieves – two men dressed in Boston P.D. uniforms – were witnessed by some St. Patrick's Day drunks at about 12:30 a.m. parked in a hatchback about a hundred yards from the entrance to the museum. At 1:20 a.m., the thieves pulled up outside the side entrance, parked, walked to the door, and rang the buzzer, which connected them to Rick, the twenty-three-year-old guard. Rick let them into the side entrance where he was told to call Randy down from his rounds. When Randy arrived, both guards were restrained with handcuffs, at which time the thieves indicated they were there to rob the place. The guards were then marched down to the basement and cuffed to a steam pipe and work bench."

"Were the guards investigated for collusion?" Darius asked.

"Absolutely. And it's generally assumed that Rick's movements during his shift just prior to the thieves' arrival may have had something to do with preparation for the robbery. I've read a blog post with FBI photos that indict Rick as an accomplice, but no conclusive proof was ever found, and at the time the FBI believed the two guards were too incompetent to have pulled off the crime."

"The motion detectors must have left a record of movements through the museum, correct?" Darius continued. He was listening as a security systems expert, and the reminder of our relative positions on the subject of art theft made me squirm a bit in my seat.

D nodded. "It took eleven minutes to subdue the guards, but the first movement in the Dutch Room wasn't recorded until thirteen minutes after that. There, they smashed the glass on two Rembrandts, *The Storm on the Sea of Galilee* and *A Lady and Gentleman in Black,* by throwing them on the marble floor, then cut the canvases off their stretchers."

If D noticed the look Darius shot me, it didn't halt his story. I noticed it though, and the look sent a slithery feeling down through my stomach which subdued any butterfly that dared take flight at how close we sat to each other.

D continued. "Three minutes later, one of the thieves left the Dutch Room and went down the hall to the Short Gallery where he tried to steal the Napoleonic flag, but he couldn't manage the screws, so he just took the finial from the top of the flagpole. The other thief joined him there, and they also took five Degas sketches from that room. From the Dutch Room they took Vermeer's *The Concert,* Flinck's *Landscape with an Obelisk,* a small Rembrandt self-portrait, and a Chinese vase. The final painting that was stolen, and the one most confounding, was a Manet from the Blue Room."

The slithery feeling wound around my spine when Darius *didn't* look at me and instead leaned forward intently. "Which Manet, and why was it confounding?"

D sat back and finished his beer in a long gulp. Darius raised his hand to the bartender for another and avoided my eyes as he focused his attention on the craggy-faced reporter in front of us.

"You've seen the small empty frame under the larger Manet in the Blue Room?" he asked us. We both nodded. "That used to hold a painting called *Chez Tortoni.* The entire painting, frame and all, was removed from the wall the night of the theft, but the frame was left on the museum director's chair, and the motion detectors recorded no footsteps in the Blue Room while the thieves were in the museum."

The bartender set another dark beer on the table in front of D, who raised it in a toast to both of us. "Eighty-one minutes the thieves spent in the Gardner Museum that night. Eighty-one minutes with no police, no security cameras, and no guards to interfere. The side door was finally opened at 2:40a.m. and again at 2:45a.m., after the thieves took time to remove the cassette tapes from the perimeter camera feeds and data printouts from the motion detectors."

"The hard drives were still in place though, I assume?" Darius said.

"They were, which is how we have the timeline we have. The thieves also made a point to check on the guards to make sure they were comfortable before they left with thirteen stolen artworks."

"No leads on who the thieves were or where the artwork ended up?" I asked. I didn't look at Darius, but my foot accidentally brushed against his under the table, and I nearly jumped from the electric current that passed between us. I was acutely aware of his profession, his attractiveness, and his interest in the story D was telling us – all of which made him completely, dangerously compelling.

The veteran reporter shrugged, clearly blind to the tension that had been building between Darius and me. "There's always Whitey Bulger to blame, especially now that he's dead."

I barked a laugh that seemed to startle both men. "Did you know that Whitey hated his nickname? He preferred to be called Jim – which is a *terrible* name for a mob boss-turned-FBI-informant, by the way. Also, he did three years in Alcatraz, but liked it so much there he went back as a tourist with his girlfriend. And when he was in prison in Alabama, he volunteered for the CIA's MKUltra program to take time off his sentence. They injected him with LSD as part of a mind control experiment. He didn't know that's what they were doing – nobody did – and when he found out, he made plans to assassinate the guy in charge of the program."

D leaned back in his chair and chuckled in appreciation. "I knew about Alcatraz and the nickname, but not about MKUltra. You a journalist?"

"No," I said happily, giving myself a point for stumping the reporter, "I just don't sleep much."

D looked at Darius as if checking for confirmation, and I wasn't sure whether to be insulted or complimented by it. Darius had a strange look on his face, and his knee brushed against mine, zinging me with another electric shock.

"Well," D said, still chuckling, "there were a lot of dead ends, a couple of mob connections, and a chop shop or two that were investigated. Consensus now seems to be that the heist was probably planned as a way to get insurance against prison time."

"Insurance against prison time?" I asked.

D shrugged. "Mid-level mob doesn't have the connections to move big money art. But they could use it to negotiate a deal when they got caught for stupid low-level stuff that carried stiff sentences."

I looked at Darius, and his eyebrows had risen as high as mine had. "Just what Junior tried to do."

D's eyes narrowed. "You have something new on the heist?"

I shook my head. "I had a bounty offer me some info if I'd let him go."

"You didn't take it?" D practically gasped.

"I'm a bounty hunter, not the D.A. I don't make deals with bail jumpers," I said sharply. That earned me a speculative look from Darius and a frown from D.

"Well, if you ever do stumble on something solid about the Gardner heist, I'd appreciate a call. It's one of the Holy Grail stories for Boston reporters."

Darius stood, and when I started to get up, he pulled my chair back in a total Disney prince move. "We appreciate your time, Mr. DeAngelis, and if anything does come up, we'll certainly call you," he said.

I took out my card and wrote a name on the back of it. I handed it to D and said, "This is the name of my bail jumper. He's worried about his mom because his sister has had some trouble. If you want a crack at Junior's information, I'd suggest playing a compassion card with him. You might have some luck."

D took the card with a grateful nod. "Thanks. I appreciate the tip." Then he shook Darius's hand and pulled a black-and-white photograph out of his coat pocket, which he handed to me. "Here's one of the original crime scene photos of the Dutch Room. *The New York Times* reprinted it as part of a book review in 2015. It's hard to find online without a direct link."

I glanced at the photo, and my gaze slid right past the two frames and smashed glass on the floor to the open wall panel. "There's a door on that wall?"

D settled back in his seat and lifted his beer to us in a toast. "There used to be."

The docent in the Dutch Room was a friendly middle-aged woman named Amber, whose short, spiky hair was tipped in a deep red that matched a beautiful knit scarf she gathered closed with an Irish cloak pin.

I stopped to admire Amber's pin in a tactical move to open a dialogue, while Darius strode across the room to examine the fabric-covered panel behind the empty frame that had held *The Storm on the Sea of Galilee.*

"I've heard there was a door behind that panel," I said to Amber, nodding to the place where Darius studied the wall.

"They turned it back into a window when they tore down the annex building," she said with a helpful smile.

"The annex?" I asked.

"Where they used to do restoration and repair on the artwork. Now that's all done in the new wing." Amber said.

Darius turned to join the conversation. "The hinges of the wall panel are cleverly concealed behind the fabric," he said to me.

"This door was only used when art pieces were moved in and out of the laboratory. The staff who worked in the annex used an outside entrance."

I opened my mouth to follow up with a pointed question about the night of the heist, but Darius beat me to the next sentence, which he uttered with perfectly casual interest that actually impressed me with its sincerity.

"Have you worked here a long time then?" He flashed his perfect Disney prince smile, and I had to shush the instinct to smile back, or throw myself on him, because both were real.

Apparently Amber was similarly affected, at least in the returned smile department. "I started as an intern—" she looked around with all the subtlety of a bad spy and whispered, "the year before the heist."

I saw the sharp glint of steel flash in his eyes as he upped the wattage on the princely smile. "You must know *all* the stories ..."

I could practically see the ellipsis hanging in the air after his words, inviting her to finish the sentence with *all* the stories.

Amber's smile faltered just a little bit as she leaned in closer to us to whisper. "We're ... discouraged from speaking about it. They actually give us a script to follow when people ask."

I totally called it. I leaned forward too. "What if we don't ask about that night at all? What if we just ask what it was like to work here that first year? I mean, you must have some great stories from that time. I know my mom does," I lied, totally not knowing anything at all about my mom's time working here. I was sure if I did the math, I could figure out when exactly that had been, but Darius's expression of approval as he looked at me completely prevented any mathing.

"Oh! What's her name? I might know her," Amber said, all traces of nervousness gone from her voice. I shot Darius a quick glance and he gave a tiny nod.

"Sophia Kiriakis. She was a student at MassArt."

Amber's expression scrunched up like she was struggling to remember. "I feel like I know that name, but I'm not sure."

"What about her sister, Alexandra? Alex Kiriakis."

Amber's eyes opened wide. "Alex? Yeah, I remember Alex. She went to all the parties."

I stared at Darius, then quickly shifted my attention back to Amber. "There were parties here, in the museum?"

"Oh yeah, almost every weekend. When the new museum director – she's gone now – when she didn't move into the fourth floor like all the others had, a couple of the guards started having impromptu jam sessions with their band out in the courtyard. It was pretty great, actually."

"It sounds like it. Kind of like the movie *Night at the Museum*, except without all the animals that come to life," I said, picturing Rembrandt stepping out of his portrait to go chat with the Madonna next door.

Amber laughed. "Oh the animals definitely came to life back then. There was one boy, one of Ricky's friends in the band, I think, who taught a couple of the others how to play sensor tag."

Another docent entered the Dutch Room and waved Amber over. Her expression shuttered. "Damn," she whispered under her breath. "It was nice talking to you both," she said in a professional voice as she walked toward the man who'd entered the room.

I watched her greet him carefully, and then I tugged Darius' hand. "Come on, we won't get anything else from Amber today. She's getting spanked for talking to us."

Darius glanced at the man, and I knew he understood. I took us on a circuitous route around the room, playing the happy tourist for the security people. It wasn't until we finally wandered out of the Dutch Room that I realized I still held his hand – or he held mine, I wasn't sure.

It was nice. Way more than nice. It was also electric, zingy, zappy, and confusing as hell.

He must have realized it too, because he dropped my hand like it was a live wire.

"Sensor tag?" I said, to crowd out the other words that my instinct for self-preservation prevented me from saying. "Like trip a motion sensor, and tag, you're it?" I took a step back from him so the current between us could diffuse.

"Exactly like that, I think." He considered the room for a moment, his eyes taking in every camera, every motion sensor, every fire alarm and sprinkler. "Come," he said finally, and walked down the corridor to the Short Gallery. Damn, he was sexy when he got all bossy and professional. I had to keep reminding myself that his profession was actually still diametrically opposed to my one and only foray into thieving, no matter how much fun this investigation of a thirty-year-old mystery might be. I also reluctantly reminded myself that the Gardner heist had nothing to do with Madame Auguste, and she was the whole reason I was at the museum in the first place.

But who was I kidding? Solving the old mystery was a game I could play that let me spend time with Darius without the risk that he'd have me arrested, and Darius seemed to prefer playing it too. So I followed him as we went in search of the next clue.

Once we were inside the small gallery, he studied the cabinets on either side of the room. "The pieces stolen from here were drawings from the cabinet and the finial from the top of the Napoleonic flag."

I watched him move around the gallery, his natural grace making the khakis and casual sweater he wore look expensive. I could be wearing an evening gown next to him and he'd still look more elegant. He wasn't especially tall – probably six feet or so – and his athleticism looked like it came from rowing or swimming rather than gym equipment. I thought I'd heard him say that his spirit animal was a jaguar. That felt right. He prowled the room with stealthy grace, and I found it ironic that he'd make a great thief.

Except I was the thief.

And even if thief wasn't my usual job, I had the brain, eyeballs, and a few of the skills of one, so maybe it was time to put all that criminal potential to use.

"What was the timeline of the heist?" I murmured to him as I came to stand next to him in front of the cabinet where the missing Degas drawings had been kept.

"If DeAngelis' information is correct, the sensors apparently logged quite a bit of back and forth activity between the Dutch Room and this one, but the Dutch Room had all the high-dollar-value paintings, and these were just sketches," he said quietly. The docent that stood just inside the Little Salon could see into the Short Gallery, but he was paying attention to a young couple with a toddler who wanted to touch all the tapestries.

My shoulder just barely touched Darius's arm as I studied the contents of the cabinet. "There's a Michelangelo in there," I said, pointing.

"And so many lovely little pocketable things, and yet they only took five drawings," he said.

"They must have had a list," I finally said. "Given to them by whoever planned the job. And if anything else went missing, it would come out of their cut."

Darius turned to me, studying my face as he thought about that. "Drawings are easily transported and easily hidden. But why this room? The thieves came all the way across this floor of the building to get here, and they went back and forth to the Dutch room several times, according to the motion sensors."

I went back to the door we'd entered and stood with my back to it. An older man with a cane excused himself and I let him pass by, then I studied the Short Gallery for a few seconds before walking across it to the window. The view looked down onto Palace Avenue and the main entrance, and suddenly I understood.

"This was the lookout station. One of them checked for police while the other grabbed the paintings from the Dutch Room."

Darius came to join me at the window. "Of course. Whoever planned this thing sent the thieves in here to watch for cops, and also gave them their list of drawings to take." He smelled so good that I had to take a half-step back, just so I didn't throw myself at him.

"It makes more sense that it was planned rather than opportunistic," I said, because talking was more socially acceptable than sniffing the man, "otherwise whoever was on lookout would have raided the cabinet for any drawing by a recognizable name. And Michelangelo is pretty fricking recognizable."

The ghost of a smile passed over his lips, and I gave myself one point for cleverness, one point for self-restraint, and a half a point for whatever it was that made the man's mouth twitch.

Darius's cell phone buzzed in his pocket. He checked the screen before muttering under his breath that he had to take the call. He left the room, and after a moment's hesitation, I followed him out. He was already walking down the stairs to the East Cloister where he finally paused at the railing that overlooked the courtyard.

I waited until he'd finished his call before I approached. He looked up from his phone with a serious expression.

"I need to go meet Markham Gray." His eyes searched mine, presumably looking for guilt. I had none where his client was concerned.

"Can I come?"

That surprised him, and I gave myself another point. "Why?" he asked.

I smiled. "I've heard he has great art."

Darius stared at me in complete shock for one very long moment, and then he burst into laughter. I gave myself three whole points and a very stern talking-to about falling for the opposition.

# [ 24 ]
## DARIUS

*"Is the collector of stolen goods more or less culpable than the thief?"*

– DARIUS MASOUD

I left Anna at the museum talking to the chatty young docent Crystal, who had just come back on duty, and met Dan O'Malley in the lobby of Gray's offices. The building had likely been a bank at one time, and just as Anna had surmised, there was art.

My art education was limited to the requisite undergraduate art history class, so I wasn't particularly well-versed in the styles and periods, but even to my untrained eye there didn't appear to be any particular method to Gray's collection, other than that everything in it could be attributed to a recognizable name. There was an O'Keefe hanging near a Warhol and what looked like a Miró near something that may have been a Sargent.

"You looking at the art?" Dan came to stand next to me and spoke quietly.

"If they're originals, they're worth several fortunes," I murmured back.

He shot me a quizzical look. "He's got the dough and the swagger. You think they might not be the real deal?"

I shrugged. "I've had some interesting debates about authenticity recently, and what I think is that I don't know nearly enough about the art world."

Dan gave our names to the receptionist, who could just as easily have been a model as an economist, and after a hushed phone call we were politely directed upstairs.

Another beautiful woman, this one slightly older than the receptionist, met us at the elevator.

"Mr. Gray is just finishing a call with his son," she said as she ushered us into an office that contained even more valuable art than the lobby had. To my eye the paintings were more classically European and would have fit right into one of the rooms in the Isabella Stewart Gardner Museum. Gray hung up the phone and came around his desk.

"It's good to see you again, O'Malley," Gray said as he shook Dan's hand. With me he was less jovial. I got a nod, not a smile, with my handshake. "Masoud, my son tells me your system failed."

I could feel Dan bristle next to me, but I kept my voice even and unaffected. "My system did exactly what it was designed to do. The thief exploited a weakness in the *type* of security it was, not in the system itself."

Markham Gray was in his late fifties and had the build of someone who still took his fitness seriously. His custom-made suit fit him perfectly, and everything from shoes to watch was designed to project class, elegance, and power. He was not a man who appreciated contradiction, no matter how mildly it was delivered.

He turned his attention back to Dan. "I expect that Cipher Security will find and return my painting to me."

"I understand the painting wasn't insured," I persisted. Gray either didn't know or didn't care that he was poking a bear by speaking to Dan as though he were an employee.

"You can't insure sentimental value," he snapped at me.

"Wiring and alarming a painting inside a panic room seems a bit more than sentimental," I said casually. The corner of Dan's mouth lifted wryly, but I didn't think Gray saw it. He was too angry at me to notice that Dan had started pacing around the room looking at the art in it.

"I knew the artist," he ground out through clenched teeth. "Her family will want to know the painting is safe."

"Is that so?" I didn't have to feign interest. "Perhaps I could speak to the artist directly?"

"She's dead," he said, with what sounded like anger.

"What's her name? Someone in her family might know something about the painting's disappearance."

He glared at me, and his right hand flinched as though he resisted clenching it into a fist. "Find the thief and you'll find the painting." His voice held menace, and Dan looked up from a Picasso sketch.

"Art's only worth what someone will pay for it, unless it's made of glitter paint and your kid did it in pre-school – then it's priceless. So either it's worth money, or someone thinks it's made of glitter. Tell us who the artist is, so we have a place to start," Dan said. It was a remarkably astute observation.

Markham studied Dan through narrowed eyes and didn't look at me at all. Finally he gave a quick shake of his head. "No, she doesn't matter. It was a long time ago, and if the painting's gone, it's gone. Now, get out of my office. You're fired."

Dan's eyes hardened, but he kept his expression neutral as he nodded once. "Right."

He looked at me and then quickly around the room, as though directing my eyes to all the things I'd already taken in - cameras aimed at all the art, and the faint red glow of the motion sensors in the doorways. The office art was better protected than the painting in the safe room had been, and I said as much to Dan when we were finally outside the building.

"He let the painting go too easily," Dan said. It wasn't an answer, but I'd felt the same.

"First the son pitches a fit to me about no police and threatens me with the wrath of dad, and then when we want to know more about the artist, we get told to leave it alone and mind our own business." I pulled my phone out to call for a ride and noticed a text from Shane. It was the names and address of Anna's parents in Rockport, MA.

Dan looked up at the building which housed Gray's office, a thoughtful expression on a face more suited to menacing glares. "He's hiding something big, and he's an asshole."

I thought about the break-in at the Gray mansion, and the woman who was likely a thief waiting for me at the Gardner Museum. She'd lied and then disappeared when her lie was discovered. She was embroiled in a mysteriously hidden Manet, and she continued to lie by omission about how she'd found it. I had enough proof from her own lips to go to the police, but not enough to get a conviction on the theft of a painting Gray hadn't insured and didn't want the police to know about.

"There are mysteries here – a couple of them. About Gray, about the woman who may or may not have stolen his painting, about the painting itself, and even about a thirty-year-old art heist that may have nothing to do with anything, but is damned compelling," I said to Dan, who raised an eyebrow but said nothing. "I have a couple of sick days accrued. I'd like to stay in Boston to look into some things here, if you don't mind."

Dan considered me for a moment. "You said the kid threatened you with Gray's wrath if the painting wasn't found, yeah?"

I nodded. "He implied that the senior Gray had connections in the Chicago press with which he wouldn't hesitate to smear Cipher."

He grunted and scowled in response. "I'm not taking your sick days. Sometimes you muzzle the fuckers with the law, and some-times you muzzle 'em with the truth." His gaze found mine again, and his smile had an edge to it as she shrugged. "He fired us. As far as I'm concerned, anything you find is a muzzle."

## [ 25 ]
### ANNA

*"Are you criminally-minded just because you can plan the crime?"*

- DARIUS MASOUD

C rystal was a delight. I spent the hour that Darius was gone trailing her around the museum as we whispered stories to each other about the art. Her imagination was enough like mine that we had a shorthand for our theories about why Isabella had hung certain pieces together, or what the placement of the different columns could mean.

She showed me her favorite corners, where she could stand and see into three completely different spaces, and I invented stories about the patrons who came through the rooms where she was supposed to be working.

"There are only really ten people in the world," I said under my breath as I practiced staying out of the line of sight of the cameras in the room, even though Darius had said they weren't manned. It was a habit – a game that I'd always played with myself. Spot the cameras, then avoid them, just because it's what Honor would do.

"Okay," she said, nodding to a patron who stood admiring the portrait of a beautiful redheaded woman who hung high on a wall of the Blue Room, "who's that?"

The patron was a handsome middle-aged man, and his gaze up at the painting was thoughtful as he stood for several minutes, utterly still.

"King Arthur, the Clive Owen version from the movie. He accidentally stepped through a time travel portal in the Tapestry Room and has been wandering around the museum trying not to freak out, until he came in here and saw the portrait of Guinevere. And now he wonders if he'll ever hold her in his arms again or if he'll be stuck in this awful time for the rest of his life."

Crystal tilted her head as she watched him for another moment before he finally moved on to Madame Auguste. "I can see that. And now he's making sure that the witch he imprisoned in the painting will stay locked in there."

I grinned at Crystal. "The subjects of the paintings walk the halls at night, don't they?"

"Totally," she said with utter conviction. "I would never want to work as a night guard, especially because—" she dropped her voice and looked around nervously, "because of the heist. I'm pretty sure the place is haunted now."

"You think?"

"Sure. I mean the guy in *Chez Tortoni*," she nodded toward the small empty frame that hung beneath Madame Auguste, "he flew out of the room without leaving a motion detector footprint behind."

"But the thief left his frame on the museum director's chair, right? That's kind of a big F-you to the establishment and is a little more rebellious than your average ghost." I said.

"Know a lot of ghosts, do you?" A voice came from behind me. His voice. Just hearing it brought back the sensory memory of his hands on me, his mouth kissing down my body. I shivered with it and met his eyes.

"Apparently, I do."

He had an odd expression on his face as he looked at me, and I felt unequipped to decipher it. Then he turned to Crystal with a smile. "I hope we didn't get you into trouble yesterday."

She smiled in return. "It's fine. They just don't like us to dwell on the heist, even though it's the thing that keeps the tourists coming in. Everyone wants to solve it, you know?"

Darius met my eyes for a brief, conspiratorial moment that I felt all the way down to my toes. "I admit to a degree of fascination with solving mysteries myself." I tried to ignore the stress his words inspired as he chatted with Crystal for a few more minutes. I impulsively hugged Crystal goodbye, then headed to the door.

I stopped in the doorway and looked down at the motion sensor just inside the frame. "Do you think this was the type of sensor they used thirty years ago?" I asked Darius.

He studied it. "If not this, then something similar."

"But the placement is right?" It was about set about seven inches above the floor.

"The sensor is aimed into the room. At that height, the average person wouldn't be able to jump over it and land outside the sensor's reach, so yes, it is adequately placed for the job."

I stepped back and looked at the door from outside of the room. "Look at that," I said, pointing to a decorative metal piece set above the door frame with a ring attached. I jumped up and grabbed it, ignoring Darius's stunned expression when I hung from it for a moment before dropping back to the floor. "I'd run a rope through that ring, get a running jump, and swing into the room over the sensor. It would be tougher to come back across carrying a painting, but *Chez Tortoni* was small, so maybe the thief tucked it under his shirt." I shrugged, then started down the hall toward the museum entrance and bag check.

When I realized Darius wasn't next to me I stopped and turned to face him. "What?"

He was looking at me in a way I couldn't interpret. Finally he shrugged and joined me. "Nothing," he said.

I was silent for a while as we walked in the cool Boston afternoon to my crappy rental car. "How was your meeting?" I finally asked.

"It was ... surprising," he said in a voice that told me it was all I was going to get.

I took a breath and bit back the snarl that threatened.

I had spent the night before in a hotel room as crappy as my car, definitely not sleeping because I alternated between the sweats (from stress) and heat (from thoughts of him). I had used up my quota of cheerfulness playing imagination games with Crystal, which had allowed me to spend more time in close proximity to Madame Auguste, but hadn't otherwise netted me new information. So I was tired.

"Feed me tacos, and I'll tell you a story," I said, in a bid to push tired and annoyed back into the closet.

I apparently surprised him, because it took him a minute to respond. "Have you ever had Iranian food?"

A little grumpiness fell off me and wriggled into the cracks in the sidewalk. "No. What is it?"

"Kebabs, stews, rice and vegetables. I don't know if you remember your seventh grade social studies lessons, but Iran was the original bread basket of the world."

"There are parkour schools in Iran just for women," I said. "And Iranians used to be able to vote at fifteen."

He smiled. "I actually knew that. Come," he turned down a different street, "I scouted a restaurant today that looks like it has good food. And maybe while we're eating, I'll tell you a story too."

# [ 26 ]
## DARIUS

*"Fairy tales are more than true: not because they tell us that dragons exist, but because they tell us that dragons can be beaten."*

– NEIL GAIMAN

She ate with her fingers, talked with her hands, and she laughed with her whole body.

I had been raised in a household with five-piece settings for every meal by a mother who forbade elbows and open mouths and conversation while chewing. My mother had perfect posture, perfect manners, and perfect etiquette, and she made very sure her sons did too.

The woman who sat across the table from me moaned in appreciation for the piece of grilled lamb she had just popped in her mouth with her fingers. She was so wrapped up in the eating and talking that she didn't notice that I hadn't been able to take my eyes off her lips.

"I've never met Markham Gray," she said, after licking her thumb clean. I shifted uncomfortably, but she didn't notice. "Colette knows Sterling, of course, because her ex was his architect."

"So that was all true?" I asked in surprise.

She shot me an eye-roll. "Of course. There's no way *I* could've scored an invitation to the Gray mansion. I'd never met the guy or his dad. I have to say, from everything I've read about the guy, Markham sounds like a jerk."

"He is. I'd never dealt with him face to face before today, but his reputation isn't helped by proximity."

She giggled and bit into an olive. "You speak like an English school boy." I raised an eyebrow, and she added, "The English are the best at making an insult seem like a compliment, otherwise known as baffling them with b.s. I bet you're good at it."

I smirked. "My mother said I should have been a lawyer."

She sipped her wine and added another lamb kebab to her plate. "A good lawyer knows the law, a great lawyer knows the judge."

"Exactly why I didn't go into law," I said, still struggling not to be distracted every time she licked her fingers.

"Did you ever want to be a journalist like your parents?" Her question caught me off guard. I'd been prepared for a discussion about Gray and his painting, not anything personal about me.

I thought about it for a moment as she watched me. "Investigation has always appealed to me, but I've never felt that I connect well enough with people to be good at anything that requires getting someone to open up to me."

"I think it wouldn't be hard for you to get people to trust you. You have principles – people like that. It's pretty rare to meet someone who knows what he stands for, and I think people would respond to it." She spoke the words as though they were obvious, as though everyone knew that what she said was true. It was a degree of certainty I'd never had about myself.

"Sometimes," I sighed, "I feel like my principles are all on paper."

She frowned as she considered me over the piece of pita that she was tearing into bite-sized pieces and dipping into toum, the Lebanese garlic sauce that came with the kebabs. I took a bit of my own food to distract myself from her mouth.

"You mean," she finally said, still frowning, "that you think they're a good idea, but you can't back them up?"

"Something like that," I said, surprised at the accuracy of her simple translation.

She thought for a moment. "I think belief is like that. You decide which ideas fit your world view, and you believe them." Then she shrugged. "Who's to say your principles are any more or less valid than the idea of the Ten Commandments or the Four Noble Truths? The point is that *you* believe them. If they work for you, and nobody else gets hurt because of them, that's all the back-up you need."

Her casual words felt solid and substantial in a way I hadn't expected from this woman whose exuberance couldn't be contained by something as corporeal as her skin. Her hair was evidence of that. It moved as though it was as alive as the rest of her – restlessly, relentlessly. I wanted to gather up the curls in my hand and then watch them slip through my fingers, just to see all the different paths they took to get free.

"What do you believe in?" I asked, completely aware of the potential minefield such a question presented.

She took a sip of wine and smiled.

"I actually made a list once, when I was sick and holed up in a hotel in New Delhi, contemplating the fact that my stomach seemed to rest on the bed outside my pelvis when I lay on my side. I think I was trying to decide if getting up for water was worth the effort, which was really just me figuring out whether *anything* was worth the effort of moving. I needed the list to remind me."

She held up her fist and ticked her statements off on her fingers. "I believe in throwing your hat over the wall and then figuring out how to get it. In saying yes, in making time, and in learning as you go. I believe that fear and excitement produce the same physical symptoms, so why not decide something is exciting instead of scary, and I believe that travel is the best education money can buy." She waggled the fingers of her open hand as if to make sure she had remembered everything, sat back in her seat, and only then did she take in the expression on my face. "You look surprised."

I shook my head, then nodded. "I didn't … I am."

Her smile slipped a little, and it made me inexplicably sad to see. "You don't agree. That's okay. That's the cool thing about believing in things; other people don't have to believe for it to be true for me."

"It's not that. I just … wish I believed as you do. I want to trust that I'll learn as I go, and to say yes even when I don't know how it could be possible. In my experience … I just don't."

"I'm sorry," she whispered, as though it actually were her fault.

I shook my head in wonder. "Where did you come from?"

She shrugged, and I could see confusion on her face. "From everywhere. Anywhere that would have me, really. I mean, I grew up in Rockport, but once I left home, I was gone. What about you? Where did you grow up?"

"Tehran. London. New York. Chicago." My voice sounded flat to my own ears. Each city had had its own culture and rules and structure, and I'd had to learn each one like a language in order to navigate life there.

"That sounds so much more cosmopolitan and sophisticated than Rockport, Boulder, Nevada City, and Zion," she said.

"And yet the view seems so much better from those places."

She smiled a little dreamily. "They do have pretty great views. Have you ever been to Zion? The colors in those canyons are surreal – like the earth was formed in a giant taffy pull from all the colors of the sunset. The sandstone isn't really great for climbing, but if you look for them, you can find just enough footholds to feel like you've fallen into a Willy Wonka candy world. Almost like you could lick the wall and taste lemon and orange and strawberry, except it would taste like fire and wind and the ripple of heat over the desert floor."

I felt as though I should only ever travel with this woman from now on – that her view of the world was so fascinating and unique that listening to a tourist guide would be a pale fragment of the experience I'd have seeing the world with Anna Collins.

But then the sound of her full name in my head pulled me away from visions of multi-colored taffy walls and back to the land of the larcenous Collins sisters.

"You said you grew up in Rockport?" I said with what I hoped was casualness.

The fanciful look in her eyes faded. "I promised you a story, didn't I?" Her tone was more statement than question, and I regretted that I'd caused the playfulness of her tone to disappear.

The waiter came to remove the plates, and I signaled him for the check. Anna noticed and pulled her wallet – a slim metal card case – from the back pocket of her jeans.

"You did," I said, noticing the way her eyes had gone stormy gray in the dim light of the restaurant.

"Once upon a time there was a family with two daughters," she began. She watched me as she spoke, but warily, as though she would run at any sudden movement. "One daughter grew up knowing she would become a princess, and her whole life was spent preparing for the job."

"Princess is a job?" I asked with a smile, because I hadn't been expecting a fairy tale.

"You've seen how hard Kate and Meghan work? And yeah, I know they're both duchesses, not princesses, and I know Meghan isn't doing the official gig anymore, but there are rules, and it's a job," she snapped back.

I held up both hands in surrender. "Sorry, please continue."

She sighed. "One sister was princess-in-training, so the other one became a thief."

My eyebrows shot up, and her eyes narrowed, but she otherwise ignored me.

"The thief was named Honor, and she wasn't really an actual thief, she just had mad thief skills. Everyone wanted to be friends with the princess, but a couple of the lesser-known villagers realized that the thief played the best games, and her hide-and-seek plans were always legendary. She was the best at capture-the-flag because she was ruthless and could anticipate every move the opposition would make. They called her a thief because she stole every game she played with the villagers, until finally even they wouldn't play with her anymore."

Anna paused to take a sip of water as I picked through her words looking for recognizable landmarks. Colette was the princess, obviously, which made Anna the thief, Honor. I might have smirked at the irony, but she wasn't laughing.

"Eventually, Honor learned to play games that didn't need playmates, and to use her thief's brain to catch real thieves rather than become like them. She traveled the world playing solo games and catching thieves and pretending it was enough."

She had her hands wrapped tightly around her wine glass and was swirling it gently to watch the red wine dance against the sides. Another man might have taken her hand to comfort the lonely girl she'd been. I wouldn't have taken her hand, even if one had been free, because that would have meant letting go of something I couldn't stop holding on to.

She exhaled and didn't meet my eyes as she continued speaking. "One day, in a hiding spot only she could find, she found a letter addressed to her containing a request that only she could fulfill. It was a quest, noble and honorable, and a way for a thief to distinguish herself. A treasure was hidden in a dragon's lair to keep its rightful owner captive. If Honor could take the treasure from the dragon, the captive could go free. Honor knew the history of the treasure, and she knew that it didn't belong to the dragon, so she decided that stealing from a thief wasn't stealing at all, especially if it freed someone she loved."

She looked at me then, and her eyes were sad. "But when she took the treasure from the dragon, she found another treasure hidden inside, and suddenly it felt very much like stealing, and maybe the dragon had been the thief, or maybe someone else had been, but she didn't know who the hidden treasure belonged to, and putting it back would be much, much harder than taking it had been. And so she was afraid."

"Of getting caught?" I asked carefully.

She smiled, not very convincingly. "Oh, she's Honor among thieves, and everyone knows that thieves are just one bit of bad luck away from getting caught."

She pushed herself back from the table and stood. "I should go find the waiter to pay my bill." Her voice caught, and it sounded almost like a swallowed sob.

"Anna, let me help you," I said quietly.

"You can't," she whispered. "You have principles that won't let you, and that's good." She smiled, and her lips trembled. "I'll let you pay for dinner though, thank you."

She tucked her little metal wallet back in her pocket as she strode through the restaurant to the door, wiping her eyes as she went.

# [ 27 ]
## ANNA

*"The minute you walk through that door you're no longer a guest,
so help yourself."*

- SOPHIA COLLINS

I needed to find someplace else to sleep. I sat in my crappy rental car where I had parked it for both of the days I'd gone to the museum and searched up *places to stay in Boston that don't make you itch.*

I disliked crying. I especially disliked doing it where anyone could see me. I was not a particularly tall person, but I was strong and athletic and could do enough things well that I rarely felt vulnerable – except when I cried.

Analyzing my distaste for tears was much easier than figuring out why I was upset, so I indulged in self-analysis while entering a new search for *comfy beds for cheap in the greater Boston area.*

Kids in America grew up with "cry like a girl" and "only babies and sissies cry" as the standard taunt for tears. The average girl could just shrug that off as par for the course. *I am a girl, ergo I cry like one.* Boys, tomboys, and girls who identified with the male gender generally had a tougher time with such teasing, as it was meant to belittle and hurt. I pretty much self-identified as a tomboy, mostly to counter my sister's girly-girl status, and as such, I didn't cry.

Except when I did.

I finally got a hit on *bed and breakfasts that don't break the bank in Massachusetts*, except it wasn't a Google search hit, it was a text.

Mom: Colette said you're in Boston. Come home.

Me: Hi Mom. Thanks, I will.

See? A hit. Bed, breakfast, and about sixty minutes and a world away from Boston. Plus laundry facilities and a place to send the underwear I'd be buying online.

I thought about stopping at the police station to check on Junior on my way out of town, but it was already dark and I was tired, and the prospect of bribing my way past cops who should know better than to take my bribes was a little more than I could handle after a dinner with the principled Disney prince.

Sigh. Why couldn't I have fallen for someone who saw the world with a few more shades of gray? Darius Masoud had the kind of principles that would never let him see what I'd done as anything other than the darkest black in a checkerboard world, and frankly, I felt as far away from the black queen as a player could get.

My phone paired with the rental car stereo, and as I drove out of downtown, it rang. I checked the number and hit the button that put me on speaker phone.

"Hey, Sister."

"Hey," she said. "How's Boston?"

"Weird," I said as I passed a cop who had pulled over a Chevy. I checked in with my conscience and it felt clean – no racing pulse or sweaty palms at the sight of the flashing lights.

"You're weird," she said automatically.

I smiled. "No, you." It was a game we'd played since we were kids, and playing it with her reminded me that I had – and was – a sister.

It was an antidote to *alone*.

"What'd you find out about the Manet?" she asked. The room had a slight echo around her.

"Dude, what if someone else had been in the car with me? And p.s., are you on the toilet?"

I could practically hear the eye-roll in her voice. "You're always by yourself, and I called you, which means I'm definitely not on the toilet. I'm doing my make-up."

"But if I'd called you and you were on the toilet, you would have picked up?" I tried to ignore her comment about my aloneness, but it stung.

"Even mid-push. That's how much I love you," she said, with the open-mouth sound that meant she was putting on mascara.

I laughed and gave her a point for it.

"So? What'd you find out about Madame Auguste?" she prompted.

"Well, she's not missing from the Gardner," I said, but even I could hear the lack of easy confidence in my voice.

"But ...?"

"But our Madame Auguste is pretty much a dead ringer for the one on the Blue Room wall."

There was silence on the other end of the phone. I tried to picture my sister studying her reflection in the mirror as she thought about what I'd said, but all I could see was *WTF* written all over her expression in black Sharpie.

"So one of them is a forgery," she said in a hushed voice.

"But which one?" I answered back as quietly.

"Dude."

"Right?"

Single word sentences were also in our communication style guide. Translation: *Are you freaking kidding me? How did we end up with a possible forged, or worse, real Manet painting?* Answer: *I know! I can't stand this much longer. What the hell are we gonna do?*

"Why would Mom and Alex stretch *The Sisters* over Madame Auguste – real or forged?" she finally said.

I hadn't had a chance to talk my theories through out loud with anyone because, of course, Darius was the only other person who knew about Madame Auguste, and we were still talking in fairy tales around each other where the paintings were concerned. "Well, either they reused a frame and just wanted the Madame August to stiffen up the canvas on their own painting, or they did it to hide Madame Auguste. Or *they* didn't do it."

"You think it's possible Markham Gray used *The Sisters* to hide a Manet?"

I shrugged as I pulled onto the expressway. "It was in his possession, and it was the only art hanging in his panic room."

"But why— no, never mind. If he's the one who hid Madame Auguste, it's probably because she was stolen," Colette finally said.

"And if Alex or Mom hid it, it's because they shouldn't have had it. The only explanation that doesn't get people into trouble is that it was just a copy on a frame that they re-used."

Colette was silent for so long that I thought the call had dropped. "You still there?" I asked.

"Yeah. I'm just wondering if I should ask Sterling about it."

"What? Why would you do that?" I had to swerve to avoid a dead raccoon in the road. Not because I had any particular affinity for raccoons, because I definitely didn't. They were trash pandas and chicken killers, and I sent a mental "That's right" to the universe, as I did whenever I passed a dead one. But this one was recently dead, which meant it would likely squish under my wheels unpleasantly, and at the rate my luck was going, I'd get a flat and then have to pick through raccoon guts to change the tire.

"I'm seeing him tonight," my sister said. Her voice sounded odd, or maybe it was just the words that sounded odd to my ears.

"I'm sorry, I was avoiding trash panda guts. Could you please repeat that?"

She sighed, and then sounded annoyed. "I'm going out with Sterling tonight. On a date. To a private gallery opening."

"Wow, he's actually taking you out in public?" You could have infected the whole state with the snottiness in my tone.

She hung up on me.

I counted to five and then the phone rang.

"Sorry, that was bitchy," I said when I answered.

"It was."

We stayed on the phone in silence for a long moment. I could hear her thinking. She could hear me grinding my teeth. It's what we did when we didn't want to say the thing that needed to be said, and it was also in our communication style guide. Finally, I took a breath and tried for calm.

"Do you have actual feelings for the guy? Because what you're doing is really dangerous, Sister."

"It's only dangerous if you get caught," she said. "And you won't, because you're smarter than they are. And besides, Sterling said they didn't even call the cops."

I thought about the grim expression on Darius's face when he set up his meeting with Markham Gray. "Why wouldn't they call in police?"

"I don't know, except his dad has been freaking out on him since the painting went missing, and now he's threatening to cut him completely off if he doesn't get it back. Basically, turn him out of the house, his job, the company - everything."

"Sterling's job isn't our problem." I said. Neither was Darius's job, I thought to myself, even as my conscience twinged.

"Are we sure Markham didn't have a right to *The Sisters?*" she asked.

"Mom and Alex painted each other, worked on the painting together, and then it disappeared. The artists are the owners of their art until they sell it. Mom didn't sell it, and Alex didn't have the right to give it away without her permission, so no, it wasn't Markham's to keep. And honestly, if he's that freaked out, it makes me think he's the one who hid Madame Auguste. Because let's face it, if our Madame Auguste is the real thing, she's worth millions."

Colette sighed the long-suffering sigh of the reasonable sister. "Well, maybe we should find a way to get Madame Auguste back to them if that's the reason Sterling's dad went psycho. Then the heat will be off."

I barked a laugh. "How do you propose I give it back? Should I break back in and staple her back into the frame? Or are you going to drop her off behind a dumpster at the mansion next time you go to Sterling's for a booty call?"

"Don't be ugly," she said.

"Don't be stupid," I snapped back.

"You're stupid," she snapped, but there was a hint of a reluctant smile sound in her voice.

"No, you," I groused. And then, because I was seriously sick of arguing with her, I said, "I'm on my way to Mom and Dad's."

"Tell Mom to look for a package from me," she said. "How long are you staying?"

"I don't know. If the police aren't looking, maybe I can come back to Chicago."

"What about the Cipher guy?"

Yeah, what about him? I heard his quiet words in my head – *let me help you*. I didn't need help; I was the strong one, I was the one who went on quests, the boy my dad never had. I didn't cry because thieves don't cry.

"The Cipher guy will do what he does, and I'll stay out of his way," I finally said.

"Well, give him a couple more days to forget about you," my sister said.

I swallowed the hurt, and then swallowed again to make my voice work. "Yeah." I let the sounds of the road fill my ears and numb my brain. "I'm going to do some more digging into Madame Auguste, maybe ask Mom for help. You know where to find me if you need me," I finally said.

The old-fashioned doorbell sounded in the background. "Just think about what I said, please. If it goes back, it's not our problem anymore." Colette disconnected the call and there was silence.

"Bye," I said to no one in particular, and the word tasted sour in my mouth.

# [ 28 ]
## ANNA

*"Show me where you're from and I'll tell you who people think you are."*

- FROM THE T-SHIRT COLLECTION OF ANNA COLLINS

My parents' house sat high above the rocky shore, but the windows in my old bedroom had been cracked open for fresh air, so I'd slept with the sound of the sea and woken up with the pale eastern light illuminating the familiar space.

I'd long since determined that I was a morning person. Growing up with an east-facing bedroom had probably been a major contributing factor to my tendency to rise with the sun. Colette's room was on the west side of the house, and she had taken those night owl proclivities and turned them into a thriving social life – something people who are usually in bed by nine don't have.

My dad had waited up the night before to make sure I made it home, so I doubted I'd see him for a few hours. I could hear mom in the kitchen, talking to her dogs. We'd always grown up with at least one dog in the house, but since Colette and I had moved out, mom had started fostering rescues for the local shelter. She said it was because our dad still traveled for work and she wanted the dogs for protection, but we knew it was for the company they gave her.

I pulled on yoga pants and one of my dad's T-shirts and padded downstairs in bare feet with a handful of my clothes. "Good morning," I said as I entered the kitchen. "Can I do laundry?"

"Good morning. Yes. Add it to the pile on the machine," my mom said while measuring out dog food into dishes on the counter.

I counted five dogs seated around her waiting with expectant faces for their food dishes. Two or three of them had looked over at me when I entered, but at least two – a beagle I didn't know and a black lab named Timmy – had eyes only for my mom.

"Help me with these, would you?" she asked, indicating two of the bowls.

I grabbed the bowls and followed her out to the sunroom that had been added onto the hundred-year-old house sometime in the fifties. With time it had become sort of a glorified mud room. Coats hung from hooks on the walls, and a line of boots and clogs stood sentry beneath them. A big orange construction bucket held umbrellas and walking sticks, and a stack of beach chairs leaned against one wall, with towels draped to dry over them.

"You can put those two over there for Conor and Lucas, the two corgis. They're brothers and they share everything, even if they have to wrestle for it," my mom said, indicating two handsome little corgis with wiggling tail stubs. She put bowls down for Timmy, the beagle, and a shepherd mix I vaguely remembered was called Maggie. "Come," she held her hand out to me when all the dogs were eating, "let's fill thermoses with coffee and take them down to the beach."

At the word "beach," Timmy looked up at mom and wagged his tail adoringly before finishing his food. She laughed and gave him a pat before heading back into the kitchen.

I got two thermos mugs out of the jumble of random coffee cups and promotional mugs mom saved from every convention my dad ever went to. He was a sales rep for several different building supply manufacturers, all the while living in a house that had been built before WWI and was in its original condition. She filled the mugs with fresh coffee from the pot, and I had just pulled on my dad's sweater when the doorbell rang.

All five dogs swarmed to the front door, barking like a pack of rabid hunting hounds, while Mom waded through them to open it. I'd started the laundry and gone back into the sunroom for a pair of clogs when Mom finally returned from the front. "Anna, there's someone here to see you," she said with a smile in her voice.

I looked up just as Darius entered the kitchen, herded there by several dogs and holding a large FedEx box. "You can just set that on the counter over there," Mom told him as she pulled a knife from the butcher block.

I stared at the scene in shock. "What are you doing here?" I gasped to Darius, somehow afraid my mom had pulled the knife on him. But then she got busy cutting into the FedEx box, and I could refocus my shock on its intended recipient, who looked far too handsome to be standing in the kitchen of my childhood home looking at yoga-pants-and-dad-sweater-wearing me.

"I actually came to talk to your mum."

*Oh, well that's better*, my brain sneered.

"Did you bring that?" I nodded toward the FedEx box.

"No, it was sitting outside the door when I drove up," he said.

I leaned back against the kitchen counter with my arms folded tightly across my chest and suddenly became aware of what my body language must be saying when he stepped closer to me and said quietly, "I'm not stalking you, Anna. I really did just come here to speak to your mum about her time at the Gardner Museum." His eyes searched mine.

"Why?" *Why did he come here? Why talk to mom? What did he see in my eyes?* "What could Mom's internship possibly have to do with the Gardner heist or the Manet?" I murmured. *Or even The Sisters painting*, my mind whispered.

"Oh!"

I tore my gaze away from his, and we both turned to see what had startled my mom. The cardboard box and a wad of bubble wrap lay discarded on the counter, and in her hands she held an ornately carved wood framed painting. Her eyes filled with tears as she turned it to show us.

"I never thought I'd see this again. My sister and I painted each other for a class we were taking at MassArt, but it was stolen from the annex at the Isabella Stewart Gardner Museum on the night of the heist."

# [ 29 ]
## DARIUS

*"My fucks dispenser broke, so I had it removed."* – Sophia Collins

The most interesting part of that remarkably interesting statement was that my eyes went immediately to Anna's face. That she was as pale as a ghost and wouldn't meet my eyes was less fascinating to me than the fact that I apparently cared more about her reaction than my own.

To be fair, my own reaction was more *of course* than *what?!?!?*

"What's wrong, Anna?" her mother said, sounding worried as she set down the painting and came over to her daughter. I hadn't seen the resemblance until that moment, but then I saw that they had the same shaped eyes framed by the same thick lashes and arched eyebrows that looked like wings.

Anna looked frantically at me, then back at her mother. "Why was your painting at the Gardner Museum?

Sophia Collins looked startled, as if she were surprised that she'd said what she did. Then her eyes met mine. "I'm sorry, Darius is it?"

Anna met my eyes, and when I didn't immediately answer the

question, said, "Mom, Darius Masoud is an investigator for a security firm in Chicago. He and I have been …" she faltered then, and I finished the sentence before I could think too much about it.

"We're tracking down the provenance of a painting. Anna received a tip from one of her bail jumpers that led her to the Gardner, and the more we look into things there, the more all roads seem to lead back to the Gardner heist."

Anna's expression was unreadable. Then she looked back at her mother. "He actually came here so we could ask you about your time as an intern there."

Her mother looked back at me, and the concern in her expression faded into a smile. Again I saw her daughter in her face. "Well then, pour yourself a cup of coffee, Darius, and let's talk on the beach."

Anna gave me a rueful smile and pulled a travel-style mug with a K&P Janitorial logo off a shelf and filled it with coffee, while her mother called all the dogs together and headed out to a sunroom. "Bring the bag of tennis balls, Anna," she called as she stepped outside.

Anna's worried gaze followed her mother until she was out the door, and then she seemed to visibly relax. "Good," she said, "she didn't take a towel."

"Why is that good?" I asked, though there were a million other questions that were more pressing.

"Because it means she won't take her usual topless dip in the sea."

I laughed, and Anna looked sharply at me. "You think I'm joking, but I'm totally serious. My mom believes her daily dip keeps her young. Colette and I just think she's an exhibitionist who knows she doesn't look like the fifty-year-old frumpy matrons in town."

"She doesn't," I said, thinking how similar mother and daughter were in build.

"But topless?" her nose wrinkled in distaste. "She's my mother."

I shrugged. "My mother always said, 'look at her mother before you marry her, because that's the person who taught her how to be a woman.' It seems as though you had an interesting teacher."

She sighed. "My lessons were from my dad - I was the son he didn't get. I pretty much fail at anything remotely female."

She picked up her coffee and turned to leave the room. I followed her through the sunroom, admiring the view her yoga pants revealed as she walked. "I must disagree," I said to myself.

The house stood on a cliff overlooking the ocean, and the path down to the beach was a wide, sandy one, anchored by scrubby brush and rocks. It wasn't a private beach – it stretched out of sight on either side – but it felt remote, and Sophia and her dogs were the only things moving on it that I could see.

We were about halfway down the path when Anna stopped and faced me. "You don't lie. Why did you tell my mom we're working together?"

"Are we not?" I asked. "We may not be standing on the same side, but the end goal appears to be the same."

"I don't know what the end goal is," she said, a note of desperation creeping into her tone. "I thought it was simple – get Mom's painting back for her from the guy who had it."

"Her painting was the treasure, and Markham Gray is the dragon," I said quietly. "How do captivity and freedom come into it?"

Anna sighed in what seemed like defeat, and then turned to continue walking. "I'll show you the letter from my aunt when we get back to Chicago," she said over her shoulder. I tried not to notice how much I enjoyed the sound of the word 'we.'

The dogs came racing over to us when we reached the beach, and Anna pulled the sling bag off her shoulder to fish out a couple of tennis balls. She handed one to me, and then hurled hers down the beach with the form of a baseball pitcher. The dogs went off in a mad race for the ball as we walked to where Sophia was picking seaweed off the sand and tossing it up to the rocks.

I took a sip of coffee and watched Anna and her mother navigate the dogs, the ball, and the seaweed without words. They were at ease with each other, and they seemed to know each other's rhythms as they cleaned the beach and took turns throwing the ball.

"You know, I never thought to look on the box. I assume the painting came from you girls," Sophia finally said to her daughter.

Anna shot a quick glance at me, and then she nodded. "I found a letter from Alex in my studio. It was written about six months before she died and addressed to me."

Sophia said nothing as she looked far down the beach at nothing in particular. "What did the letter say?" she finally asked.

"She told me about the painting, that Markham Gray had it, and how she'd tried to get it back for you but couldn't. She said maybe you'd understand why she did what she did if you got it back."

"Markham Gray," Sophia whispered.

"You know him?" Anna asked, though the question held no surprise.

"I ..." she smiled nostalgically, "I had a crush on him." But then the smile fell. "Alex left Boston with him. She knew I liked him, and she went with him anyway. After I met your dad, I realized it would never have been good with Markham, but still ..." Her voice faded as memories crowded in, but she found it again when she looked at Anna. "My sister chose a man over me. That's the part I couldn't forgive."

"Did she ever explain why?" Anna asked.

Sophia shook her head. "We never spoke again. I didn't answer the phone, and she eventually stopped calling."

Anna's thoughts seemed far away as she threw the ball for the black lab, so I stepped in to continue the conversation.

"Why was your painting in the annex of the Gardner Museum at the time of the heist?" I asked Sophia.

She looked at me as though she'd forgotten I was there for a moment. Then she smiled quietly. "The annex was where all the restoration and repair work was done. They had the most interesting paints – oils in colors that are no longer made, and brushes the old masters and Impressionists once used. Occasionally, the interns from MassArt would be allowed to work with the restoration artists, and the one in charge at that time liked Alex, so he let us use their supplies to work on our painting. Sometimes we'd come over at night and work on it then."

Anna's head whipped around. "Were you there the night the art was stolen?"

Sophia shuddered. "God, no. What a nightmare that would have been. They fired all of us anyway, of course, after the theft – just changed the locks and dumped the contents of our lockers into paper bags, which we couldn't pick up until we'd spoken to the police. I tried to get into the annex to retrieve our painting, but they wouldn't let me in. Finally, the restoration artist let Alex in, and when she came out, she told me it was gone."

"Could it have been thrown away by the museum staff when they fired everyone?" Anna asked her mother.

"That's what I'd always assumed happened. It may not be an actual Chasseriau, but it's painted like one, with the paints and brush techniques that were used then, and thieves might not have known the difference. The museum didn't know we'd been working there, so if it had been stolen, no one would have missed it but us. "

The sound of the waves filled the silent spaces as Anna continued to throw the ball for the dogs, and the lab continued to drop it at her feet. I wondered if she realized how adoring his gaze was when he looked at her. I wondered if she knew how many men probably looked at her the same way, or if I made the sort of eyes at her that a dog did.

"Mom, was there another canvas on the stretcher behind your painting?" Anna had just stooped to pick up the ball the beagle had dropped for her, so she didn't see the startled look on Sophia's face, but I did.

"Yes, there was."

Anna jerked her head up to look at her mom. "There was?"

Sophia looked as though she would rather say nothing, but she couldn't evade her daughter's question, so she nodded. "I'd wanted to try my hand at copying a real Impressionist, so I'd been working on the Manet that was hanging in the Blue Room."

"*Madame Auguste Manet*," Anna said. Sophia looked at Anna in amazement.

"Yes. Exactly. How did you know that?"

Anna darted another look at me, then swallowed. "She was stuck to the back of *The Sisters* … your painting. I was afraid she was the original. They're hard to tell apart."

Sophia's laughter sounded nervous and relieved. "No, no. I stopped working on her when Rick's parties became too frequent and I couldn't sneak down to the Blue Room to paint anymore."

Anna stared at her mother. "You worked *in* the Blue Room? Mom! What if they'd caught you?"

Sophia absently rubbed her fingers through the black dog's fur. "We were young then. We didn't think anything bad could happen to us." She smiled wryly. "We were invincible and impossible in that way young people are when they're convinced they're the first to feel or do or experience. The theft of the art shook all of us out of our privileged bubble."

"Your Madame Auguste seemed finished to me," Anna said quietly, with another look at me, "what was left to do?" I sipped my coffee and nodded at her for asking the question I would have asked.

"I painted what I could from the original that hung in front of me, but I was never brave enough to take her off the wall to see the edges. It's how you know if the copyist was in the presence of the original, you know? Because the edges of a painting are always hidden by the frame. The edges of my Madame Auguste were unfinished, and since I was never going to be able to finish her, we used the same stretcher for our painting of each other." Sophia brushed the dog dust off her hands and looked at me.

"What else can I tell you about that time?" Sophia mused. It was clear that it hurt her to remember, and I was inclined to leave Anna's mother alone with her memories, but I wasn't sure if I'd have this access again.

"Can you tell us what you know about Markham Gray?" I said, as I threw the ball for her dogs, who yipped happily as they chased it down the beach.

She nodded thoughtfully. "Markham was a couple of years older than me, closer to Alex's age, and handsome in that way that meant he never had to work too hard for girls." She looked at me and allowed a small smile. "Something I'm sure you're familiar with."

Anna scowled. "Mom!"

I was amused to see her cheeks go pink, and I didn't bother to contradict her mother with the truth of my experience as a shy boy whose only access to his classmates was through a soccer ball.

"His family had money," Sophia continued, "but they didn't support his music, so he was trying to make a go of it without their financial help."

"His music?" Anna asked her mother.

"He jammed with Rick and his band – he played the saxophone. They were the house band for the after-hours parties." Sophia scoffed slightly. "When the old director retired and moved out of the fourth floor apartment, Rick's band came in to practice a couple times a month. Some guys brought beer, and suddenly it was a party."

"Did you ever date Markham?" Anna asked.

Sophia smiled. "It was 1990. We didn't really date; we mostly just hung out."

Anna laughed. "Not much has changed."

I wondered if that's what she and I were doing – just hanging out. Investigating a crime that happened thirty years ago, avoiding the one that happened days ago, pretending to ourselves and each other that there wasn't something … there.

I shook myself out of my contemplation. Up in the house on the kitchen counter sat a stolen painting, and down here on the beach stood the thief.

Sophia looked out at the waves breaking on the shore. "We kissed a few times, and sometimes after a set he'd come find me in the Blue Room and we'd talk while I painted. He was so handsome, and he had a way of looking at me as if I was the only girl in the room, which, truth be told, I usually was. Alex would be drinking or dancing with the guys – it was always so easy for her to be free, to be fully herself – so when Markham would come and find me, I felt … special … seen."

She inhaled the cold ocean breeze deeply, then turned to find Anna's eyes. "I used to watch you hide in plain sight around Colette, and I recognized it from my own relationship with Alex. When she left town with the one boy who actually saw me – well, let's just say I'm glad you developed your own skills and passions. It's too hard to be seen next to a leading lady."

Anna shrugged as if it was nothing. "Sometimes it's just easier not to share the same stage."

I thought I saw a flash of sadness pass over Sophia's face, and I wondered if it was for her daughter, or for herself.

"In any case," Sophia continued, "I thought Markham and I had a bigger connection than we apparently did, end of story. I never saw him again after I left the museum and Alex followed him to Chicago, so I went from having a sister, a job, and a boy to fantasize about one week, to losing all of those things the next." She spoke directly to Anna. "I was angry and alone for almost a year, and then I met your dad, and suddenly I was the heroine of the story who got to live happily ever after."

Anna's mother smiled, and I could see the love in her expression – for her husband, for her children. A wet corgi chose that moment to go barreling into her, covering her with sand and seawater. Sophia just laughed and scooped him up in her arms to cuddle him. "Lucas, my love, you are a very naughty little boy. Now I'm going to have to dip in the sea to get all the sand off."

She reached for the hem of her shirt and Anna grabbed my hand and turned us toward the path in a panicked motion. "Oh no! Save yourself. The woman has no shame."

Sophia laughed. "No shame and great tits," she called to her daughter. "A lethal combination to the easily mortified. Go on and tell your dad to bring a towel down for me when he comes."

"Does he go for a dip in the sea too?" I asked Anna as we walked up the path. I could hear Sophia playing with the dogs, who swam out to join her in the water.

"God, no. He has way more sense. But he likes to photograph her, and she gives him plenty of opportunities."

I thought about the photos I'd taken of Anna which burned a hole in the hidden file on my phone, and I realized Anna's father and I might have a thing or two in common.

# [ 30 ]
## ANNA

*"I see the very best version of myself when you look at me."*

- ANNA COLLINS

D arius's gaze left a trail of pink everywhere it landed on my skin. Blushing was one of those feminine things princesses and pretty girls did, which is why I had never been prone to it. But now it seemed like the blood under my skin rose up to meet his eyes – not like a challenge, unfortunately for my sense of self-preservation, but like an invitation.

It was disconcerting and slightly mortifying because now that I'd actually admitted I'd stolen the painting, lusting after the guy who was going to bust me felt a little too Stockholm syndrome-y for comfort. Granted, he wasn't my captor, but I'd tried telling that to my traitorous skin with zero success.

We met my dad on the cliffs, already headed down to the beach with his camera and a towel for Mom. I introduced Darius to him as someone I was working with on a case, and they shook hands with a strange formality that I only ever saw in my dad when he was sizing up a business rival.

He was halfway down the path away from us when I called out to him impulsively. "Dad, can I borrow your bike?"

He stopped, looked up at me, and after a quick glance at Darius, said "Sure kiddo. Helmets are on the wall."

Until he said yes, I hadn't thought about taking Darius with me, but then it was all I could think about, and the blush on my face must have been epic, because he almost looked concerned. Almost.

"Want to go for a ride?" I asked quickly, in a futile attempt to divert his attention from my face.

"Your father has a tandem bicycle?" Darius asked, and suddenly my blush melted into a grin, and I felt my confidence slide back into place.

"Not at all. Come on, let's go chase the wind."


I took us north around the rocks and points, inland on the small, twisty roads where I'd first learned to ride my dad's Triumph, and then finally south to Land's End, where I parked the 1972 Bonneville motorcycle that my dad had rebuilt from the wheels up. Darius practically flung himself off the back of the bike, and I tried to ignore the voice in my head that said he was disgusted by me. He stood with his back to me and pulled off his helmet to look out at the view of Thacher Island, where the twin lighthouses still protected the ships from the rocky shore.

I removed my own helmet and wished we were still riding and his arms were still around me. I almost suggested we keep going, but when he finally turned to look at me, the expression on his face made me glad that I hadn't.

It was raw and hungry, and it sent a shiver of something that definitely wasn't fear up my spine. I suddenly realized it might not have been disgust, but desire that sent him off the back of my bike. Like being pressed against my back, with his arms around me, had been too much. It had been for me. I looked away to compose my face into something that didn't scream *I want you*, and when I looked back a moment later, prepared to say the words out loud, his expression had slipped back into something cool and detached.

"You ride like the motorcycle is a part of you," he said, with about as much investment as if he were discussing the sunny day. Okay. Two could play at this game.

"My dad started teaching me on a dirt bike when I was little and on this one when I was fifteen," I said, my tone carefully neutral as I kicked the stand down and stepped off the bike.

His eyes jerked toward the lighthouses. "Why are there two?" he asked roughly.

"They're twins," I said, with a small smile at the memory of picnics on Thacher Island when we were kids. "And when they line up together, they point you to true north."

Darius's eyes reflected wry amusement as he contemplated the view. "Do they still operate?"

I nodded. We'd learned the history of the lighthouses from Dad, who grew up in Rockport and was part of the association involved in their preservation. "They were built in 1771 by the British, and rebuilt in the 1860s. For a while after the Coast Guard took over, they only lit the south tower, but when they relit the north tower, they became the last twin lighthouses in the U.S."

"Did you grow up here?" Darius asked when he turned back to face me.

I nodded. "My dad used to take me out there in his kayak because Colette was never brave enough to go on the ocean in such a small boat. He said that back in the late 1700s, the lights were called "Ann's Eyes" when they lit up stormy nights. That's how I got my name. Mom chose Colette for the firstborn twin, so Dad chose Anna for me. I've pretty much been his ever since."

"That explains the handshake," Darius muttered.

"What handshake?" I asked.

"The one with which your father nearly crushed my hand." I must have looked concerned, because Darius chuckled. "I guess I should be flattered that he felt the need to warn me."

"To warn you about what?" I'd noticed the odd competitiveness of their handshake, and if Darius could explain it, I was all ears.

Darius's gaze slid away from mine and back out toward the light-houses. "That I'm not to hurt you."

"Oh."

Too late.

Actually, to be fair, he wasn't the one who hurt me. Working with Darius over the past few days, I had let myself dare to hope for something more than just sex.

"I'm sorry, Anna."

He still didn't look at me. I liked how my name sounded in his voice, but not the carefully blank expression on his face.

I pasted a cheerful smile on with thoughts of corgi butts and tumbling kittens. "So," I said, "how does this go now? You go back to Chicago, give my name to the police, and my mom's painting back to the Grays? Will you give me enough warning to get out of the country, or do I need to change my identity and run?

"Anna—"

I looked away, toward Thacher Island. "I always thought the name Anna was too boring for who I wanted to be. Anna isn't a skydiver, or a mountain climber. That's Parker, or Scarlett, or Shane." I smiled a little at that. What if I changed my name to Shane and became a P.I.? Except for that whole stealing-someone's-identity thing, not to mention the fact that we looked about as related as an Afghan hound and a shih tzu.

"Do you know what a shih tzu is?" I asked him. "It's a zoo with no elephants or zebras."

I reached for my helmet, but Darius grabbed my hand before I could take it from the seat. He pulled me around to face him, and all I wanted to do was lose myself in his gaze. I *had* lost myself in it – that was part of the problem.

He searched my eyes, and then his eyes went to my lips and lingered there. It seemed like it took effort for him to meet my eyes again.

"Anna," he said again in a hushed voice, "I don't know how this goes now. Cipher doesn't work for Gray anymore, he fired us, so my responsibility to him is done. But I still work for Cipher. I need to tell them what I know – what we found out – and see where they want to go from there."

His hand was wrapped around my wrist, and I knew he could feel my pulse tripping along like a busy little jackhammer. I let ten beats go by without moving or saying anything, and then I nodded.

"When?" I asked. "I'll meet you there."

"You'll—" he frowned, and then something that looked like respect crossed his face. "Monday morning. Ten o'clock."

"Okay," I said as I pulled my phone out of my back pocket and entered it into my calendar. "Cipher Security. 10 am on Monday. I'll meet you in the lobby?" I looked up to see him gazing at me with an expression that looked something like confused wonder.

"Yeah. That's fine." He shook his head a little like he was trying to clear his vision.

I stuck my phone in my back pocket again and tried not to look forward to having his arms around me again on the bike. Tried, and failed, and then laughed at myself for thinking it would ever be easy. "Okay," I said to redirect my focus, "now, are you hungry? Because I'm starving, and the world's most perfect fish and chips is a six-minute ride from here."

His expression gradually softened into something less surprised and more … relaxed. "The *world's* most perfect? Are you sure you want to make that claim to a man who lived in England?"

I narrowed my eyes at him. "Perfectly deep fried fish is all about the batter, and everyone knows the best batter can only be found at Marisma in Puerto Vallarta, Mexico and at the Fish Shack in Rockport."

"*Everyone* knows," he countered as he reached for his own helmet, "that the best ingredient in fish and chips is the ink from the English newspapers the fishmongers wrap it in."

I opened my mouth to respond, but then quirked my head at him. "Gray actually fired you?"

Darius looked a tiny bit chagrined, and then he shrugged. "Yes. My boss didn't seem particularly worried though."

"Worried about what?" I asked.

He exhaled quietly. "Gray threatened to kill us in the court of public opinion unless we were successful in retrieving the painting of your mother and aunt. Apparently he has the connections to do so, but that didn't seem to worry my boss. He has let me stay to sort out what I can on the heist, and on the Manet."

"Well, the Manet is a closed case. Mom said she painted it," I reminded him.

"She also said it was unfinished," he said seriously.

I flung my leg over the seat of the bike and faced backward, then gestured to him to the seat. "Sit." After a moment of hesitation, he did, and despite scooting as far back on the seat as he could, there was less than a foot between us. "What haven't you told me?"

His expression did a rapid-fire shift, from something guarded to something resigned, and I didn't like either, so I was glad when he settled on something neutral. "I did a cursory examination of the frame that was left behind in the panic room."

I noticed that he was careful not to say "that *you* left behind," which I appreciated.

"There were, as you obviously know, the remnants of two canvases left between the stretcher and the frame," he continued.

"Right. *The Sisters* and Mom's copy of the Manet." I tried not to sound impatient, but I really was hungry, and he sat so close to me that it was fifty-fifty which hunger I'd try to satisfy first.

"Your mother said her Manet was unfinished. She never painted the edges."

I waited for him to continue speaking, but he didn't until he'd looked into my eyes for a long moment, like he really wanted me to get what he was about to say. "The edges were black, Anna. They'd been painted."

The Roadrunner in the Looney Tunes loop in my brain screeched to a halt, and I stared at Darius, unable to process what he was implying.

"The edges of both canvasses in the panic room were painted black."

# [ 31 ]
## ANNA

*"You can't scare me. I have two daughters."*

- MAX COLLINS

D arius left my parents' house soon after we got back from our ride. He'd been quiet during lunch, and it was clear that whatever he thought about the Manet, he wasn't going to share it with me. I was a thief, after all, and he didn't trust me. Fair enough.

I was in the garage wiping down the Bonneville when my dad found me.

"Hey, kiddo," he said, grabbing a shop towel and kneeling at the other side of the motorcycle to help. "Everything okay?"

I shrugged. "Not really."

He was silent for another minute. It's how we'd always talked – working on something, with long silences between the words. "Your mom said you got an old painting of hers back from the guy who caused the rift between her and Alexandra. Seems like it meant a lot to her."

I nodded but didn't say anything. Dad must have caught the motion, because he nodded too. "You take it?"

"Yeah," I said after a minute.

Dad sat back on his heels and studied me. That rarely happened. Most of the time our hands were too busy for our eyes to look. "He catch you?" he finally asked.

I knew he meant Darius. My dad and I had a shorthand that had never really required too many words, which might explain why I sucked at being a girl sometimes. I didn't use the requisite number of words most of the time, or I used too many, and they were the wrong ones.

I sighed. "Yeah."

More silence. I finished wiping down my side of the bike and moved next to him to get the parts he hadn't gotten to yet. "That his job?" Dad finally asked.

"Yep. He's good at it too."

"Hand me the chrome polish," he said, already reaching. I tossed it to him and got a clean rag to polish what he applied. We polished the chrome in silence for a few minutes, and I was glad to have something shiny to focus my attention on. My reflection in the pipes distorted to something fantastical and freakish, but the story that would usually spin its way out of my brain didn't come, and the fantasy faded into something flat and strange with no magic at all.

We finished the chrome, and my dad stood up with only a slight wince.

"He wants you," he said.

The words startled me, and I shook my head. "No. He might have if I hadn't lied to him."

He studied me. "You lied?"

"Yeah."

"About a life or death thing?"

I shook my head and scoffed. "A freedom thing maybe, but not life or death."

"Same thing to some." My dad took the shop towel out of my hand and turned me around to face him. Then he opened his arms, and I stepped into them for a hug. In my dad's arms was the one place I ever felt like I could be vulnerable, and I let myself relax into his hug.

"Thanks, Dad," I whispered into his sweater.

"Your mom's already got that painting up above the fireplace," he said after a long moment.

"How attached are you to the purple sofa?" I asked.

He chuckled at that. My mom was known to change all the furniture in a room to highlight a new piece of art. There was no question where my sister had gotten her decorating skills.

"I could never give your mom her sister back. You did that."

"Colette and I did it together," I murmured.

Dad stepped back so he could look at me, and he wore a wry smile. "She might have had a little something to do with it, but we both know who did the taking."

"I'm not sure how I'm supposed to feel about that, Dad. Flattered that you think I'm capable, or insulted that you're so sure I'm the one with the criminal tendencies."

He laughed and pulled me back in. "Both. But not insulted." Abruptly, he let go of me and busied himself cleaning up the shop towels. "Your sister is a princess, and God knows, she has her own way of getting what she wants."

I smiled at that. "She does, doesn't she?" I had to admit I was kind of proud of her for it.

My dad studied me. "But you think outside the box like there is no box, and you're the only one creative enough to see that."

I sighed and hung the helmets on their hooks on the wall. "I'm not sure what to do next. Taking the painting has opened a whole can of worms that I don't know how to close back up again."

"Here's the thing, kiddo. Right and wrong aren't as simple as black and white, because there are about a million shades of gray in the world."

"You think?" I scoffed, because that was exactly what I thought. And exactly what Darius didn't.

He sighed as if he wanted better words. "You're who you are because of the life you've had. You had advantages and an education

209

that shaped you – you've traveled the world and done some pretty incredible things. What's right for you might be a couple of shades different than what's right for someone with different experiences."

I nodded. "Yeah, I can see that." I thought about what Darius had said about building three hours into his travel schedule because the sound of his name fit a profile. Meanwhile, Colette could talk her way out of a ticket just by smiling.

My dad continued. "That doesn't mean there isn't a hard line on things that hurt other people, but you know what your own code is. You know what you can live with and what you can't, and I like to think you were raised to make workable choices."

"I've never had a problem with that, Dad. I'm pretty clear on where my hard lines are." I had realized when I was a kid, choosing Honor as my D&D character, that my personal code felt a little like a mix of Robin Hood and Mulan, with an unfortunate dose of Sid, the filterless sloth.

"So, work with what you've got," my dad said as he organized his impeccable workbench. "Trust your gut, protect yourself and the people you care about, don't hurt anyone, and stay true to what you believe in. At the end of the day, there are a lot of things more important than a couple of swirls of paint on a canvas, even if they make your mom happy."

"Thanks, Dad."

He swept a hand over his spotless work bench and headed for the door, but turned back just before he left the garage.

"Anna?"

"Yeah?"

"You bring people to life when they're with you. Choose someone who does the same for you."

# [ 32 ]
## DARIUS

*"Art isn't the answer, it's the reason."*

I made it to the museum just before it closed and went immediately to the Blue Room to study the Manet. The docent on duty was the woman from the Dutch Room, Amber, and she greeted me with recognition and a smile when I walked in.

I had spent the drive from Rockport pointedly not thinking about Anna. Instead, I used the time to look at the problem of the forged Manet from every angle I could see. First, if the painting behind the Kiriakis sisters was the original *Madame Auguste Manet*, then Anna's mother and aunt were implicated in its theft. That it hung in Markham Gray's panic room implicated him in the theft as well – an idea that troubled me less. Theoretically, an unknown thief might have hidden the original Manet behind a painting that had been stored in the annex, but that didn't explain its presence in Gray's panic room. But the constant through all of it was that Anna herself was implicated – not because she had necessarily stolen the Manet, but because she'd been responsible for the uninvited liberation of the Kiriakis sisters' painting from Gray's mansion and was now likely in possession of a stolen masterpiece.

The option that I continued to hope for, but which seemed less and less likely in the face of the circumstantial evidence, was that the Manet on the wall of the Blue Room was the original, and the one in Anna's portfolio was just an excellent copy painted with period paints and brush techniques by her mother.

I stood in front of *Madame Auguste Manet*, staring up at the stark black-on-black of her dress, when I felt someone approach. I looked over to see Amber standing next to me. She studied the painting as she spoke. "Manet painted this just two years after he painted the nudes that made him infamous. I wonder what his mother thought of them?"

"She looks formidable," I said, "as though she had opinions and wasn't shy to express them."

Amber laughed. "Apparently, Manet had a close relationship with his mother, who was a great supporter of his art, even when his father had pushed him into studying law. Mrs. Gardner bought this painting from Manet's stepson, who inherited it from Madame Manet herself, and she may have been his grandmother, if the speculation that Manet was his father is true." Amber looked at me with sparkling eyes. "Art history was my favorite subject. It's why I came back here after ..." She trailed off as she looked around the room.

"After they fired all the guards and interns?"

Her eyes darted to mine again. "Yes, exactly."

"I had a chance to speak with my friend's mother, Sophia, who also interned here then," I said quietly.

Amber moved to another painting, and I followed as though our conversation was purely about the art. "I thought about your friend's mother and realized I did remember her. She was a talented artist herself and spent a lot of time in this room copying the Impressionists."

"She told us that she painted in here after hours, when Rick and his band played in the museum."

Amber smirked and shook her head. "Those were very different times."

We moved on to another painting, and I continued speaking in quiet tones, as though asking about the art. "Do you remember a young musician named Markham Gray?"

Her eyes darted to me in surprise. "Markham? Of course. Everyone knew him. He's the one who invented sensor tag and was the best at playing it. The games we used to play here after hours horrify me now. The priceless art we put at risk just because we were bored—" She shuddered. "As awful as it is to say, the heist was probably the best thing that happened to this place. Attention was finally paid to proper security, which definitely put an end to the shenanigans, and the empty frames and the mystery of the missing art have become a huge draw for the public."

We had walked all the way around the room and were back in front of the Manet, with the small, empty frame beneath it.

"Sadly, some invaluable artworks remain lost to the public because of it," I said, studying the sad little frame.

"It's very lucky that *Madame Auguste Manet* was in the annex that night for repair. I'm certain it would have been the thieves' target if it had been here." Amber said, studying the painting once more.

I failed to control my expression when I asked her, "You mean to tell me she was in the annex?"

Amber seemed confused by my shock. "It was a scheduled restoration."

"The door to the annex from the Dutch Room was open that night," I murmured.

She stared at me in surprise. "It was?"

"There's a crime scene photo showing the open door. The *Times* printed it a decade ago."

The docent exhaled quietly. "I didn't know." She was pale as she gazed up at the formidable woman looking down at us as though in judgment. "That makes it even more remarkable that she wasn't stolen. She's far more valuable than *Chez Tortoni*."

Indeed.

# [ 33 ]
## ANNA

*"The door to possibility isn't locked."*

- FROM THE T-SHIRT COLLECTION OF ANNA COLLINS

The Cipher offices had no obvious entry points beyond the front doors, which were watched over by a trained security guard and six cameras, and the elevator, which presumably went down to the parking garage and more cameras. My escape route assessment was automatic, and the guard at the desk seemed amused when I gave him my name.

"Darius said you'd look for the exits. Did you find the staircase?"

I narrowed my eyes at the man behind the desk. He could have been mistaken for a younger Idris Elba, and his British accent added authenticity to the resemblance. His smile seemed genuine, not mocking, so I decided to play.

"The obvious one is next to the elevator, but I assume the cameras cover it." I looked around the wood-paneled lobby, and my eyes lingered on a large potted palm on one side of the lobby, well away from the main entrance. "There," I said, nodding to the palm. "That's meant to draw eyeballs away from the seam of a door panel."

I studied it more closely. "Not an outside door. Either a staircase or a closet with another elevator." I turned back to the guard. "Probably goes to the roof, where I'd put a helicopter pad if it were my building."

An eyebrow arched, and Idris-ish looked impressed. "It's a staircase, and it took me three months to spot it. I'll let Darius know you're here."

He picked up a phone, and I walked over to the panel behind the potted palm to study the seam of the hidden door. It was cleverly done and was similar enough to the panic room door at the Gray mansion that I thought it might be Darius's work.

A minute later the elevator dinged, and Darius stepped out into the lobby. He wore a gray suit and white shirt with no tie, and he was gorgeous. My breath caught, and I was instantly self-conscious of my jeans, engineer boots, and Alice-in-Wonderland T-shirt that proclaimed "To Live Would Be an Awfully Big Adventure" across the front. At least I'd swapped out the leather jacket for a black cashmere sport coat I'd found in a second-hand store in Los Angeles.

But Darius didn't seem to notice my outfit. His eyes were fixed on my face as he walked toward me, and my heart started trying to climb out of my throat, apparently to embrace him. A heart with zero self-preservation instinct was a liability I didn't need to bring into a meeting at Cipher Security, but the smile on my face didn't get the memo.

"Hi," I said, approximating the cleverness of a frog.

"Hello," he said with a smile in his voice and eyes. His expression was pure business though, and if I hadn't seen the sparkles, I would have been a little bit crushed.

I bit the inside of my cheek to get my smile under control, but then Darius whispered, "Stop biting your cheek," and I poked him in the side, and then I was officially twelve years old.

Idris-ish saw everything – he had that kind of casual attention that made it seem he wasn't watching when he was actually aware of everything in his environment. Darius walked me to the desk and introduced us.

"Anna Collins, this is Gabriel Eze. He's been working with Cipher for what, about a year now?" Darius directed the question to Gabriel, who stood and held out a hand to shake mine.

"It's nice to properly meet you, Anna. Welcome to Cipher." Gabriel's hand was as warm as his voice, and I half expected "Bond, James Bond" to come out of his mouth.

"Nice to meet you too," I said. I should probably have been nervous and twitchy being in the lion's den, but the lions all seemed very nice and far too pretty to be as dangerous as they probably were.

"We have a meeting with Dan and Quinn in the conference room on three," Darius said to Gabriel. "You can reach me there if any calls come in."

"Got it." He looked at me. "That room has the best coffee, so don't be shy."

"I can be a lot of things," I said with a smile I actually felt, "but shy isn't in my repertoire. Awkward and dorky I have covered, and I could draw a map to Mortification Central, but I won't, because that's the kind of place you have to stumble into."

Even Gabriel's chuckle held warmth, and I had the sense he was a genuinely nice guy. "I've been there, but you make it seem like fun."

I waved cheerily as Darius guided me to the elevator. I felt the barest touch of his hand on the small of my back, and it sent prickles of awareness through my skin. "We can't take the secret stairs?" I asked, looking pointedly at the hidden door by the potted plant.

He hesitated for a fraction of a second. "You saw them?"

"I found them when I looked for them. I'm intrigued by things that are hidden in plain sight," I said.

Darius threw a smirk in Gabriel's general direction then led me over to the hidden door. "Okay, Smartypants. Find the access."

The wall was paneled with honey-colored wood, and each three-foot section had a seam, so it was clear where the door was, but not how to open it. There were no visible latches, depressions, or hinges, which meant it probably opened inward, and nothing hung on the panel that could be used to hide a catch. There was, however, a wall sconce on the panel to the left of the one I thought was the door. I reached up and felt around the base of the sconce. I found a button that I knew wasn't the switch for the sconce because sconces like these would be controlled by a master switch with a dimmer, so I pressed the button and voilà, the panel gave a little click as the latch opened. I shot Darius a triumphant look and caught the raised eyebrow of surprise.

"Did you know to look for that too?" he asked.

"You designed it, didn't you?" I asked, with only a little bit of awe.

There was pride in his smile. "Yes."

"It's cleverer than at Gray's," I said without thinking. His expression shuttered in the next instant, and I scowled at myself for reminding him of what I'd done, and who I was – or wasn't – to him.

"Gray doesn't appreciate clever," was all he said in response. He opened the door and gestured for me to enter the narrow staircase ahead of him. I began climbing as he closed the door behind us with a quiet snick.

"You didn't like him much, did you?" Despite everything it had and could still cost me to have him know my part in the theft from Gray mansion, I was happy to be able to speak honestly. I actively disliked lying, even by omission. I preferred to save my energy for things like climbing mountains and icy ocean swims.

"Malcom Gray tried to have me removed from his project when I wouldn't give him priority on a set of door locks that had been ordered for another client. He tried to bribe me for them first, and then he tried to have me fired." Darius's voice came from behind me on the staircase, echoing slightly in the empty space. I could almost feel the echo in my stomach because the disgust in his voice was so visceral.

"Right. Your thing with greased wheels," I muttered.

"Right. That." His teeth were gritted, and that echoed in my stomach too.

"If we're still friends later, can I meet your parents?" I said, making the conversational swerve of the century.

There was a long pause, and I was glad not to be able to see his face so I couldn't tell if "Ah, hell no" was written all over it.

"I ... suppose so," he said carefully as I reached the third floor landing.

I tried not to notice how hard the words were for him to say, and I changed the subject so I didn't have to think about it too much.

"Can I just open the door," I asked, indicating a simple metal fire door, "or do I have to tap three times and spin around in a circle?"

Whatever expression had been on Darius's face at the start of my question was replaced with the quirk of a smile. "The latter."

I grinned, then tapped three times on my own head and wiggled around in a circle as if there were a hula hoop around my hips. It was absolutely worth the look on his face and went a long way toward replacing his usual intensity with something more playful.

I liked playing with Darius.

He might have even liked it too, considering that he got way too close to my face as he reached past me to open the door – the kind of close that sometimes resulted in lip collisions. Sadly, this one did not.

I stepped into the hall a little more breathless than I would normally be after three flights of stairs, and Darius led the way to a conference room dominated by the kind of table people took shelter under in earthquakes.

"Would you like a coffee?" he asked, moving to a machine on the sideboard.

"I think I'd better, in case Gabriel asks," I said, looking around the room. "This table is bigger than my first apartment."

He smiled. "When we lived in London, the first place my parents rented was a bedsit in Chelsea."

The sound of the coffee machine filled the room with a pleasant hum. "What's a bedsit?"

"It's a flat so small you have to literally sit on the bed to wash your face in the sink. We lasted one month before my brother and I were ready to climb out the window just to get enough air in our lungs to complain."

He smirked. "Of course, we weren't allowed to open the window because of the drug deals happening in the alley below us."

"Nice neighborhood?" I asked. I'd accidentally rented a guest room in an interesting part of Hollywood once, and since then had learned to do my research.

"Right around the corner from a strip club. But the price was right while my father made his connections with the Iranian community that eventually led to work as a teacher."

"Is that what he does now?" I asked as Darius set another coffee cup in the machine.

"How do you like your coffee?"

I smiled. "Surprise me."

He considered me a moment, then reached under the counter and pulled out a bottle of almond flavored syrup. He poured some out and steamed it with milk while he answered my question.

"My father drove a taxi the whole time we lived in London and for the first few years we were in Chicago. Disgracefully, a professor's salary at a junior college is not enough to support a family."

"In Luxembourg, the beginning salary of a teacher is higher than the highest teacher salary anywhere else in the world," I said, and then scoffed at myself for the random fact outburst.

"Don't do that," Darius said, with the beginnings of a scowl.

"I know," I said, "my trivial-trivia nonsense gets exhausting."

"No. I love your trivia. Don't dismiss yourself for the things you say. It's diminishing." He set the almond cappuccino in front of me.

"Thank you," I said automatically, while my brain spun on the things my ears had just taken in.

He looked at me oddly. "What are you thinking?"

"I'm not. I got hung up on 'love' and 'diminishing.' Aaaand ... now I'm just going to insert my foot the rest of the way into my mouth and know that at least I do self-humiliation perfectly."

Darius smiled at the expression of mortification on my face. "I get hung up on love too, if it's any consolation."

"Oh, phew. I'm just going to step right over that as if it never happened. But explain diminishing. How do I diminish myself for owning my own ridiculousness?"

"You don't. You diminish anyone else who thinks what you just said was interesting, or thinks you're fascinating for knowing such a thing."

"Oh." I'd never thought of that. I looked at him while I sipped my coffee, which was sooooo good, by the way. "So, self-deprecation is a bad thing?"

"It can be," he said.

I had just opened my mouth to dispute that when the door opened and two men came in. The timing was unfortunate on so many levels, not the least of which was that my open mouth resulted in a relaxed jaw, which, at the sight of their majesties Alpha Male One and Alpha Male Two, became an unhinged one. When I realized I was staring, I snapped my mouth shut, but not before I caught the glint of amusement in the shorter man's eyes.

Darius stepped forward and spoke to the men. "Quinn, Dan, I'd like to introduce Anna Collins. Anna, this is Quinn Sullivan," he indicated the taller of the two men who looked like he was made of steel and kidskin leather, "and Dan O'Malley," he said, nodding at the other man, who was more cast iron, bull hide, and ink. "They own Cipher Security."

I stood and shook each man's hand. "You must be very good at your job," I said to Quinn before I could stop the words.

He raised an eyebrow. "I am. But I'm curious why you would say so?"

"Because you're scary and intimidating and too handsome to be real." I clapped a hand over my mouth and squeezed my eyes shut. "I just said that out loud," I murmured through my fingers.

Dan barked a deep, rumbly laugh. "She's got your number."

I opened my eyes to see that the man of steel wasn't scowling. He wasn't smiling either, but I hadn't been kicked out of the room yet, so that was something.

I inhaled. "Let me try that again. Hi, I'm Anna. Thank you for letting me crash your meeting, and sorry-not-sorry I stole from your ex-client."

Quinn's not-scowling expression froze very slightly, and Dan shot Darius a look. "This is your thief?"

"She is," Darius said quietly.

"Maybe we better sit down," Dan said seriously.

I returned to my seat and took a fortifying sip of my coffee. Dan nodded at it. "What kind did you get?"

"Almond cappuccino. What's your favorite?"

"Hot, strong, and on demand." He shot a look at Quinn. "Do not say what you're thinking."

"Can I?" I said, yet again opening my mouth without the control of my good sense.

Dan smirked, I smirked, and the phrase *like my women* was said without words. It was oddly satisfying to have an inappropriate mental dialogue with a stranger. "So," Quinn said, looking at Darius. That was all. Just, "So." That's what power looked like. One word.

"Anna did indeed take the painting from Gray's panic room. Apparently there is some question about the legitimacy of Gray's claim to it, but for the moment, that is not the primary issue," Darius said. He spoke to both of his bosses but managed to include me in the conversation with his gaze.

"Ownership is what determines whether the crime includes theft or is restricted to breaking and entering," Quinn said.

"I have the materials to back up the ownership issue," I said.

Quinn gave a curt nod of the head. "Good." His gaze returned to Darius. "What is the primary issue, then?"

"A second painting was found behind the first, stretched on the same frame. This second painting is, to the naked eye, indistinguishable from a Manet that currently hangs in the Isabella Stewart Gardner museum in Boston."

Eyebrows on both men went up, but they waited for Darius to continue. He looked at me, so I picked up where he left off, proud that my voice was steady.

"I swear on all the corgi butts in the world that I did not know I was taking that painting. The painting I meant to take, *The Sisters,* belongs to my mother. She and my aunt were both the artists and the models for it, and my aunt wanted me to take it back from Gray, which I can prove. I had no idea the other painting was there until after I'd left the Gray mansion, and then, well, I couldn't exactly put it back."

"I'm just gonna go with corgi butts as a solemn oath," said Dan, with a smirk.

I shot him a quick smile of gratitude and continued. "We've figured out that there are a couple of factors that tie *The Sisters* painting to the Gardner Museum. One," I ticked off on my fingers, "my mom and aunt worked as interns at the museum thirty years ago. They painted *The Sisters* in the annex of the museum, where repairs and restorations of the museum's holdings were done. Two, their painting went missing from the annex around the time of a big theft from the museum in 1990."

"Holy shit, I know that heist," said Dan, the surprise evident in his voice. "Word on the street was a couple of guys working for Merlino did the job."

"Merlino went down for an armored car robbery and died in prison," Quinn said.

"Right," Dan nodded, "which is why I had my doubts about Merlino as the kingpin."

"Apparently it's been speculated," Darius said, "that the stolen art was being kept as insurance against prison time."

"So if he had three hundred mil in stolen art to trade, it makes no fucking sense that Merlino died in prison," continued Dan.

I held up three fingers, which got the men's attention. "The third thing that ties the paintings I took from Gray to the Gardner is that my mom had painted a copy of the Manet but never finished the edges of it. She didn't see it as having any value, so she and her sister just put their painting over that one to save having to use another stretcher. "

Dan shrugged. "So what's the problem? The painting underneath is your mom's copy."

223

"Except I saw the edges of both paintings left behind in the frame in Gray's panic room, and they were finished. Both of them." Darius took a sip of his own coffee – black, I noted – and watched his bosses' expressions.

Quinn got it immediately, and his eyes narrowed at Darius. "You're suggesting that the painting on the wall of the Gardner is a forgery, and the one behind *The Sisters* is a real Manet."

Darius nodded, and then glanced at me to drop his next bombshell. "Apparently, the original *Madame Auguste Manet* was in the annex for repairs on the night of the Gardner heist."

"No sh—?" I managed to stop the word from forming, but not the thought.

"No sh—." Darius mimicked back to me.

"And that is surprising because?" Quinn asked.

"Because there's a crime scene photo that shows the secret door to the annex was left open on the night of the heist," I said, still staring at Darius. He pulled a manila folder out of his bag and opened it on the table for Quinn and Dan. Inside was a copy of the black and white photo, a picture of the Madame Auguste painting, and copies of the photos we'd taken comparing the one from behind the sisters to the one hanging on the wall of the Blue Room. He also surprised me with a close-up photo of what was left behind in the frame in Gray's panic room after I cut the paintings out of it. The edges of both paintings were clearly visible, and both were painted black.

"How does Gray fit into all of this," Quinn asked grimly.

"He knew my mom and aunt when they worked at the museum. He was in a band with one of the guards, and they apparently practiced their music and had parties after hours at the museum in the months before the theft. There are a lot of factors that point to an inside job, and it seems like Markham Gray was tight with the guards who opened the door for the thieves."

"Most damning is the fact that the two paintings were wired and alarmed to the wall in his panic room," Darius added.

I tried to meet his eyes, but he didn't look at me. Quinn studied the photos before his gaze found mine. "I'd like to see whatever proof you have of ownership," he said.

I nodded.

"Where are the paintings now?" Dan asked.

"My mom has the one she and her sister painted. It's hers," I said with a decent amount of fierceness in my tone. "And I have Madame Auguste."

Quinn still studied me through narrowed eyes, and I met them squarely. It was either that or run away yipping with my tail between my legs. I forgot to close my mouth, though, and accidentally whispered in my best Dr. Evil voice, "Frickin' laser beams."

The corner of his mouth trembled, and I wondered if he was having a seizure. I spent thirty seconds picturing the paramedics, the gurney, and all the heroic measures people would go through to save his life, until he finally spoke. "Is the painting safe where it is, Ms. Collins?"

"Safe as long as no one knows I have it," I said.

"Make it safer than that, please." He had already turned to speak to Darius when I interrupted.

"Can I just ask what you plan to do about me?"

Quinn's gaze returned to me. "Is there something to be done about you, Ms. Collins?"

I exhaled, and I felt about as able to lie to Quinn as I did to Darius. "You know I stole the painting, and the police could probably find something that'll get me convicted for breaking and entering at a minimum."

"Are you a criminal?" Quinn asked in the same, almost-bored tone of voice.

"Not generally."

"Do you feel the need for punishment?" he asked.

"Are you offering?" I said before I could smack a hand over my face.

Dan laughed, Darius scowled, and Quinn just looked at me in silence. I would have been way more uncomfortable in that moment if I hadn't been counting prime numbers to myself, just to keep from saying the next idiotic thing that popped into my head.

"What do you do for a living, Ms. Collins?" Quinn asked, interrupting me at 239.

"You can knock off the Ms. Collins stuff, you know. Normal people don't say each other's names in conversations, they just, you know, look at each other. Your 'Ms. Collins' this and 'Ms. Collins' that is designed to intimidate me with how very polite you can be while you twist my arm up behind my back. My name is Anna. I talk too much, have no filter, and clearly should not be out in public without a gag order. Also, I'm a bounty hunter."

The corner of Quinn's mouth twitched again, and I gave the seizure up as wishful thinking. He was laughing at me. One twitch at the corner of the man of steel's mouth was the equivalent of a full belly laugh from a normal person.

"We would appreciate any help you are willing to render us, *Anna*," he said, emphasizing his use of my first name.

"Help doing what?" I asked, trying not to sound belligerent.

"Discovering the truth," he answered.

"Why? Gray was your client – doesn't that pose ethical problems for you?"

"In my experience," Quinn said, "it's better to be slapped with the truth than kissed by a lie. I prefer to see the hand coming so I can control how hard it lands."

I realized that I respected Quinn Sullivan, and actually liked Dan O'Malley. Dan laughed at the things I didn't say out loud, and Quinn said things I hadn't considered. Not a bad potential working environment. "What's it take to get a job here?" I asked.

"A clean record," Quinn answered without hesitation.

Damn.

"Cool." I said quickly. "I'll bring you what I have to back up my mom's ownership of *The Sisters*." I stood up and turned toward Darius, who looked at me with an odd expression on his face. "Let me know how I can help, and I'll do what I can while I'm in town."

"You have plans to travel, Ms. ... Anna?" Quinn said carefully.

226

I shrugged. "I always have plans to travel. It was interesting to meet you both."

Darius exchanged some indefinable look with his bosses that I didn't try to analyze because I was too intent on leaving the room. He caught up to me at the staircase.

"Can I come with you?"

"You don't trust me to bring the docs back?" I shot back, more defensively than I intended to.

"I'd like to see where you live," he said simply.

I had turned to face him, ready to do battle, but all the fight blew out. "Um. Okay."

He smiled and held the door to the hidden staircase open for me. "Who else uses this way?" I asked him.

"Just me," he said, "and now you."

# [ 34 ]
## ANNA

*"My idea of housework is to sweep the room with a glance."*

W e didn't say much to each other on the ride to my studio. I was weirdly nostalgic to be back in Darius's Land Cruiser. I tried not to pet the dashboard but failed. Darius was too distracted to comment or even smirk, and I wondered what was fueling the little hamster on the wheel in his head.

"You'll have to find a spot on the street," I told him when we pulled onto Burton Street. "It's why I don't keep a car."

"Where do you park your bike?" he asked.

"How do you know I have a bike?"

He gave me a side-eye, but said nothing.

"There's a spot by the dumpster behind the building. It's protected and mostly hidden, and I make sure the garbage guys get cookies a couple of times a month."

"Cookies?" He sounded incredulous and ... annoyed.

"It's not a bribe," I said quickly. "It's a courtesy. They're considerate of my bike, I'm considerate of their stomachs."

He lapsed back into silence, and I wondered which one of us was being unreasonable. He found a spot a block away, and I told him the history of the building as we walked.

"My aunt left me her space at the Carl Street Studios, which was what Carl Miller and Sol Kagan called their design project in the 1920s and 30s. Carl Miller was an artist who mostly worked in architectural design, and a lot of the things he became famous for were first tried in this building."

I led the way into the old Victorian mansion and compound that had been converted to twenty-two individual spaces. Mine was a small studio on the third floor, and I watched Darius's face for his expression as I opened the door.

He didn't disappoint. The hamster wheel stopped spinning in his brain when he stepped inside my studio, and I saw his imagination engage. I looked around, trying to see everything through his eyes. The space was a single room with a soaring ceiling and tall windows with stained glass accents that made the walls glow with jewel tones. The wood floor was laid with contrasting strips of ebony, walnut, and ash, and the fireplace which dominated one wall was surrounded by art deco tiles in all the shades of green. I had set my bed up on a platform under the window, and the heavy tapestry I threw over it during the day, plus big pillows against the wall and a thick rug on the floor, gave it a distinctly divan vibe. A small galley kitchen and same-sized bathroom occupied the other side of the studio, and an old wardrobe that I'd inherited with the space, which held my small collection of jeans, T-shirts, boots, and two dresses, dominated one wall. The only other thing of Alex's which had remained in the studio was her easel, which stood in the corner holding the painting she had been working on when she died.

Darius strode directly to the easel. It was a portrait of two women, nearly identical to *The Sisters* painting in style and use of color. The only real difference was that the subjects weren't my mom and Alex, they were Colette and me. She'd used a photograph my dad had taken of us when we were home for Christmas a couple of years ago.

"The letter Alex left for me was taped to the back of the canvas," I said, as Darius examined the faces. I'd spent a long time doing the same. He picked up the snapshot from the easel where I'd found it and flipped it over to read the inscription on the back. "*Sophia misses you every day*," he read. "Whose handwriting is this?"

"My dad's. I'm not sure my mom ever knew he'd been in touch with her sister, and I've never asked him about it."

"The painting is beautiful, Anna."

"It is, isn't it. She didn't finish the edges." The edges of the canvas that stretched over the wooden frame were still white, and it made the painting feel more like a print than something a paintbrush had ever touched.

He studied the edges then walked around to peer at the back of the canvas. "Single canvas?"

"Yeah. I checked."

"Can I see the letter she left you?"

I fished it out of a drawer in the wardrobe where I kept things that were precious to me, and Darius saw what else was in the drawer before I could shut it.

"You have a T. rex costume?" he asked as he looked over my shoulder.

I snorted. "You don't?" I shut the drawer before he could see the rhinestone tiara.

He laughed and wandered away from the painting. "The tile baseboards are cool."

"Right? Only a few of them repeat, and all of them were hand-fired in a kiln that was kept downstairs for all the artists to use."

"I like the heart," he said, pointing to a tile I loved near the fireplace.

I tried not to swoon as I handed him the letter. Swooning was poor form when corsets were not involved. They were par for the course when corsets *were* involved, but that was not a story that bore repeating.

"Do you mean to say such lovely things to unsettle me, or are you really a guy who thinks hearts are cool?"

He looked surprised. "Sorry?" He gaped slightly, then seemed to realize he was doing it and stopped. "You do remember I was denied membership in the man club of manly men, right?"

"And yet, here you are – undeniably male." I waved my hand in an up-and-down motion that denoted my clear thoughts on the matter of his attractiveness.

"And here I am," he echoed, as though wondering why.

I studied my aunt's handwriting as he read her letter. She had nice handwriting, sort of architectural and blocky, and I wished I had gotten letters from her my whole life.

"May I photograph this and the painting?" he asked carefully.

I shrugged. "Sure."

I plopped down on my bed to wait for him as he pulled out his phone and took the photos. When he was done, he refolded the letter and handed it to me, then sat on the edge of the bed next to me and looked around the room.

"I expected to see books."

I leaned over him to pull my kindle out from under my pillow. "I travel too much to buy paperbacks, and the studio isn't really big enough for bookshelves."

"It's beautiful here," he said quietly.

"Thank you. I think so too."

We sat side by side, but not close enough to touch, and finally, Darius sighed. "Why did you ask to work at Cipher?"

I did not expect that question and looked over in surprise. "I like your bosses."

He didn't meet my eyes, but nodded. "They're good guys. Quinn's intense, but his wife makes him human. She reminds me a little of you in some ways."

I smirked. "She jumps out of planes and climbs Half Dome whenever she gets a chance?"

He smiled, still not looking at me. "No. Her filter is … odd."

"Ah, but she has one," I wagged my finger. "Not the same."

He was silent for another long moment as his eyes wandered the room, settling on a mirror I'd hung on one wall that was almost completely obscured by my collection of postcards from my adventures.

"I have Sunday roast, Iranian-style, with my family every Monday night." He looked over at my mouth, already open to protest the ridiculousness of that statement, and laughed. "Yes, I'm aware of the irony – Iranian food for a quintessential British meal, served on Monday instead of Sunday. It's a habit left over from my father's taxi driving days, because everyone else had Sunday roast taxi needs, and Mondays were typically quiet."

"Makes sense."

He inhaled. "Why did you ask to meet my parents?"

I hadn't quite formulated words to go with the request when I'd asked, so I winged it now. "You've met my family," I watched his face and was happy to see the upward quirk of his lips, "and that probably filled in some of the colors of your picture of me."

He smiled properly at that. "One or two," he said.

I wondered what color my mom's topless dip in the freezing ocean added to the picture of Anna Collins, then decided I hoped it was hot pink or sunset orange.

I met Darius's eyes. "I want to add some colors to my picture of you."

His eyes searched mine long enough for my inside voice to start whispering self-consciously. "Would you like to come with me tonight?" he finally asked.

I sighed. "I do realize I just put you on the spot. I could meet them at your boat, or at a café. If I go to a family dinner, all kinds of awkward assumptions could be made about the non-existence of our status."

"You said we're friends. That's a status, right?"

"Of course it is," I said impatiently. "Some of my best friends are … friends." I couldn't help the smile at my own nonsense, and Darius finally lightened up to smile too.

"The restaurant we went to in Boston was good, but my mum's cooking is much better. Come. They enjoy meeting my friends."

His expression had shifted from carefully neutral to friendly-ish.

It made me want to tickle him, just to see him laugh, but I resisted the urge. Barely. It was a close one though.

"Sure, I'd love to. Thank you for inviting me," I said formally, in an attempt to quell the tickling instinct.

"Great," he said, standing up. "I'll pick you up at six?"

"Sure. Is this okay?" I said, looking down at myself. "It's either this or a dress. I don't really have other options besides jeans."

He smiled. "You look good in whatever you wear, and yes, jeans are fine."

I walked him to the door and tried not to skip for joy at the compliment, because really, I could take a compliment without doing backflips. He turned to take one last look at my studio. "This really is a great place. The color, the light, all the quirky bits and unexpected beauty - it suits you."

He turned and left, and it probably was my imagination when, on his way down the stairs, I heard him say, "It *is* you."

# [ 35 ]
## DARIUS

"*Mechanic (noun): Someone who does precision guesswork based on unreliable data provided by those of questionable knowledge. See also Wizard. Magician.*"

- FROM THE T-SHIRT COLLECTION OF ANNA COLLINS

I was nervous. It was ridiculous, and it made me feel like I was sixteen, but I couldn't escape the fact that I was nervous to bring this woman home to dinner with my parents.

My parents were generous and gracious, so I thought they would overlook the jeans and boots Anna was wearing. A dress would have been too much though, because that would've looked like I was bringing my girlfriend home to meet Mum and Dad. She was not my girlfriend, and she couldn't be. Too much stood in the way of a relationship with her, no matter how my heart raced when she laughed, or how hard I got at the memory of our day on my boat.

My parents lived in Sheridan Park, in a small single-family home on a big lot that had survived suburban subdivision. My father had built a boat-sized garage which currently housed his latest restoration project. My boat had been his first project, and this one was for my brother, Reza.

I parked my Land Cruiser in the driveway and pointed through the windshield to the garage, where a light shone through the windows. "My father and brother are likely still working on Reza's boat, and will be until Mum calls them in for dinner. It's slightly smaller than mine, but newer and faster, so the restoration has revolved around the mechanics of it rather than the aesthetics."

I sounded inane, even to my own ears, so I opened the door before I could say something even less interesting.

"Can we go see it?" Anna asked, startling me enough that I stumbled on my step out of the truck.

"Uh, sure." I hated how uncertain I sounded. Anna was my friend. Certainly she was an acquaintance with whom I was friendly. If friendliness included watching how the expressions on her face lit up three feet of space around her, or actively forcing my hands not to reach for her hair, or the itch in my fingers to touch her skin, trace her lips, feel the soft roundness of her hips in my hands.

I pulled the mental handbrake on that train of thought. Attraction did not override common sense. And my common sense would not allow me to want a woman whose code of honor was so different than mine.

She was out of the passenger side of my truck before I could open her door, and I had to resist the urge to take the wine from her hands. We were just friends. She wouldn't welcome opened doors or carried things, and if I insisted, it might send the wrong message.

"I can hear you thinking all the way over here, Darius. What's going through your head?" She sounded concerned, and I didn't want that concern directed anywhere near me.

"I'm fine. Just thinking about the case." In fact, I had been thinking about the case. I'd given the photos of the painting and Alex Kiriakis's letter to Quinn and Dan, and the three of us had spent an hour hashing through every issue, every problem, and every potential pitfall for Cipher around the two paintings and the break-in to steal them.

"And? What did you all decide?"

Anna Collins was astute. She knew I would have spoken to my bosses. "Cipher Security has no official position on the theft and current whereabouts of the painting known as *The Sisters*, which was removed from the panic room of Markham Gray's residence. If, at some future time, Gray were to file a police report on the theft, Cipher would be obliged to comply with law enforcement as per our contract with Gray, which was in effect at the time the painting was taken."

Anna's expression was as guarded as she knew how to make it. I didn't like the uncertainty that shone through her eyes. "And what about Madame Auguste?"

"That's not something we're prepared to pursue at this time in light of the fact that we've been released from our obligation to our former client who never made us aware of its existence." My voice sounded cold to my own ears, and she tensed.

"So," she said, in a tone of voice that was meant to be light, "do you have any suggestions for what I should do with a painting that may or may not be an authentic Manet? Because, you know, keeping it in my studio is probably not the best idea for someone with a fifty-fifty shot at being arrested for B&E at a minimum."

We stopped outside the garage door, and I dropped my voice to just above a murmur. "I want to help you, Anna, but I don't know what I can do."

She looked up at me with so much sadness in her eyes that I wanted to pull her directly into my arms and never let her go. "It's not your job to help me. I'll figure it out," she said with a tenderness in her voice that almost broke me. Then she touched my cheek and smiled at the sound of my brother's voice in the garage as he cursed in frustration. "Sounds like he could use our help though. Come on, introduce me."

I tried to hold her gaze for a moment longer, but she looked away, so I reached past her for the side door into the garage and opened it to let her in.

My father looked up immediately and grinned at us. "Welcome!"

He opened his arms wide as he stood to greet us. My father was in his mid-fifties and looked very much the same as he always had. He was my height and had the same lean muscle I'd inherited from him. His hair was black and silver, and his skin was darker brown than mine, like my brother's.

Dad came and hugged me, then turned to Anna. "You must be Anna. Welcome to our home."

Anna shook his hand, and her smile was bright and genuine. "Thank you so much for having me. I'm sorry it was so last minute."

"Nonsense," he said. "Any guests of my sons are guests of ours."

Reza stood up and stretched his arms over his head, a move I'd seen him do around women for years. His T-shirt rose at the hem so that six-pack abdominals greeted whoever was looking. If I was the Disney prince, as Anna called me, then Reza was the muscle. He was an inch taller than me and had at least twenty more pounds of muscle on his frame, which wasn't a surprise given that I'd run cross-country in high school while he'd played rugby.

He held out a hand to Anna that was black with grease. "I'm Reza," he said.

Anna took his hand and shook. "It's nice to meet you. I'm Anna." She didn't wipe her hand on her jeans when he let go, and I saw speculation in my brother's eyes when he noticed.

"What are you working on?" I asked, to interrupt Reza's perusal of my guest.

"Trying to get the right timing." Reza turned back to the marine engine. "I can't quite dial it in, and Dad's hands are too big to help me."

That was another thing we'd both inherited from our father – strong hands that seemed almost too big for our build. Reza fit his hands better than I did, though mine had been useful for turning wrenches as I worked on engines.

"What do you need help with? Holding the timing light or turning the cap?" Anna asked as she set down the wine bottle she carried and pulled off her leather coat.

I was surprised to see that her normal T-shirt had been replaced by a white linen shirt that looked crisp and elegant in a way I hadn't expected from her.

"Turning the cap, but it's fine. I've already gotten you dirty," Reza said with a gleam in his eye that made me want to punch him.

Anna looked at her hands, which did indeed have black smudges on them, then down at the white shirt. She then looked at me expectantly. "Could you unbutton me so I can work without getting oil on my shirt?" She held up her hands in explanation.

My brother was suddenly very interested, and even my dad looked a little speculative.

"It's fine," I said to her, "I'll help him."

Anna smirked. "I've seen your hands – they're too big. All of you," she said, looking around at the three of us, "have great hands that probably suck for all the fine tuning you have to do on carburetors. I, however," she waggled her fingers where I could see them, "have excellent hands for working on engines. Now, will you please help me so I don't go in to dinner looking disgraceful in a stained shirt?"

"I'm not going to unbutton your shirt, Anna," I murmured to her.

She rolled her eyes. "Well I can't, and he can't," she indicated Reza, "so it's either you or your dad. Sorry, Mr. Masoud," she said, cutting her eyes to him, "would you be so kind as to help me?"

"I've got it," I said quickly. I reached for the buttons on the front of her linen shirt and tried to ignore the catch in her breath as my fingers grazed her skin.

"I'm wearing a tank top, so relax," she said.

I realized my jaw had been clenched, and I forced myself to relax so I could work the buttons. My brother seemed frozen, and I seriously wanted to punch him for looking at Anna the way he did. My dad busied himself with the tools, and I tried not to notice how the pulse beat in her throat as I unfastened her buttons.

She was indeed wearing a white tank, and when I pushed the linen shirt down her shoulders and she shrugged the sleeves off, I saw she had strong arms like a person who had spent a lot of time in garages working on engines.

She moved around Reza and kicked a crate over to stand on so she could reach into the engine compartment of the boat. "Okay," she said, "hit the engine." She nodded at my dad who looked momentarily nonplussed as he hit the ignition button. The engine roared to life, and I could hear the roughness in the idle.

Reza got over his own surprise and connected the timing light to the battery. I draped Anna's white shirt over my shoulder and picked up a flashlight to shine on the distributor cap so she could see what she was doing.

She reached over the belts and moved the cap a couple of millimeters to the left, then paused, listening to the idle for a moment. Reza opened his mouth to speak, but Anna shook her head, deep in concentration. Then she moved it back a millimeter to the right. The idle smoothed out, and the engine purred as quietly as a marine engine was capable of.

Anna looked at me and grinned. "Good, right?" She bit her bottom lip as if she was seeking my approval, and I wanted to kiss her so badly I took a step backward.

I nodded and said, "Good," but not before the pleased look on her face dimmed to something merely pleasant.

My father found a clean-ish shop towel and poured bottled water over it to hand to Anna. "Thank you for your help, Anna. Where did you learn engine timing?"

She wiped her hands and took her shirt off my shoulder to put it back on. "My dad taught me. First it was motorcycles, but he made me help with my uncle's sailboat engine too."

"You sail?" my father asked with real interest.

Anna nodded. "I love being out on the ocean." She shrugged. "I love being out, period. I'm at my best when I'm climbing something, or jumping off something, or when I'm just chasing the wind. What about you? When did you fall in love with boats?"

She had re-buttoned her shirt, and I missed the sight of her collar bones. My dad was able to meet her eyes again though, and it was clear he appreciated the question, because he smiled at some memory as he answered. "Fell in love ... hmm, yes, I suppose that's what I did. When I was a boy, my family spent holidays at my grandparents' villa by the Caspian Sea, and my grandfather taught me how to sail. It was wonderful to spend all day on the water with him, fishing and singing, returning only when it was nearly dark." He shook his head, laughing. "My grandmother always sighed the sigh of the long-suffering when we came in bearing baskets full of fish, but she always fried one for me in butter with lemon, and it was always the best thing I'd eaten that day."

I'd heard my father's stories of sailing with his grandfather, but I never tired of the happiness that shone in his eyes when he told them. Anna was just as captured by his memories as he was, and her eyes met mine just long enough for me to see the smile in them.

"By the time the revolution came," my father continued, "I'd become a competent sailor, though I wasn't able to boat again until we lived in London. The villa and boat were confiscated by the ayatollah's government a few years later. I remember my father's shock at the time, though in retrospect, the political heat had been getting higher and higher, and we were the frogs slowly cooking to death without even realizing it."

He shook his head at the memory and continued to clean the tools that lay near him. "The revolution in 1979 actually caused a social and political regression, which had been an unexpected outcome for some. My mother wore lipstick and high heels to work before the revolution, and she was one of those who marched against the veil afterwards. But my sons never saw a woman's hair uncovered in public until we left Tehran."

"I don't even remember living there," said Reza as he emerged from the engine compartment. Anna handed him the cloth she'd used on her hands, and he smiled in thanks.

I still wanted to punch him, but Anna distracted me by speaking. "Do you remember?"

I nodded. "I was seven, so it's just impressions. A lot of black clothing mostly. My parents' friends were over a lot, and the best thing about that was the leftover food."

Reza grinned and threw the shop towel at me. "You and food." I grabbed it out of the air and hurled it back, and since he was looking at Anna – again – it hit him in the side of his face. I smirked, he growled, and he would have launched himself at me except Anna stepped between us.

"Someone please take me into the kitchen to meet your mom so I can help with the food." Her tone was too sweet, and I knew it was a ruse to keep us from fighting.

"Go on, you two," my dad said to me and Anna. "We need to clean up in here and change."

Anna looked at their jeans and shirts and then at her own. "How much changing are you going to be doing?" Her eyes narrowed at Reza suspiciously.

"Sunday roast is the one time Mom makes us wear real clothes."

"And jeans aren't real clothes?" Now Anna's suspicion was directed at me.

"Jeans are fine," I said quietly. "We're just not allowed to wear them."

Anna held my gaze a moment longer, then closed her eyes and exhaled. "Right, well, hopefully the wine's good enough."

# [ 36 ]
## ANNA

*"My personal style these days is 'I didn't expect to get out of the car.'"*

- ANNA COLLINS

It shouldn't have surprised me that the mother of the Disney prince was a queen. She was gorgeous, elegant, refined perfection personified – and I was pretty sure that when this night was done, I was going to kneecap Darius for letting me come underdressed to dinner.

"Mum, this is Anna. Anna, this is my mother, Silvana."

Silvana had long, dark brown hair with thick, glossy waves. Her eyes were lined with black, and her lipstick was the kind of matte red that Parisians, and apparently Iranian queens, wore effortlessly. She wore an apron over a silk blouse, perfectly tailored black slacks, and high heeled black pumps with red soles that matched her lipstick. There were small gold hoops in her ears, and a gold chain around her neck with a teardrop-shaped ruby hanging from it. She beamed at her son and spoke to him in rapid Farsi that seemed to be all 'you're here, I've missed you, and give me a kiss,' because he beamed back and they traded a trio of cheek kisses with nary an air kiss or red smudge in sight.

I couldn't even begin to compete with that, so I didn't bother to try. When Silvana's gaze shifted to me, I broadsided her with the biggest smile in my arsenal. "Thank you so much for allowing me to come to your home, Mrs. Masoud. I apologize that I didn't dress up, and if I'm ever invited back, I promise to do better next time."

Silvana laughed and leaned in to give me the three-kiss treatment her son had gotten. "Welcome, Anna. I'm delighted that you've come. Darius, please take Anna's coat and put your things in the sitting room. I need Anna's help in here."

I handed Darius my coat and avoided his raised eyebrows as I immediately rolled up my sleeves and washed my hands at the sink. "Please put me to work."

She eyed my white shirt and pulled an apron out of a drawer for me. It looked like a very girly 1950s dress with pockets, and I looked up in surprise. "I don't even think my dresses are this pretty."

Silvana smiled. "Pretty things are never an indulgence. They are a necessity that bring joy to every task."

I put on the apron and tied it behind me, and then Silvana put me to the task of seeding a pomegranate. It was cold from the refrigerator, which, she explained, was the only way to keep them past January.

"This is the last time I can make proper *fesenjan* until the pomegranates are ripe again in September," she said, giving a heavy pot on the stove a stir.

"It smells amazing," I said.

"It's one of Darius's favorites. He is the one who usually helps me in the kitchen and has become an excellent cook himself. Has he made any of his specialties for you?" The way Silvana asked the question was meant to sound innocent, but she was clearly fishing for the status of our relationship.

And if I thought lying to Darius was hard, lying to his mother was impossible. I looked up from the pomegranate and met her eyes. "I'm very attracted to your son, but I don't think I'm right for him."

My forthrightness seemed to surprise her. She glanced back at the pot she was stirring, then spoke. "If I may ask a personal question, why do you believe you're not right for Darius?"

I continued seeding the pomegranate, grateful to have something to do with my hands and eyes while my mouth tried to form words that made sense. I inhaled and hoped for the best. "I lied to him once – it was by omission, but it was on purpose, and it was enough to change his opinion of me. Since then, he has seen that there are things I do that don't fit his code, and it doesn't work for him that my code allows them."

She was silent for long enough that I looked up from my work. "My son was a serious boy who grew into an even more serious man." She seemed to reconsider whatever she was going to say, but then she met my eyes. "Things had been dangerous for us for years before we finally fled Iran, and Darius spent the first years of his life listening to adults speak of concerning things. Our dinner conversations with our journalist friends were about human rights violations, corruption, and all the lies that were being spoon-fed to people who wanted to believe them."

Her eyes took on a distant look, and there were lines of anger around her mouth that hadn't been there before. But then they softened, and Silvana's memory playback shifted. "When Reza was born, it was Darius's job to protect his baby brother, and when we left Tehran, Darius had to comfort him in a new place where nothing was familiar to any of us. There wasn't much time for play in our lives then, and to be honest, it wasn't until my husband began teaching in London that we found things to laugh about. It is a reason our Sunday roast tradition is so important to us – those Monday dinners in our tiny flat when I would make the Persian food of my youth and Basim would tell the boys stories from *One Thousand and One Nights*. We were able to let down our guard and be a family."

Again, Silvana's eyes were distant as she replayed the memories, but this time her expression was peaceful.

I brushed all the broken pieces of pomegranate skin into my hand and dropped them into the garbage. "I've seen Darius play a little," I said quietly. "It's an awkward thing, like an old dog pouncing on a tennis ball and sending it flying across the room. But it's beautiful too, because it feels rare and precious to hear laughter in his voice." I looked at my hands, covered in pomegranate juice where engine grease had been before. "I learned to play in self-defense," I finally said. "It was a way to be noticed as different from my sister, who was everything beautiful, elegant, and proper." I looked up and met Silvana's eyes. "Kind of like you, only not as regal."

Silvana laughed. "Regal? What a delightful word. I quite like the idea that I could be regal."

The kitchen door opened, and Reza and his dad entered, with Darius right behind them. Basim went to her and kissed her cheek. "You are regal like the moon, my love, queen of everything you oversee."

Silvana made a scoffing noise that sounded like "don't be an idiot" plus "go on, tell me more." It was an excellent noise that I resolved to practice for my own repertoire.

"Go wash up. Dinner is ready."

The two men left as Darius eyed my apron with a raised eyebrow. "It looks much better on you than it does on me."

I burst into laughter at the picture he would make in the pretty apron, and he smiled as if he was pleased with himself for making me laugh. Then I shook my finger at him. "Just so you know, I've decided to wear this the whole night."

Now it was his turn to laugh. "Why?"

"Because you said jeans would be fine, but they're not fine, and since this is a nicer dress than what I have, I'm borrowing it." I turned to Silvana. "May I borrow this for dinner?"

She grinned at me. "You may wear whatever you like to my dinner table, Anna. You called me regal, so you are granted immunity from my Sunday roast dress code."

"Thank you," I said with a side-eye and smack for Darius's hand when he tried to reach for a pomegranate seed. "I accept my immunity, but I'd still like to wear the apron. It's like getting to be girly without the commitment." I eyed Silvana's shoes with a mock shudder. "I actively suck at high heels."

She, meanwhile, moved like she'd been born in them, and she kicked up one shoe to show me the red sole. "There are marble stones in Iran, from the Safavid period, on which women would place their feet while henna was applied. Engraved on the marble were words that roughly translate to, *Is that the color of henna on the bottom of your foot, or is it the blood of a lover you've trampled underfoot?*"

My eyes widened as my gaze went from the red soles of her shoes to her face. "That is a truly excellent reason to own red-soled heels and is almost worthy of the walking lessons I'd have to take to wear them."

"I prefer your boots," Darius said as he snatched a pomegranate seed from the stash I was no longer guarding. "You walk with confidence in them."

I considered my engineer boots, which were like the ankle version of motorcycle boots and way more comfortable. "They're useful for keeping my ankles from being burned on hot exhaust pipes, and they add a little extra whoop-ass to my perp-kick."

"Whoop-ass to your perp-kick?" Reza asked with a laugh as he entered the kitchen, having changed into khakis and a long-sleeved shirt, similar to what Darius wore. "Are those words that actually mean something?" He leaned over to kiss his mother's cheek as a distraction while he snagged a few walnuts from the bowl next to her.

"Anna's a bounty hunter. Apparently, she has a special kick she reserves for intransigent bail jumpers," Darius said as he poured the contents of the heavy cast iron pot into a serving tureen. Did he have any idea how sexy his kitchen skills and fifty-cent words were?

"As one does," I muttered, just so I wouldn't be caught staring.

"Dang," Reza said, with an inflection that was the total opposite of Darius's classy way of speaking. "That's hot."

Darius handed Reza the tureen with a grumpy, "Take this," and Silvana handed Darius the bowl of rice she'd plated earlier.

"Come, Anna, now it's the men's turn to work." She led the way to the dining room where Basim was lighting candles on a table already set with beautifully glazed dishes. The two men followed behind us, bringing bowls of food that smelled amazing. I was seated to Basim's right, next to Darius. He was on my right, and Reza sat across from me, with their mother between them.

"Who was the last bail jumper you caught?" Reza asked as soon as he sat down. I glanced at Silvana to see if there was something special that needed to be done, but she just smiled encouragingly and passed the bowl of rice to Darius, who passed it to me.

I took spoonfuls of the rice and the chicken, walnut, and pome- granate stew, and told Reza the story of catching Junior. Basim and Silvana seemed equally invested in my tale, but I kept it pretty light on the details because Darius had already heard it. He surprised me by asking leading questions that prompted me to answer with specifics.

"What kind of handcuffs do you carry?" he asked after I'd described my takedown of Junior in his crappy apartment.

"You would ask about handcuffs," his brother snarked.

I flushed, which Silvana noticed. "Zip ties are easiest," I said, meeting Darius's eyes. "I have some in my back pocket if you need to use them on your brother."

He smirked. "I'll keep that in mind."

I turned to Basim before anyone could ask me more questions. "Darius said you've been a teacher since you lived in England. Do you still teach?"

He nodded. "At least one journalism course each semester, and one political science. This year I'm also teaching a class on the art and literature of the Middle East."

"Anything to use *One Thousand and One Nights* as a textbook, right Dad?" Reza said.

"Would you tell us a story from it, like you did in London at Sunday roasts?" I asked.

"He told them in Farsi," Reza said. "I don't even know if he knows them in English."

Basim gave his son a quelling look. "Perhaps you'd like to tell Anna the story of the three apples?"

Reza shrugged, "I don't remember that one." The gesture made him seem like an overgrown teenager, and I was about to change the subject again when Darius's voice near my right ear made liquid heat pool in my stomach.

"*The Three Apples* is essentially a murder mystery," he said. "A chest is discovered with the dismembered body of a woman locked inside. The Caliph then charges his vizier with finding the killer—"

"Which he doesn't – the killer comes to him to confess," interrupted Reza, who apparently did remember the story.

Darius continued as though he hadn't heard his brother, "—and the Caliph hears the confession of a young man who tells a story of his loving and dutiful wife and three rare apples she asked him to find for her when she was ill. He traveled far and wide and finally brought her the apples, which he took from the Caliph's own orchards, but then she was too ill to eat them. Later, the man discovered a passing slave with one of the apples, and when asked about it, the slave said his girlfriend gave it to him as a gift after her husband traveled for more than a month to find it. The man went home and killed his wife, cut her into pieces, and stuffed her into the trunk. Later, his young son confessed to stealing the apple, which a slave had then taken and run off with. The Caliph feels sorry for the man and pardons him, but then sends his vizier to find the tricky slave and bring him to justice."

"He pardons the murderer and goes after the slave?" I asked, incredulous.

"Right?" Reza said, clearly amused by my horror. "Nice priorities, big guy."

"In the end," Darius continued, "the vizier discovers it was one of his own slaves who lied about the apple. He asks the Caliph for forgiveness for his slave, which the Caliph grants."

"And," Reza adds, "the Caliph feels so sorry for the guy who killed his wife that he offers him one of his own slaves to marry as a consolation prize."

"So," Basim said, "who is the victim in the story?"

"Clearly it's the wife, since she's dead," I said.

"Not the Caliph?" he asked, apparently serious.

"Why would the Caliph be the victim?"

"There are some people," he said, in full professor voice, "who would argue that the Caliph was the real victim – as it was from his orchards that the apples were taken. And yet he still found it within himself to forgive the husband and the slave for their transgressions."

"Not only did he forgive them, he gave them a reward," I said in disgust.

I saw the shutters go down on Darius's face and knew I'd just said something wrong. No one else at the table seemed to notice this though, and conversation shifted to the contemporary retellings of various *One Thousand and One Nights* tales.

When the dishes had been washed and dried, and Darius was talking through a boat mechanics problem by the kitchen door with his dad and brother, Silvana handed me the pretty apron I'd finally taken off. "It suits you," she said.

I smiled and tried to hand it back. "It actually doesn't. I'd feel like a fraud."

"Are you a fraud?" she asked in a way that reminded me of her son.

The question was too personal, too bold, and definitely should have been approached with the wariness I had for snakes. But I'd been second guessing whatever I could have said that pissed Darius off, and I didn't want to mess around with complex answers.

"As a person, no. As a woman?" I shrugged. "I guess it depends on the things you think are important."

"What do you think is important, Anna?" Silvana's voice was quiet, but I had the sense Darius had heard her question. I *felt* him listening, though his dad and brother were arguing about boat throttle timings.

"Loyalty. Standing up for people who need help. Family." I took a deep breath. "I think what you *do* defines you more than what you believe."

"And ideals? Are those worthless?" Darius's voice had a sharp edge to it. I refused to bite back in front of his family. Instead, I set the apron down on the counter and met Silvana's gaze.

"Thank you so much for your wonderful hospitality. The food was so good, and I really enjoyed meeting you all." I included Basim and Reza in my gaze, then I turned to Darius. "You should stay and hang out with your family. I'll call a Lyft to get home."

"Don't be ridiculous," he muttered. He leaned over to give his mother a kiss on the cheek, then shook his dad's hand and clapped his brother on the shoulder. I reached my hand out to shake Silvana's, but she pulled me in to kiss my cheek.

"You are a lovely young woman, Anna," she murmured. It felt like a benediction, but I appreciated the sentiment anyway.

I decided that if meeting a person's parents added color to their portrait, she was the red in the picture of Darius Masoud.

# [ 37 ]
## DARIUS

*"Be careful with your words, once they are said they can only be forgiven, not forgotten."*

"I am ridiculous, didn't you get the memo?!" Anna exploded at me as soon as the door closed on my truck.

I inhaled deeply. "I apologize. You are not ridiculous. I was angry."

She glared at me. "You were angry." It was not a question. "You've been angry all night. Your anger makes me tired, Darius."

We rode in silence until the silence was louder than the unsaid words cycling through my brain.

Finally, Anna spoke again. "What did I say that made you shut down?"

"It doesn't matter," I said, attempting to believe my own words.

I could feel her watching me, and I deliberately avoided her gaze.

"Then you're a liar, Darius. The very thing you condemn me for."

White hot anger pounded through my veins, and I ground my

teeth against the words that threatened to explode from me. "I don't lie," I breathed out.

"So that time you said we were friends wasn't a lie? Because shutting me out and then pretending it doesn't matter are not the actions of a friend. For that matter, neither is setting me up to look disrespectful to your family. That actually sucked. I felt stupid and sloppy and even more clumsy than usual, so thanks for that too."

A wave of shame swept the anger away and I felt sick. "Anna ..." I began, but then couldn't find the next words. I looked over at her, but she wouldn't meet my eyes. I tried again. "I didn't set you up, and they don't think you're disrespectful at all. They like you." I exhaled. "That's the problem."

"Because I'm just so awful?" Her voice broke on the word, and she turned toward the window.

There were so many things I should have said. She wasn't awful. She was the opposite of awful. She made me want things I couldn't want, to be something I couldn't be. Her voice had woven through my dreams, her scent was on my pillow, her laughter was under my skin. *She* was under my skin, and like an itch I couldn't scratch, all I wanted to do was tear my skin off.

"Who is the bad guy in the three apples story?" Anna asked in a small voice that made my heart hurt. "Was it the guy who killed his wife and chopped her into little pieces, or the slave who tricked the guy with the malicious lie about his wife's fidelity?"

"Or maybe it was the Caliph who forgave the criminals their behavior and gave them a second chance?" I said, feeling the anger seep back into my veins.

"What are we actually talking about? The fact that I think the Caliph is a misogynistic jerk?"

"He should never have forgiven the crimes, isn't that right?" I said.

"The husband murdered his wife over a rumor," she spat out. Obviously her anger was rising too.

"And because he forgave the murderer, he's now complicit in the wife's death." I knew she didn't deserve my anger in this, but I *was* angry.

"Yes!"

"Exactly." Saying the word took the fight out of me. It was everything I knew, and everything I believed, and yet it made me inexplicably sad.

I felt her gaze return to me for a long moment, and then she turned her eyes to the play of streetlights on the dashboard. She traced the path of light with her hand. "We're not talking about the Caliph at all." The light disappeared and then reappeared with the next lamp. "And that's why you withdrew tonight at dinner. Because you're the Caliph. I broke into your orchard and stole the apples growing there. And no matter what other crimes are revealed later, it falls on you to investigate and judge." She inhaled, and then sighed. "And if you forgive me, you become complicit."

I turned onto West Burton and stopped my truck outside her building. I didn't put it in park or turn it off, and Anna unbuckled her seatbelt and turned in her seat. The streetlight cast half her face in deep shadow as she studied me for a long moment. She was unendurably beautiful.

"I didn't know you existed," she said, "and now I do, but I don't get to have you, and it hurts. A lot." She sighed, and I felt her sadness creep into me. "I wouldn't change what I've done, but I would change who I've done it to. I'm sorry." Her last words were a whisper, and then she got out of my truck and walked in front of my headlights and into her garden gate, and was gone.

I drove mindlessly around downtown Chicago for a while, until the wildflower scent of her that still lingered in my car had faded. The parking lot at the harbor was nearly empty, as usual, but I recognized the old Bronco in a space near the pier gate.

My brother wanted to talk. I hoped he'd brought beer.

He lay on my bed reading a time travel fantasy, and I had to bite back a surge of anger that he could be erasing the last of her scent with his own. "Reza," I said as I hung my coat on a hook near the door.

"Dar," he said, without looking up from the book. "Mom sent *fesenjan*. It's in the fridge."

I checked the fridge and found a big tub of the stew, some rice, and a six-pack of beer. I grabbed two beers, opened them, and put them on the table as I kicked off my shoes and sat. "You can borrow the book," I said, staring at the label on my bottle as if it held all the wisdom in the world.

He came out of the bedroom, grabbed a receipt to use as a book-mark, and dropped onto the bench seat across from me. "So, Anna," he said as he took a swig of his beer.

I sighed. It couldn't have been boat engines or a problem at work that inspired my brother to show up at ten o'clock at night?

"Do we need to talk about this tonight?"

Reza leaned back, sipped his beer, and regarded me. "We don't ever need to talk about it, but if you're not going to keep her, can I take a shot?"

"Fuck off, Reza."

A smile crept along the edges of his smug mouth, and I wanted to wipe it off with my fist. I'd never punched my brother, not even when he had begged for an attitude adjustment, but he was finally bigger than me, and my degree of self-loathing was such that I actually wanted the fight.

"I think she's the best thing to happen to you since you bought this tub," he said, gesturing around him. He loved my boat and had spent long hours helping me strip and sand the wood.

"She's gone," I said, glaring at him. "And she's not for you, either."

The smugness disappeared, and he sighed. "What'd you do?"

Sometimes I hated my brother for his ease with himself, because it shone a spotlight on everything I struggled with.

What *had* I done? And worse, why had I done it? "I let myself forget what I believe in for a little while – told myself it didn't matter, because whatever it was ..." I trailed off, because I knew exactly what it was. "The attraction between us couldn't be real."

"The attraction is visceral, man. It sparks the air between you like electricity, but ungrounded, like a live wire."

He was right. It was dangerous.

I picked at the label on my beer while I chose the words I hadn't even said to myself. "If I let myself be with her, it would make what our parents stood for, what they left Iran for, what I built my own ethics from, a lie."

Reza scowled at me. "What is she, man, a terrorist?"

I huffed a mirthless laugh. "No. With her it's not one big thing. It would be death by a thousand cuts every time she bribed the police with coffee, lied for information, traded a favor, asked for forgiveness rather than permission."

"She's a bounty hunter, right? Isn't that what they do?" It was so easy for Reza.

I peeled the label off the bottle in one continuous strip and found the words to explain. "It's more than her work. She lives by her own code, and if I let myself play by her rules, I'll lose my own."

My brother was silent for a long time, turning the bottle in his hands. "Who made your rules?" he finally asked. "Because it seems to me that you made them yourself a long time ago, maybe even when you were a kid."

Reza had been a toddler when we left Iran. All his memories came from other people's stories, and yet he continued. "You heard the things people said, people who were afraid and maybe justifying their choices to leave Iran, and your little seven-year-old brain decided what was right and wrong, and how the world should be." He held my gaze as though making sure I heard every word.

"You were three, Reza. You don't remember," I pushed back.

"I know the stories. I remember the dog ..."

I flinched and he pushed harder. "You've been living by a seven-year-old's rules, probably since the day we left Iran, and seven-year-olds don't have the full picture of the world."

Reza stood. "I don't know about you, but kids don't get to make the rules for me."

He drank the last of his beer, grabbed the book off the table, and clapped me on my shoulder as he headed for the door. "Good talk," he said, and was gone before I could have the last word.

# [ 38 ]
## ANNA

*"I'm allowed to hate my sister, but nobody else is."*

- ANNA COLLINS

C olette was asleep on my bed when I got in, which was good, because it meant I wouldn't be tempted to cry, but annoying, because my pity party was not for sharing. But then I saw the mascara trails on her face, and all inclinations to self-indulgence disappeared.

"Colette," I whispered. "What happened?"

It wasn't that late, and my sister was a night person, which meant she'd cried herself to sleep. She cracked an eyelid open and then rolled away to face the wall.

"I'm going to make some hot chocolate," I said as I got up and turned the kitchen light on.

"Do you have any whipped cream?" Her voice sounded raw.

I scoffed. "No."

"What good are you then?" she said, and I was glad to hear the snark.

"I have marshmallows," I said as I got the milk out of the fridge and poured it into the pot from a fondue set that I used as a saucepan.

"Homemade?" She rolled over to watch me.

"Who *are* you? Do you know how hard marshmallows are to make?"

"Lazy."

"*You're* lazy," I said as I whisked good chocolate into the milk.

"No, you." There was a smile in her voice, and it made the tension in my chest let go enough for normal breath.

She got up off the bed and went into the bathroom. "Well, that's pretty," she said, presumably to her reflection. Then I heard the sound of running water, and when she emerged, her face was clean and bare of make-up. She looked at my outfit with a raised eyebrow. "You had a date?"

"Why do you say that?" I countered, because it wasn't a date.

"Because that's an actual shirt, not a snarky T-shirt."

"I have actual clothes."

"You're avoiding the question. Who'd you go out with? Cipher man?" she asked as she parked on a barstool across from me.

"Why were you crying?" I countered, and then immediately regretted it. Her expression clouded, and she looked so vulnerable I wanted to drop-kick whoever made her feel like that.

"I need the Manet," she said quietly.

"Colette," I said with a sinking stomach, "what did you do?"

"Why do you assume I *did* anything?" she shot back defensively.

"We think it's the original," I said, ignoring her outburst.

"Who the hell is 'we'? You and I are 'we,' not you and Cipher man, or whoever you're sharing a bed with."

She was hurt, and I'd just poked a stick into the wound. I took a deep breath and started again. "I met with Cipher man and his bosses today. Sterling's dad fired them, so they're not actively trying to bust me, but they do want whatever we can get about why Markham Gray might have a stolen Manet hanging on his wall."

Colette closed her eyes as the fight seeped out of her. "I asked Sterling why his dad was freaking out so much about the painting.

He said he didn't know, but that it looked like there'd been another painting behind it."

"Did you tell him we had it?" I asked.

Her eyes flew open. "No! He still doesn't know about you. He can't, because then he'd know we stole it."

"But ..." I prompted, and Colette closed her eyes again.

"His father knows something. I don't know what, but something," she whispered. "Sterling took me to meet his dad for lunch today. He was in town for a meeting." She took a deep breath for courage, I thought. "When Sterling left the table to take a call, Mr. Gray told me that he didn't know how I'd done it, but he knew I was involved in the theft of the painting, and if I didn't give him back what was his, he would plaster my naked butt on every billboard and in every interior design magazine in the city."

Her naked butt. The butt she'd exposed to his security camera to give us both an alibi. "He'd do that to his own son?"

She barked a laugh that had no humor in it. "Apparently so. A Sterling Gray sex tape would probably help his career, but it would sink mine."

I turned the stove off and poured the simmering hot chocolate into two mugs, then put a bag of gourmet marshmallows between us.

She scoffed. "You do have good marshmallows."

"No point in bad wine, cheap chocolate, or crap marshmallows."

She dropped two of the cubes into her cup and raised it to toast me. "Truth."

"I'll figure something out," I said as I blew across the top of my drink.

Her eyes got wide. "What?"

I shrugged. "Not sure yet. Some variation on what we did before, probably."

She wrinkled her nose. "I'm not going on camera again."

"No, but you guys go out, right?"

"Yeah, sometimes."

I gave her my best side-eye. "Just sometimes? Are you sure you're not just a booty call for the guy?"

"He introduced me to his dad," she said, defensive again.

"Who proceeded to threaten you when he conveniently left to take a call." I sighed. "Sterling Gray was supposed to be the booty call. You were going to love him, leave him, and never take another call from him again."

"I like the way he treats me," she said. "He thinks I'm funny, and he's interested in things I have to say." She took a sip of her chocolate and pondered the melting marshmallow. "It may not seem like much to you since guys always treat you like a real person, but he sees me for more than my face and my body."

She'd surprised me. I needed a minute to think about her words, so I took my cup and walked over to the window that looked down into the garden. The only thing moving down there was my neighbor's cat.

I thought about the Disney prince – how he laughed at my jokes and rolled with the crazy things I said. He argued against my self-deprecation and said he loved the random bits of trivia I knew. I felt seen and known and understood in his eyes. It was a heady feeling.

"I get it," I said, turning back to Colette. "It's addicting to feel like a whole person in someone else's eyes."

"You're a whole person to me, Sister," she said. "I always feel a little anemic next to you."

I scowled. "You're the beauty, I'm the badass. Or maybe more accurately, you're the princess, I'm the thief."

"You do realize we're identical twins," she said.

I turned to look at Alex's painting of us. "I know Alex meant this painting for Mom, but I really like it. Even though she didn't know us, I feel like she kind of got who we are."

Colette came to stand next to me, sipping her chocolate. "It's weird that she didn't finish the edges though. I mean, how hard would it have been to paint them?"

I looked at her in surprise, then I put my cup down and took the painting off the easel. "Let's do it. What should I use to get this off its stretcher?"

"A flathead screwdriver to get under the staples."

"There's one in the kitchen drawer, and I have black paint and brushes in the medicine cabinet."

She scowled at me, opened her mouth, then shook her head. "Nope. Not going to ask."

Colette handed me the screwdriver and then went for the little tub of black acrylic paint I kept in the bathroom for face painting when being a panda or a skull was called for.

I laid the painting face down on the rug and started pulling up the staples. Colette held out her hand for the staples as I pulled them, and in a few minutes, I'd removed them all. We carefully peeled the canvas back from the wooden stretcher. "I have newspaper to put on the floor—" My voice trailed off as I saw tiny words, handwritten in the distinctive architectural writing of Alex Kiriakis, revealed around the entire canvas as we pulled it free.

"Is that—?" Colette began.

"A message from Alex," I finished.

The words had been perfectly placed so they were directly behind the one-inch-wide wood and therefore invisible until the stretcher was removed.

"Where does it begin?" Colette asked as I threw away the staples and got a flashlight.

I knelt next to her. "Here," I said, shining the light on a small infinity sign in the upper left corner. I read out loud as I deciphered the writing.

*"If you have retrieved our painting from Markham, you will have found the Manet. He believes it is the real one. The Gardner heist was his plan, but he wasn't in charge and had to follow orders about what to take, so to get anything for himself, he had to make sure it was never reported. Sophia's copy of the Manet was the perfect cover for stealing the original, and I made some bad choices for love. I was to finish her edges, which I did, and switch the paintings in the annex, which I didn't, though I told him I did. He's a vindictive man, and I'm afraid he could go after your mom if he discovers my lie and thinks I told her about his role in the robbery. I stayed away from all*

*of you to protect you from my mistakes. Please tell Sophia I always loved her, and I'm so sorry."*

I met my sister's shocked eyes, knowing mine looked the same. "He can't know we know about any of this," I said.

"I think Alex was right about Markham's vindictiveness. If he knew he was duped, he could still go after Mom. We know he's capable of it, and since she painted the forgery, it's his word against hers that she wasn't involved in the heist itself." Colette looked genuinely afraid as she worked through the ramifications.

Hysteria bubbled up through my chest and came out as laughter. "Holy heist, Batman, I have to put the painting back."

## [ 39 ]
### ANNA

*"Grown-ups are complicated creatures, full of quirks and secrets."*

- ROALD DAHL

I hated that I was so nervous as I walked into the Cipher Security building the next day. Gabriel was at the front desk, talking to a tall, beautiful woman I realized was Shane, and I almost turned right around and left.

Shane saw me though, and she waved. "Anna, it's good to see you again."

"Funny, it's intimidating as hell to see you, Shane of Cipher Security," I grinned, not joking even a little bit. "How are you?"

"I'm good," she laughed. "Have you met Gabriel?"

I nodded. "We met yesterday." I looked at him. "You were right; the coffee in that conference room is excellent."

The look Shane gave Gabriel sent a wave of pure jealousy washing over me. Not because I particularly wanted either of them, but because I wanted that look for myself. It didn't help that I was about to put myself at the mercy of the guy I wanted it from, or that the only looks I was likely to get from him at this point would be cold and disapproving once he heard why I was there.

So I steeled myself and asked, "Is Darius in yet?"

"He is," Shane said, then turned to Gabriel. "You want to call, and I'll take her up?"

He was already picking up the phone and dialing when Shane walked me toward the elevator. "Sorry about ratting you out to Darius after the D&D game," she said casually. "I'm glad Gray fired us though, so it turned out okay."

I looked at her through narrowed eyes. "It's not weird for you to be friendly with someone who broke into one of your systems?"

She laughed as we stepped into the elevator. "I met Gabriel because I did a little unauthorized money transfer from one of his clients. Turned out the client was shady as hell, so it all worked out in the end."

I scoffed. "This client is shady as hell too. Kind of makes you wonder about the people who need private security."

"Quinn has moved toward corporate security. A lot of these guys are hold-overs from when he and Dan were just starting out."

The elevator doors closed and Shane turned to me. "Dan told us a little about what happened. I just want you to know that I don't see things as black and white as some people do, and there is a lot of stuff that happens in the gray areas that I'm fine with. If you and I happen to run into each other at Sparky's D&D nights, I want you to know that I'm just a nerd who wishes I were as cool as you."

My scoff was far bigger this time. "You're the cool one, and I'm the dork with aspirations to Shane-ness."

She laughed and held out her hand to shake mine. "Excellent. I look forward to our next campaign."

The elevator doors opened and Darius stood there, looking impossibly handsome in a gray suit with a lavender tie. The man was so elegant I might as well have been wearing cut-offs and flip flops in comparison.

His eyes searched my face for a brief moment, and I wondered what he was looking for. Evidence of tears, of anger, of defiance? "Anna," he said quietly.

I turned to Shane. "Thanks for bringing me up. I'll see you at Sparky's this week?"

"Yes you will," she said with a smile as she walked away.

Then I turned back to Darius. "I'm sorry for dropping by without calling. Can we talk? It won't take long."

Something in his expression shifted from searching to shuttered, and whatever warmth had passed between us a moment before was gone. He led me to a small room with two sofas and a coffee table between them.

"Is this room someone's office?" I asked, looking around. It felt warm and cozy, like a nice place to nap or play board games with friends.

"There are a few spots around the building that are designed as mixed-use work spaces. I often find a hacker asleep in here when I come in early." He gestured for me to sit on one sofa, and he sat on the other across from me.

I leaned forward. "I need to put the Manet back into Gray's panic room."

If my statement surprised him, he did a good job of controlling his expression. "Why?"

"Because he threatened Colette. He doesn't know about me, and he doesn't have proof she was involved in the theft, but the only way he'll let it go is if the painting goes back."

This did surprise him. "With what did he threaten your sister?"

"He has the sex tape. He threatened to make it public."

Darius's expression went stony, and I wasn't sure what triggered his disapproval. "And why not send the painting to him or leave it someplace he'll be certain to find it?"

I shot him a look. "You clearly don't have enough experience thinking like a criminal. There's no way to send it that doesn't include a trail leading right back to us. The minute we add someone else into the mix, we expose ourselves to greed or fear or whatever means he uses to compel people. And leaving it someplace is too risky. There are too many unknown variables, and I don't want my sister in his crosshairs if he doesn't get it back."

"So you believe he knew the Manet was behind you mother's painting?" Darius asked. I tried not to find too much pleasure in the fact that he admitted the painting I'd taken belonged to my mom.

I inhaled. "We found a message. It was hidden behind the stretcher on the back of the painting my aunt did of me and Colette. Apparently, Markham was the mastermind for the whole Gardner heist, and he planned it for the night the Manet was in the annex for restoration. His plan was to switch my mom's copy of the Manet with the real one so he could steal it for himself without the head honchos knowing. It was my aunt's job to finish the edges to match the original and swap the canvases. According to her message, she finished the edges but she didn't make the switch. Markham thinks she did, and it made her complicit enough that he figured he didn't have to worry about her turning him in. But now that she's gone, if he realizes Alex duped him, and then connects Colette to Alex's family, we're all at risk."

Darius huffed in surprise. "Alexandra Kiriakis certainly played a long game, didn't she?"

"I have no idea. I never got to meet her."

A hint of sympathy came into his eyes. "I'm sorry. She was your aunt, even though she left your family thirty years ago."

"She left to protect her family. She made a mistake, and then moved away to keep the mistake from hurting my mom." I was getting defensive, so I took a breath and sat back.

"And now you find yourself in a similar position," he said quietly.

I regarded him for a long moment as I tried to control the pounding of my heart. This was why we weren't possible in his mind – he saw my theft of my mom's painting as my mistake.

"It wasn't a mistake to take that painting." My words hung in the air between us until they crumbled into dust and drifted away. Our eyes held until I finally spoke again. "I need to know how to disable the alarm on the frame so I can remove the old stretcher."

He looked away then, as though my words hurt him. "I can't help you, Anna."

I nodded, exhaled, and stood up. "I think I knew you'd say that, but I had to try."

He stood and walked me to the door, where I stopped to face him. "You'll do what you need to do." I went up on my toes to kiss his cheek. "Goodbye, Darius."

I didn't look back to see whether he watched me walk away.

# [ 40 ]
## ANNA

*"Friendship is so weird. You just pick a human you've met and you're like, 'Yep, I like this one,' and then you do stuff with them."*

- ANNA COLLINS

I flew to New Mexico for a fugitive recovery, and the local sheriff who took custody of Madge when I brought her in was exceptionally helpful in pointing out how easily my license could be taken away if I put one foot out of line. I guessed he wasn't excited about the fact that it took me eight hours to find a woman they hadn't found in eight months.

But I was in a crappy mood after that, because he wasn't wrong. The bail bondsman and bounty hunting licenses I'd collected from various states were pretty heavily regulated – for good reason. Nobody wanted the guy, or gal, with the propensity for law-breaking and violence to have arresting rights. Until recently, my propensity for law-breaking had been entirely theoretical. If I was even charged with a crime, I'd lose my licenses in at least five states, and my reputation would be severely damaged in the others. Despite the fact that

271

I'd basically fallen into bounty hunting as a profession, I liked what I did, I was good at it, and I didn't want to lose my options to do it.

I made it back to town in time for Dungeons & Dragons at Sparky's loft and went early because I was sick of my own company.

"Anna-banana!" Sparky said when I lifted the freight elevator gate.

"Hey, Spark." My brain fatigue must have been audible, because he did a double-take.

"You sound like you just found out the Easter Bunny is a lie."

"My mom believed that culturally acceptable lies are still lies, so she always said she believed in the magic of Easter and Christmas, and how sad for anyone who didn't. Technically, the Easter Bunny is magic," I said.

"Dude, your tone of voice lacks the inflection appropriate to the message delivered. What's *up*?"

I sighed. I really did love Sparky for being such a bro. "I have to figure out how to extract a wooden frame from a bigger one that's wired to a wall, and do it without getting caught."

He scowled. "That's not hard, but the not getting caught part sounds like maybe it's something you shouldn't be doing?"

I sighed again like a moody teenager. "I think my filter has finally completely broken. I think not being able to lie to a guy I like broke my filter, and now I can do nothing but tell the truth to anyone who asks."

He lit up like a neon sign. "Really? Can I try it?"

I scoffed. "Go ahead. What's the worst that could happen?"

"Okay, what's the worst that could happen?" he echoed.

Jerk. I narrowed my eyes at him. "The worst that could happen is nuclear holocaust, or barring that, a meteorite strike like the one in *The Calculating Stars*, which is an excellent book, by the way."

He smirked. "What's the worst that could happen to you if you get caught."

I glared a dagger through his heart, which he must have felt, because his grin faltered slightly. "If I get caught, I lose my licenses, might go to jail, my sister's naked ass gets plastered on billboards all over the city, and the bad guy wins."

Sparky alternately scowled, smiled, and scowled again at my list. "And if you don't do the thing at all?"

"The last two," I said glumly.

Sparky raised an eyebrow. "While I'll admit to being more than a little intrigued at both the news of a sister and the threat of her naked ass, unless it's the middle of a trilogy, the bad guy doesn't get to win."

"As far as I know, I only get the one shot at this life, so no, not a trilogy."

Sparky stood and began rummaging in his workshop. "Alrighty then, describe what you need to do *exactly*."

By the time Taylor and Ashley wandered in with Ashley's newest recipe for sparkly rainbow unicorn cupcakes, Sparky had designed the perfect tool for the break-up and extraction of the stretcher I'd left behind in the frame in Gray's panic room. And when Shane got there with homemade hummus and flatbread, he'd sketched the parts for a new, portable frame that could be assembled on the spot, which he would 3D print for me in the morning.

I kissed his cheek with the enthusiasm of a much-improved mood. "Thank you! I'll see what I can do about a picture of my sister's best side for you."

He grinned, and Shane raised her eyebrows at us, not having been privy to our earlier conversation. "Your twin sister?"

Now Sparky gaped at me. "Like, identical twin?"

"Shhh, pretend you didn't hear that," I said, putting a finger to his mouth in a distracting, nonsensical gesture. Then I turned to growl at Shane, though my mood was too good to put any teeth behind it.

"Thank you for that. I don't need to figure into any twin fantasies."

"Twin fantasies," Sparky said in a dreamy voice, which ended in a bark of indignation when my elbow caught him in the stomach.

"Taylor," I began, in a desperate bid to change the subject, "thank you for the intro to D in Boston. He had some great information on the Gardner heist, and I really appreciated the time he took to meet with us."

"Oh yeah," Taylor said, "D said to tell you thanks too. The guy you connected him with came through with the name of a guard who wasn't working the night of the heist but knows something he apparently needs witness protection to share. D's tracking that down for an article on the thirtieth anniversary."

"Cool. He must have done something nice for Junior's mom to get that much from him."

Taylor grinned. "D can be a charming guy when he isn't playing a crusty old reporter."

"What does the Gardner heist have to do with the case you were in Boston to do?" Ashley asked.

So, I told them, minus the bits about *The Sisters* painting, the Manet, and Markham Gray, because apparently I could still omit, I just couldn't lie. The conversation was almost more fun than the D&D game was because no one else had even heard of the heist, and at some point during the evening, everyone's phone came out to check a fact or look at a photo. It was heady stuff to be the expert in the room.

Shane fell into step with me as we all dispersed for the night. "So, I've been trying this new thing called being friends with women. I'm pretty sure I still suck at it, and I'm definitely awkward as hell, but if it wouldn't be too weird, would you mind being one of my guinea pigs?"

"If I get to be the really cute, super soft kind and run on the wheel, I'll happily be your guinea pig. I have to warn you though, my filter is broken, and I have very little impulse control when there are inappropriate things to be said."

She laughed, then saluted me. "Noted," she said before turning down a different street. "See you next Tuesday."

"D&D's not Tues— ohhhhh, I see what you did there. *C U Next Tuesday.* Ha! You can't make me say the word just because it's the only thing my brain can hear now. GAH!" I yelled at her as she walked away laughing. "How about Tuesday, Wednesday, And Thursday?"

"Oh, well done!" she called into the night.

Sometimes adolescent humor really was called for, especially between new friends.

# [ 41 ]
## DARIUS

*"Security is mostly a superstition. Life is either a daring adventure or nothing."*

- HELEN KELLER

"Thank you for allowing me to come," I said to Sterling Gray as I followed him inside the Gray mansion.

"I still don't understand what it is you need to do, but I do agree that it's easier if you just show me." Sterling was no more or less friendly than he had always been to me, but his whole manner seemed tense, as though he were waiting for news that he expected would be bad.

"Your security system was set up," I said, leading him to the control panel in the kitchen, "with Cipher Security as the administrator, so that we could make any adjustments or repairs that you determined you needed once you'd lived with the system for several months."

I punched in our admin code, cleared it, then stepped back to give Sterling access. "There, our code has been removed from this panel. I still need to do the main computer in the panic room, so I'll get on that while you add a seven digit code to this panel to make yourself the controlling administrator. Please try not to repeat numbers or use any obvious ones like phone numbers, social security numbers, or dates of birth. I'll show myself up and leave you to it."

As nearly everyone did, in my experience, when given no warning and those instructions, Sterling stared at the panel for a long moment while trying to work out which code he would be able to remember. I probably had five minutes alone to examine the system I'd set up before he was by my side again.

I took the back stairs two at a time and noted that the cameras in the hall had been replaced with thermal imaging devices. Interesting. Also, *Moby Dick* was no longer the book pull for opening the panic room door, though before I could try all the other books, Sterling's voice came from the back stairs.

"We've had the access changed. If you'll give me a moment, I'll let you in."

I sighed, then turned to face him. "Of course. May I ask who did the work?"

"McCallum. He didn't check the admin code though. I'll have to talk to him about that." He stepped between me and the bookcase and looked over his shoulder at me. "Do you mind?"

So now we were not to be trusted. In that case, I needed to pay close attention. "Not at all," I said as I turned my back to him.

There was no sound of a book being pulled, nor any indication that Sterling reached or ducked down to press a button. There was an audible click, which to my mind was just sloppy because it meant that the tumblers were under stress from the latch placement.

I turned to see the panic room looking exactly the same as the last time I'd seen it, even down to the cat that marched in past our legs, his tail high in the air.

Sterling looked grimly at the empty picture frame on the wall. "He keeps it there as a daily reminder of my failure, and until I get the painting back, that's the sum total of who I am to him."

As far as I could tell, the frame hadn't been moved. "If and when you're ready to remove it, I'll come and detach the wiring," I said as I woke the computer from its slumber.

Sterling scoffed. "That won't happen. It's like he expects the painting to magically re-appear in its frame, as if it were all just a horrible mistake."

There was that word again: mistake. *Was* it a mistake that Anna had taken her mother's painting back from the man who had hidden it away? Did calling it that diminish her active planning and execution of a theft so clever that there was still no physical proof that she'd done it?

I pulled up the camera array and saw that two additional cameras had been installed outside, and another one on the landing where Anna had entered the building. A quick check of the logged footage showed that it had recently been copied to an external drive, and the thermal imaging in the hall was functional from all angles.

I exhaled. "Everything appears to be in order," I said as I navigated to the admin control panel and removed Cipher's passcode. I stepped back for Sterling to add his own. "I recommend a different code for this part of the system, but not a sequential one to the alarm panel. Unless you have any further questions, I'll leave you to your day."

I stooped to pet the cat and noted the new plaster patch on the inside of the bookcase door, then I went down the main staircase, noting that the original motion sensors, which were wired to the external alarm system, had not been replaced with cameras. The first floor windows and doors were, I knew, state of the art and therefore impregnable to the solo thief who didn't wield an excavator or a battering ram.

I let myself out of the Gray mansion with a sense of calm I hadn't felt for the past week and nearly collided with Colette Collins as she walked up to the door. She looked as startled to see me as I was to see her.

"Hello, Colette."

"You're Cipher man," she said accusingly.

The name earned her a wry smile. "I am."

She narrowed her eyes at me. "Don't you dare hurt my sister."

Too late. "Your loyalty to your family is a trait you both share. She has assured me that eyeballs would be removed from sockets with dirty fingernails if you were hurt."

Colette's eyes shifted to the house and back to me so fast I'm sure she thought I wouldn't notice, but I did, and I felt compelled to deliver a warning on her sister's behalf. "His fixation seems to be on returning to his father's good graces, and little else seems to be a priority."

Her voice cooled. "I have no idea what you're talking about."

I stepped closer, as if to move past her, and murmured, "Please be careful, for Anna's sake."

She looked up at me, startled, and a slow smile twitched the corners of her mouth up. "That's how we roll."

# [ 42 ]
## ANNA

*"If I tell you, then I get to kiss you,"*

I'd been surprised to get a text from Shane so soon after our D&D game, and even more surprised to find her sitting at the café with Darius. It was the kind of place that had one big, long farmhouse table in the middle, with a few four-top tables scattered around. They were seated across from each other at one end of the big table, and Shane waved me over to sit next to her.

"Hey," she said cheerily, "sit here. We're just finishing up and then let's order."

Darius didn't say anything, he just smiled.

"Are you sure?" I asked. "I don't want to interrupt."

"I'm sure," Shane said, and there was a definite finality to her tone.

I sat on the bench next to her, and she turned back to Darius. "So tell me again what, exactly, to update on the Gray file before I close it?"

My attention sharpened to a razor's edge as he answered. "As I said, McCallum added two more exterior cameras to the south side of the house – one at the door, and one aimed at the small balcony on the second floor. He also changed the cameras in the second floor hall to a thermal surveillance system and added an additional one on the landing near the balcony window."

I stared at Darius in shock. What the hell was he doing?

"Interestingly," he continued, ignoring my eyeballs, which had doubled in size, "the motion sensors I originally set into the bannister of the main staircase, two inches above every third step, beginning with the first one and continuing up to the top floor, have not been replaced or augmented with cameras. They remain tied to the off-site alarm system, as do all the ground floor windows and doors."

He was giving me the security plans to Gray's mansion, disguised as an update to a closed client file, which allowed him to keep his professional integrity and still help me. I could have leapt across the table and kissed him, except I wasn't actually sure if it would be welcome or for that matter, if my eyeballs, which were still inflated like balloons, could survive the impact.

Neither Shane nor Darius looked at me, which was for plausible deniability I was sure, but I couldn't stop looking at Darius, whose handsomeness had just increased by an exponential of google to the bazillionth power.

"McCallum also replaced the book pull mechanism that opened the panic room door. I was unable to determine the exact placement of the new mechanism, but my best estimation is that it's a push button set somewhere on the right side of the shelving unit at approximately waist to shoulder height. The new locking mechanism also seems to be made of inferior grade metal, as the weight load is insufficiently supported for silence."

Shane was taking notes in a small composition notebook, and when he paused to take a sip of his water, she looked up. "What about inside the panic room?" she asked innocently.

"The frame, which we wired to the wall and also attached to the off-site alarm system, is unchanged and remains exactly as it was when the paintings were cut from their stretcher. The computer shows the feeds of the three extra cameras and the new thermals, and the stored feeds show a record of having been copied to an external drive."

Crap. And … wow. He even checked to see if the recording of Colette's tan-line-free booty was still there and/or had been copied. He truly was a most noble prince.

"Finally, and anecdotally, Sterling Gray seems to be quite fixated on the return of the missing painting, possibly even dangerously so." And with that remarkable statement, Darius stood to leave and shot me a final, parting glance that had as much warning as warmth in it.

I quickly stood up too. "I was wondering," I said pointedly to Shane, "if we could possibly reschedule lunch?"

She looked from me to Darius with a sly smile. "Of course. You have my number. Call me anytime."

I smiled brightly, including Darius in my gaze. "I definitely will. Thank you for inviting me. It means more to me than you can possibly imagine."

I gave Shane an impulsive hug and whispered "Thank you" in her ear before turning to Darius. "I'm headed downtown. Can I give you a ride?"

"A ride?" A smile inched its way across his face. "You have a horse?"

# [ 43 ]
## DARIUS

*"Those who don't believe in magic will never find it."*

- ROALD DAHL

Anna handed me the extra helmet she carried in the pannier, and when I was seated on the back of her bike with my arms wrapped around her waist and her body pressed against mine, she turned her head to look back at me. "Where to?"

"Your place," I said instinctively. She searched my eyes for the briefest moment, then pulled her helmet on, started the bike, and drove.

It wasn't far to her place from the café, but it was long enough for my brain to spin. My reason had clearly fled with the need to keep Anna free from Gray's traps – hence the manufactured file update with Shane – but now that she knew the dangers, there was no way she would risk her freedom, so I could breathe again. Except my self-control was shattering with every moment I spent pressed against her as she sped through Chicago.

We parked behind the sprawling Victorian loft complex, and I followed Anna up the steps. She continued past her own studio to a private roof garden where potted herbs shared the sunlight with a couple of lounge chairs and a small table.

Anna stood in the sun and put her face up to the heat with closed eyes and a smile. "I love the first days of spring. It feels like the sun is elbowing its way through all the cold and gray saying, 'Okay, that's enough tough love. They've proven they can survive, now let's give people a reason to live.'" She opened her eyes and looked over at a tree that reached nearly to the roof. "It's also the time when the Minpins start to emerge from their homes in the tree to send their little ones out on the backs of the starlings to learn to fly." She turned to me. "Did you know there are only two Minpin trees in Chicago, and we have one of them?"

I kissed her then, for her Roald Dahl reference and for being free to spout every bit of nonsense that inspired her. Anna's surprise melted into heat and desire and scent and sound, and the only thing I felt was everything that was her – the whisper of her breath, the touch of her hands as they reached up my back, the scent of wild-flowers in her hair, the feeling of her lips tasting, sipping, caressing mine. She fit against me perfectly.

Then she pulled back to look at me. "Why?"

Why kiss her? Because she was the flower to my hummingbird, the island to my storm-tossed ship, and because she was air to a suffocating man.

"Why did you help me?" she repeated.

"Because Gray would've trapped you, and you're meant to be free."

She studied my face. "Thank you," she whispered.

"The firm has lawyers, Anna. We can figure out how to help your sister if Gray releases the video."

She pulled back even further, and then out of my arms entirely. "He won't release the video when I've put the painting back. He'll still have no proof Colette was involved, or at the very least he'll know she wasn't working alone, so he won't risk the information about the Manet getting out. It'll be like nuclear arms – no one strikes because we all know we have them."

*When* she put the painting back, not if. "You're still going to do this." It wasn't phrased as a question because it wasn't one. I knew – as soon as she said the words, I knew my compromise was for nothing. It didn't matter how impossible or dangerous it was, Anna would do what she was going to do, regardless of the cost to her, to her sister and family, or to me.

Understanding seemed to dawn on her face, and she took another step back. "You thought I wouldn't? You put your job and your integrity on the line to stop me from making another *mistake*." Her hands went up as though to ward me away, and I expected an eruption of anger. What I got was something completely different.

"Oh Darius, I'm so sorry."

I couldn't process what that meant. "You're sorry?"

"What you believe in is so important to you, and I'm just not worth the damage to your integrity or your identity."

She turned away. "Don't ever sell out." Her voice broke, and I could hear the tears in it. "You're too good, and I'll only take you down."

"Anna," I began, wishing I could go back to kissing on the roof deck.

"I'll take you back to work," she said without meeting my eyes.

"I'll call a car," I said dully. I stopped in front of her and lifted her chin so she'd look me in the eyes. "I couldn't bear it if they catch you."

She closed her eyes. "I know." Then she opened them again. "That's why you should go."

# [ 44 ]
## ANNA

*"Everyone knows dinosaurs couldn't read, and look what happened to them."*

- FROM THE T-SHIRT COLLECTION OF ANNA COLLINS

I spent the evening with the floor plans to the Gray mansion, acquired when Colette dated Gray's architect, and the night stumbling from stress dream to night sweats to more stress dreams, until I finally dragged myself to the shower to wash the stink of fear from my skin, which swirled down the drain like viscous snot. I had a plan – not as good or thorough as the one that had gotten me into this mess – but the details I didn't know kept sliding parts of the plan around like slippery eels that I couldn't quite catch.

I spent a few hours with Colette going through the timeline of how she was going to get Sterling out of the house. A call to a P.I. I knew in Boston confirmed that Markham Gray was at his office there and had a full schedule of meetings planned for the next two days, and a visit to Sparky put the finishing touches on my kit. I avoided all thoughts of the look of betrayal on Darius's face and focused instead on the gift of the information he'd given me about the current state of Gray's security. I knew how heavy the price tag had been for him, and I treasured it.

Finally, it was time.

I'd modified my tube harness to fit the supplies I'd packed and wore it outside a black bodysuit. I left my leather coat and helmet in the pannier of my motorcycle, which was parked in the alley one building over from Gray's mansion, and then lurked my way around to the back of Gray's property.

This was a trickier approach, but the extra cameras made it necessary. I checked my watch – Colette would be at the front door at nine p.m. to pick Sterling up for a late supper club seating. I had twenty minutes to make it to the third floor. I pulled the black silk balaclava down over my face, tucked my hair under the collar of my body suit, pulled up my big girl *I can do this* panties, and started to climb. My route over the wall and to the back of the mansion was designed to pick my way around camera views and skirt the edges of anything that could be seen from the house.

When no alarms heralded my presence, I started up the wall using window ledges and door frames as hand and foot holds. Gray's mansion wasn't a particularly difficult brick building to climb – I'd climbed worse – but there were two tough bits that required a bigger jump than I usually did without a harness. To find the courage for the first jump, I pictured my sister's naked butt on a billboard, which wasn't actually helpful because laughter isn't generally conducive to landing well. My instinct to be like Honor, my D&D rogue, kicked in and saved me from a two-story fall, and I took a few seconds to calm the adrenaline jitters.

As motivation for my second jump, I pictured Darius on his boat, looking relaxed and happy. The peace that flooded me at the thought of his happiness was more centering than all the yoga breathing I'd ever done, and I landed the jump perfectly.

"Just like Honor," I whispered to myself, and I would have patted myself on the back if death hadn't been on the line. From there it was a fairly easy grab for the small Juliet balcony that led to the third floor landing. I sent a silent thank you to the original architect of the house for his or her love of Shakespeare, hauled myself up over the railing, and crouched down next to the door to work on the lock.

I checked my watch again – five minutes to go until Colette rang the doorbell. I slid the lock-picks out from the runner's belt I wore around my waist and went to work. When I was sixteen I'd taught myself how to break into combination locks because it was something Honor would know how to do, and from there, I mastered using lock picks on a variety of household locks. The mechanism on this door wasn't the easiest, by any means, but it also wasn't the hardest, and I heard the telltale click of the tumblers opening within three-and-a-half minutes. I put the picks away, pulled on my grippy gloves, and waited.

Forty-five seconds later by my watch, the doorbell rang. I crouched further into the corner of the balcony and waited to see if Sterling passed by. He didn't, which meant he'd been on one of the two lower floors. A moment after the faint sound of an electronic snick, I opened the door and slipped inside. Ten seconds later, the system informed the house that it had re-armed, and I waited one full minute more, listening to the sounds of silence.

*Okay*, I inhaled, *time to do this*. The third floor landing was a blind spot, and the main staircase used motion sensor tech. The bannister was fair game though, so I used grippy gloves and climbing shoes to slow my backward slide down. On the second floor landing I was careful to avoid the steps as I pulled off my harness and removed all the contents except the fake Manet.

This was the part I'd worked out with Sparky to protect me from the thermal imaging sensors in the hallway. With his tech geekery and my fundamental weirdness, we'd put together the perfect, well perfectly ridiculous, plan.

I picked up my T. rex costume from among my supplies on the floor and put it on. Then I attached a portable backpacking heater to the pump and inflated the costume with ninety-eight degree air. It would make me sweat, but would also effectively create a body heat signature in the shape of a T. rex. I sauntered down the hall, in full view of the thermal cameras, like the dino-badass I was.

Finding the hidden latch for the panic room door just under the Agatha Christie shelf was only a challenge because the T. rex had stupid little T. rex arms with the reach of a house lizard, which meant I had to unzip the front, causing a momentary pressure loss. I managed to find the latch before the whole thing deflated, so my size and body shape camouflage retained some of its value. Once inside the panic room, I closed the door behind me and quickly shed Rexie so I could go to work.

I flipped the computer screen on and checked the cameras for movement. There was none, so I kept the exterior camera angles onscreen and pulled out the portable stretcher Sparky had made for me. It was quick and easy to build, and he'd even installed a clamping system that allowed the Manet to be stretched over it without staples.

Phase two involved the extraction tool he'd designed. First it cut through the original wood stretcher to create smaller pieces, and then I used it to carefully pull the pieces free from the outer frame without triggering the alarm. This process took some strength and the precision of a large scale game of Operation, but I'd been practicing since the day Sparky had made it for me.

Retrieving the old stretcher was a vital part of the nuclear arms part of the plan. I believed my intrigue-loving aunt could have hidden something inside the edges of the fake Manet when she painted them, something that could either implicate Gray or exonerate my mom, and I was taking it for insurance.

Once the broken stretcher with the attached edges of two paintings was folded up and put into the tube, I placed the newly stretched Manet into the old frame, stuck it to the wall with Command strips for support, and checked the monitor one last time.

Something moved in the image of the south side of the house, and I froze. The cameras to the south were aimed at the garages, and if a resident of the mansion came home, that's the direction they'd come from. I stared at the screen for a long moment, but the frame remained empty of anything on two legs or four, so I quickly donned my tube harness and then Rexie, which I re-inflated with hot air. I was ready to make my escape.

My plan was to climb back up the stair bannister to the third floor, wait for the alarm system to disengage when Sterling got home, and slip out the back before anyone was the wiser. It was a decent plan with a sixty-four percent chance of complete success, a twenty percent chance of at least partial injury, and a sixteen percent chance of catastrophic failure. Unfortunately, I realized I was in sixteen percent territory the second my dino-badass-self stepped out of the panic room door.

"There is a gun pointed at your head, and the police are on their way. Put your hands up or I'll shoot."

The whole thing would have been hilarious, except for all the reasons it wasn't. I genuinely tried to put my hands up, but all I could do was watch the tiny T. rex arms strain to break free of their minuscule range of motion and hope whoever was holding the gun would double over in hysterics instead of shooting me.

"Actually," said a voice that inspired the very best kind of chills, "perhaps we should let the dinosaur have a word."

# [ 45 ]
## DARIUS

*"Some of the best moments in life are the ones you can't tell anyone about."*

- DARIUS MASOUD

The expression on Sterling Gray's face when Anna turned around and he realized he held a gun on a T. rex was almost funnier than the T. rex herself.

The T. rex said something unintelligible behind the sound of the pump, and then took a step toward Sterling.

He raised his gun a little higher and took a step back at the same moment Shane stepped into the hallway behind him. I held my hand up and said calmly, "Sterling, the dinosaur is going to remove the costume so she can speak. Please lower your gun."

"She?" he asked, still twitchy and tense.

"Mr. Gray, please do as my partner asks. We both have weapons, and the T. rex," Shane had to work to keep her voice from breaking, "is unarmed … as it were."

I was less successful, and a chuckle escaped before I could catch it, which set Shane off into sputtering laughter. She had to lower her gun and put her hands on her knees to catch her breath, and that was what finally got to Sterling.

He lowered his gun and tried for stern, but couldn't quite remove all the suppressed laughter from his voice. "What the hell is a dinosaur doing in my house?"

Anna mumbled something unintelligible again, and I gestured for her to unzip her suit.

She shut the pump off, unzipped the front of the suit, and her black balaclava'd face finally emerged. "Hot," she gasped, ripping the balaclava off to reveal her beautiful face covered with a sheen of sweat.

Sterling couldn't believe what he was seeing. "You! But I just left you at the club."

Anna glared at him. "You left Colette behind at the club? What'd you do, slip out the back and leave her with the bill? Where'd you learn your manners, a kennel?" she spat angrily.

"You're not Colette," Sterling said uncertainly. Granted it was dark in the hallway, but I'd been able to tell the sisters apart within an instant of meeting Colette.

Anna sighed and her anger dissipated. "I'm not. Please tell me she's fine."

"She's fine. I told her that something didn't agree with my stomach, but that I'd be back." Sterling seemed to lose his edge as the discussion turned to such inanities. "You're her sister," he finally said.

"Yes."

"What are you doing in my house?"

She compressed her lips together for a moment, then finally spoke through clenched teeth. "Returning something. Are the police really on their way?"

"No, he didn't call them," I said calmly. "He must have installed a silent alarm on the panic room door that tripped and alerted him by cell phone."

"Why are you two here?" she said, including Shane in her questioning look.

"Stakeout," Shane said.

Anna grimaced. "I hate stakeouts."

Shane chuckled. "I don't know, Darius plays a pretty mean trivia game."

Anna leveled her surprised gaze at me until Sterling interrupted. "I really will call the cops if someone doesn't tell me what the hell is going on."

Anna sighed and pushed the button somewhere in the bookshelf to open the door. "Come on, I'll show you."

She stepped out of her T. rex costume as she walked, revealing a skin-tight body suit that appealed to every aesthetic sensibility in my body, then she bunched up the costume and shoved it into the tube she wore in a harness on her back. We filed into the small room behind her, and Sterling flipped on the light.

His eyes went immediately to the painting on the wall, as did mine. Shane was busy looking around the room.

"What the hell …?" His voice trailed off, and he looked to Anna for an explanation.

"It was behind the painting of the sisters in the same frame. I didn't know about it, but your dad did. He's the one who commissioned its theft."

"The original theft," I added for clarification, "thirty years ago from the Isabella Stewart Gardner Museum in Boston. The person he charged with stealing it for him was Anna's and Colette's aunt, because her sister, their mother, had painted an exceptionally good copy of a very valuable original."

"My aunt substituted the copy, though, and hid it behind a painting she and her sister had done of each other. Your dad refused to give that one back to my aunt, and their Cuban Missile Crisis-level stalemate lasted almost thirty years."

"You mean because they each had something on the other, so no one could force the other's hand?"

"Exactly." Anna said. "Then my aunt died and we found a letter she'd written to us asking us to get the painting back for our mom, so we did. We just didn't know about the one behind it. And since that's the painting your dad actually wants, I decided to put it back."

"In a T. rex costume," Sterling deadpanned.

I smirked, Shane giggled, and Anna just shrugged. "As one does," she said.

Sterling put his gun away in a drawer in the desk, then turned back to regard the painting on the wall.

"It isn't a very nice painting, is it," he said.

"Nope. It's a good copy though."

Sterling sighed and looked at Anna. "I presume you have proof of my dad's part in the theft of this good copy?"

She nodded. "I do. I really don't want your dad to know that *we* know about his involvement in, well, let me just say, something the police in Boston are still investigating, so I'm inclined to just tuck all of this away somewhere and forget about it."

"Which you would do if all the digital recordings from last week and tonight managed to disappear?"

Anna glared at him through narrowed eyes. "You would really have let your dad plaster my sister's naked butt all over Chicago?"

He sighed and rubbed his temples. "I didn't know about that until after he threatened her. That recording will obviously go away too."

"It better," she said menacingly. This fierce woman in a black cat suit was the sexiest, most fearless person I'd ever met.

Anna approached Sterling and stood with her hands on her hips. "Sterling Gray, my sister likes you."

He scoffed. "Despite her criminal tendencies, I like her too."

I laughed in uncomfortable awareness of the similarities between myself and Sterling Gray. He scowled at me, but Anna grinned, and my heart beat a little faster.

"So," she said, returning her attention to Sterling, "I'm inclined to pretend nothing ever happened between my aunt and your dad if you and your dad are willing to forget there was ever a painting of two sisters hanging in this room."

He looked up at the fake Manet on the wall, which, I had to

admit, looked pretty great in the fancy gold frame, and then held out his hand to Anna. "Deal." She shook it without hesitation.

"Shall I help you lose the files?" I asked Sterling.

He scowled at me then waved a hand toward the computer. "Have at it." Then to Anna, he said, "I'll have the thumb drive with *my* naked ass sent to your sister."

"Or," she said with a cheeky smile, "you can take her to a nice dinner and give it to her in person."

He checked his watch. "Speaking of, it's time for you people to leave so I can get back to my date."

I was finishing up the file erasure as Anna walked out of the panic room with Sterling. "Do you ever go dancing with the ballerina down the hall?" she asked him.

"The naked one?" he answered. "But ... it's a statue."

"Of course she's a statue. That doesn't mean she doesn't dance ..."

Their voices trailed off, and Shane turned to me with a laugh. "That woman is an absolute delight."

"She's the most remarkable person I've ever met," I said.

# [ 46 ]
## ANNA

*"A well-tied tie is the first serious step in life."*

- OSCAR WILDE

I woke up to a text from Shane summoning me to join a debrief meeting at Cipher Security. In deference to the fact that she and anyone else I encountered in the office would likely be wearing a suit, I dressed in my least holey jeans, a plain white linen shirt, and a long camel topcoat I found in a thrift store in Seattle.

A woman I hadn't seen before was sitting at the downstairs desk. She looked up when I walked in, studied me for a moment, then picked up the phone. "Anna Collins is here."

I held my hand out to her and smiled. "Hi, I'm Anna."

"I know," she said, shaking my hand. "Darius described the boots."

I smirked. "Of course he did."

"He also said you're beautiful, and fierce, and funny as hell, and he has some things he wants to say to you after the meeting, if you're interested," Darius said as he entered the building.

I turned at the sound of his voice, and then my head exploded, but I was too busy laughing to pick up all the bits. Darius wore his usual gorgeous suit and tie combo, but the tie was neon pink and covered in tiny green dinosaurs.

"Nice tie," the woman said completely without irony.

"Thanks, Dallas," he said with a smirk. She cracked a smile then, and it transformed her face from pretty to breathtaking.

He motioned for me to lead the way to the hidden door. "It's a secret staircase kind of day," he said as I opened the door and preceded him inside.

"You look fabulous," I said with genuine admiration.

"Yes, I do. I think I'll wear it to Sunday roast next Monday."

"Oh yeah," I said, with fresh laughter at the thought of Silvana's dress code for her sons. "I'd pay money to see the expression on your mom's face if you show up with a dinosaur tie."

"Good, then you'll come?" He wasn't teasing anymore, and his voice sounded ... hopeful?

I looked over my shoulder at him and giggled at the sight of the dinosaurs dancing on the shiny fabric. "Is there some deeper message to the fact that you're sporting tiny dinos?"

He raised his eyebrows and looked hopeful. "Maybe?"

I gestured for him to go on, and he took a breath. "I'm told people screw up a lot when they're learning a new game, and I never really learned how to play this one before."

"What's the game?" I asked.

He looked up at me. "Coloring outside the lines. Making it up as I go along. Hide and seek in the dark. Truth or dare," he said with complete seriousness.

The grin that spread across my face must have been catching, because he got one just as big when I said, sincerely, "I *love* truth or dare."

Then he poked my booty with a finger and said, "Go, they're waiting for us, and the sooner we debrief, the sooner we can take the boat out."

"Yes!" I ran the last few steps. "Race you!"

"Conference room," he called as I sprinted down the hall.

I beat him by a mile, and the surprise on everyone's faces when I burst into the room was worth the dignity points it cost me because I got to see Darius run.

Dan was grinning at Darius's entrance, and the twitch at the corner of Quinn's mouth gave away the hint of amusement he may have felt. Maybe.

"Now that we're *all*," Quinn looked pointedly at the dinosaur tie, "here, I'd like to close out our Gray file with the full facts as we know them."

Once we had all settled with coffees, I told the assembled Cipher team about my aunt's confession that had been written on the back of her twins painting and the threat of exposure against my sister. Quinn's scowl deepened at that, and he shot a look at Gabriel. "Follow up with Alex Greene on that will you? Let's get that file removed."

I didn't know who Alex Greene was, but the way he said "removed" made me think there might be some hacking skills involved.

Then Darius filled them in on his scout of the current Gray security system. "McCallum has been nosing around our contracts since he came to town last year," Dan said, when Darius mentioned the new thermal cameras. "I want you to keep an eye on him and his company."

"An internal case then?" Darius asked.

"Yeah. I have that itchy-ass feeling it won't be for long though," Dan said.

"You may want to get that checked," I commented before I could stop myself, then screwed my eyes shut so I wouldn't have to see the shock on anyone's face.

But then Dan laughed, and I peeked through my lashes. "Sorry," I said. "Broken filter."

"I had mine removed. Fucking thing kept getting in the way of my best lines."

"Anyway," Darius continued with the slightest of smiles, "when it was clear to me that Anna was going back into Gray's mansion to

303

return the fake Manet, I arranged for her to overhear my conversation with Shane about the modifications. We were in a public venue discussing system alterations that *we* didn't make to the system of a client that was no longer ours," Darius continued, his expression serious. "It was well outside acceptable procedure, I'm aware."

"But in this case, I believe it was warranted," added Quinn, as though that was the last he wanted to hear on the subject.

I saw surprise and a little relief on Darius's face, and I realized he had been worried about the breach in protocol. He had not only stepped over his own rules to make sure I got that information, he'd stepped over his company's rules too. I nudged his foot with mine under the table, then gave him a small smile when he looked at me as he continued.

"Shane and I arrived at the Gray mansion just as Sterling Gray and Colette Collins were leaving, so we did not witness Anna's rather remarkable free climb up the back of the house to the third floor balcony, nor did we see her entry into the house during the time the alarm was disengaged."

Dan turned to me. "You free climbed three stories?"

"It's brick. It wasn't too hard."

Darius slid a photo across the table to Dan, and I saw it was of the back of Gray's mansion and included the Juliet balcony on the upper floor. Taken in the light of day, the climb did look a little daunting.

Dan's eyebrows rose in surprise, and maybe respect. "Interesting skill set."

"It's useful for BASE jumping," I said with a shrug. "And the odd B&E when a bounty's being difficult."

Dan shot a quick look to Quinn, who saw it and seemingly ignored it to turn his gaze back to me. "Describe your plan to return the painting to its frame."

I went through the steps I'd planned and the ones I'd executed. The only raised eyebrow I got from Quinn was for the T. rex suit. Dan snickered, and Shane shared a look with Gabriel that told me they'd already laughed about it in private. Darius just looked pleased with me the whole time I spoke. He seemed ... proud of me? Like maybe I wasn't just one giant mistake waiting to happen?

Darius continued the story from the point where he and Shane followed Sterling into the mansion, and then we took turns describing the conversation with him after he'd caught me.

Quinn had a follow-up question for Darius about Markham Gray's current whereabouts, which I answered with a look at my watch. "He's in his office meeting with a Chinese investment firm about a development he wants to do in the Liaoning province."

Dan's eyebrows shot up, but Quinn actually narrowed his gaze. It was the biggest expression I'd seen on his face yet. "And you know this because ...?"

"I have a guy," I said simply.

"She has a guy," Dan smirked.

I sent Dan a shrug and a smile. "I have people. Actually," I said, including Darius in my gaze, "I got a message from a reporter in Boston. It's possible Markham Gray might have some explaining to do about his parties at the Gardner museum thirty years ago. Somehow his name came up in a conversation with a former guard who is giving information to the police."

"Excellent," said Quinn. He exchanged some indefinable look with Dan as he stood and buttoned his jacket.

I stood too, because it seemed the polite thing to do.

"Ms. Collins," he began.

"Anna, please. You know how I feel about Ms. Collins."

"Anna," he began again. "As your record remains clear, and given your rather ... interesting skill set and connections, we'd like to use your services as a consultant on a per-case basis, with an hourly or weekly rate at market plus twenty percent and expenses. Is that acceptable to you?"

"Is it acceptable to you that I may be sleeping with one of your employees?" I asked out loud, totally on purpose.

The twitch at the corner of Quinn's mouth indicated his amusement, even if his voice didn't. "As long as your activities are consensual and not conducted on my time, it is of no interest to me what or who you do."

I chuckled. "I knew you had a sense of humor under all that—" I waved my hand up and down, "alpha male. Yes, Cipher Security," I included Dan in my gaze, "I graciously accept your generous offer of consultant work, and I'm grateful for the opportunity."

Quinn shook my hand and then turned to Darius. "It seems to me that having a thief's strategic brain testing a security designer's plan could be a useful advantage."

And then Dan stood, shook my hand, and grinned. "Maybe your guys and my guys are the same guys," he said.

"Maybe," I said with a grin, "but probably not, since most of my guys aren't guys."

Shane laughed at the confusion on Dan's face as he and Quinn left the room, then she stood to give me a quick hug. "Sparky just built me a climbing foot. Will you teach me how to do what you do?"

I looked up at her. "If your arms get strong enough, with your height you'll be more Honor-able than even me."

She looked confused for exactly one second, and then she remembered the name of my D&D character. "Honor-able," she said, pronouncing 'able' like the root word of ability. "Kind of like super-abled, instead of dis-abled," she continued, with a glance down at her prosthetic leg. Then she looked at Gabriel. "I think I shall henceforth strive to be Honor-able in all things."

I could see that Shane and I were going to have so much word fun as we figured out how to be friends.

When they were gone, and it was just me, Darius, and the dino tie, I turned to face him. "You mentioned something about a boat?"

# [ 47 ]
## DARIUS

*"The truth is rarely pure and never simple."*

- OSCAR WILDE

The wind had kicked up by the time we left the breakwater and the clouds began to look a bit persuasive. "I don't think we'll be able to stay out for long," I called to Anna, who was standing at the bow, riding the deck as though it were a surfboard.

"Take us out to that buoy and around it, just so we can race the waves," she called, pointing to a red and white blob a few hundred meters away.

The wind whipped her hair around her head like Medusa's snakes, and I pushed the throttle forward until we'd found the speed that allowed us to ride across the edges of the waves instead of over them.

"Look!" she called, pointing to a pair of geese flying off the port side of the boat that seemed to be riding the same wind we were. The birds dipped and dove and seemed almost to tumble with each other in the wind, and above them I could see the formation of the rest of the flock.

Anna watched the pair with rapt attention, and the joy on her face each time a goose shifted on the currents was utterly exquisite to see. She looked back at me with wonder shining bright in her eyes. "They're having so much fun!"

As we neared the buoy marker, the pair of geese caught an upward draft and used it to rejoin their flock, settling into formation as the V continued its flight up the coast. Anna came back into the cockpit and looped her arms around my waist, snuggling in to warm herself against my body.

"Do you know that geese never leave a goose behind?" she said. "If one is injured, two will fly with it to support it until it either dies or rejoins the flock."

"And those two just came down to ride the air currents and play," I said.

"Being playful is important – vital even," she said. "You get old if you *don't* play."

I held her with one arm and steered the boat with the other, rounding the buoy and heading back in to the safety of the harbor. Anna's heart beat steadily against my ribcage, and then she slid her cold hands up my back, under my sweater.

"So it's going to be like that, is it?" I growled happily.

She looked up into my face with a failed attempt at innocent eyes. "Like what?"

"You'll go out and play in the rain, and then come home expecting me to warm you up?"

She grinned. "Yep, pretty much like that. Except when you come out to stomp in puddles with me."

I kissed the tip of her very cold nose. "It's been a long time since I've stomped in puddles."

She quirked her head and looked at me. "Why?"

I looked over the top of her head at the white-capped wind waves and thought about the conversation I'd had with Reza a few days before. I'd lain awake most of that night considering what I now realized was true, and I searched for the words to explain something that had only ever been a memory from which I flinched.

"I've told you that I was seven and Reza was three when my parents decided it was time to leave Iran?" I looked down to find her watching me intently, and I smiled to lessen the serious expression my words had put there.

"My job was to watch him when we were out of the house, as he had a particular tendency at that age to follow any dog that wandered by. A car was coming to take us to the airport, and my parents were bringing the big suitcases they'd packed full of our family's valuables out to the street. They had given us a new bouncy ball and set of jacks with which to amuse ourselves while they went in and out of the house, so we sat in the entry hall by the open door and played."

Anna's eyes were focused on my face as my words began to clog in my throat. "A puppy wandered up to see what the commotion was, and Reza ran outside to say hello to it. I remember thinking that my parents would stop him and I could just keep playing with the jacks, but they didn't see Reza or the dog, and when Reza ran up to the dog he startled it."

"Oh no," Anna whispered.

My gaze landed on nothing but the past as I continued. "The puppy ran away from Reza straight into the street, where it was hit by the car that had come to take us to the airport."

Anna gasped softly, and the pressure of her hands on my skin brought me back to the present, where I stood in the biting wind, on a cold and choppy lake, with this remarkable woman in my arms.

I kissed her lips softly and then backed the throttle off as we neared the jetty. "I remember first knowing that I'd failed at my job, and then getting so angry at Reza for not following the rules," I continued quietly. "He, of course, was devastated, inconsolable, which was my fault too. But he was also three, and very likely has no memory of the same things I still see when I close my eyes." The images of blood and fur had colored all my worst nightmares, but it had been years since I'd dreamed I'd been able to save the dog.

I shook myself from the memory. "The other day, Reza said something that really resonated with me. At seven years old, I made a decision that the dog's death was my fault. I had chosen to play jacks instead of enforcing the rules. Never mind that my parents were right there, or that any animal startled by an intent three-year-old was going to run. And never mind that I was just a kid playing a game while his parents planned their escape from a government that had killed their friends."

I kissed her again, lingering this time in the scent of her. "Somewhere along the way I forgot that a child had made the rules by which I was living," I said softly to her lips.

I reluctantly left her mouth in order to steer the boat into the harbor, and then Anna helped me dock it, tie off, and put the cushions away. The clouds had become somewhat menacing, and the wind was blowing sea spray onto the deck, so we closed ourselves belowdecks and shut the hatch behind us.

Anna was shivering when she finally stopped moving long enough to notice the cold, and her skin was red from the wind. "Come," I said, holding my arms open, "let me warm you." She went into my arms with a sigh and nestled her face into my chest. "Put your hands under my sweater if they're cold," I said, wanting the connection with her, even at the cost of my body heat.

"Actually, it's my feet that are cold," she murmured.

"All right, then, under the covers with you," I said.

She looked up at me through narrowed eyes, "Not alone, I hope."

I laughed. "Is that an invitation or a command?"

"Which will work better?" she asked with feigned innocence.

The grin on my face echoed the one in my heart. "Anna Collins, I'm going to say this out loud now, so there's no question about timing or intent. I am in love with you. Totally, completely, without question, in love, and I think I have been since the day we spent here, on this boat. And though I said I couldn't bear to lose you up on your garden roof, I've realized that if you aren't you, I've lost you already. So you be you, I'll write new rules that are me, and together we can figure out *us*."

She stepped back, frowned at me, and then kicked off her boots and unbuttoned her jeans. "You better strip down, buddy, because the last one naked in that bed has to be on top."

"Has to be?" I grinned, kicking off my shoes and pulling off my sweater.

"It's freaking cold in here," she complained, as she pulled off her T-shirt, kicked off her underwear, and prepared to leap onto my bed.

I grabbed her around the waist and she shrieked. "Too cold!"

I kissed her. "Tell me I didn't freak you out just now."

She stared at me. "Are you kidding? Those are the biggest turn-on words I've ever heard. They are like the sun, shining so brightly they're hard to look at, and like the ocean, so vast and deep they make me afraid. They're the words of fluffy bunnies and corgi puppies, of the smell of fresh bread and babies' heads, the taste of chocolate mousse and movie theater popcorn. They're every new idea, every possibility, everything hopeful and true. They're bucket-fillers, not bucket-dippers, and what you just said to me is exactly the way I feel about you. Times a thousand."

She wriggled out of my arms and flung herself on my bed, then burrowed under the covers while I finished undressing. She poked her head out and looked serious. "Tell me you restocked *Brazen and the Beast*."

I grinned at her. "Really? You think we're going to need—"

"YES!"

I slid beneath the covers and pulled Anna's naked body to me. "We are going to have soooo much fun," she whispered into my mouth. And then she kissed me, and I forgot about rules and history and the cold, and all I could be was *with her*.

# EPILOGUE
## ANNA

*"I must endure the presence of a few caterpillars if I wish to become acquainted with the butterflies."*

- ANTOINE DE SAINT-EXUPÉRY

Rexie and the dino tie were a hit at the Masoud family Sunday roast, and in the following months at least one of us tried to surprise the others with something outrageous every Monday. The best so far were either Reza's rhinestone platform boots or the silver evening gown Silvana wore the week after the dinosaurs made their appearance.

I walked in through the kitchen door, my hands covered in boat engine grease as usual, and greeted Silvana with a kiss on the cheek before scrubbing my hands at the sink. "Reza's boat is almost ready to launch," I said as I dug the black muck out from under short fingernails, "and Darius is trying to get him a slip at the marina near us."

"That's good. Reza will have the calming influence of his brother, and Darius will have another playmate to remind him not to be so serious all the time," she said as she piled roasted vegetables onto a platter already overflowing with *koobideh* kebabs, falafel, pita, and all the sauces and dips to make a perfect summer-time picnic.

"Here, I'll take that outside," I said, reaching for the platter that we would eat at a table Darius and his brother were setting up in the back yard.

"Wait, Anna, I have something for you," Silvana said, reaching for a box behind her and placing it in my hands.

"But—"

"Never argue against receiving a gift freely given. There are strings attached, but only the most literal kind," she said with a smile.

I untied the ribbon and lifted the lid. Inside was the most wonderfully girly apron, complete with ruffles and a handy pocket, made from fabric covered in pink and purple dinosaurs. "It's perfect!" I gasped. I put it on over my linen T-shirt and tied it around my waist, admiring my reflection in the window. "Thank you, Silvana."

She tucked my hair behind my ear with a smile. "Thank you, Anna. You've brought so much laughter into my family, and you've put stars in my son's eyes."

"All the better to see you with, Mum," Darius said as he kissed her cheek, then wrapped his arms around my waist. "Nice dress," he said to me with a grin.

I held the skirt of the apron out and curtsied. "Thank you," I said happily, then whispered dramatically, "I think your mom kind of likes me."

"Me too," he whispered back just as dramatically. "I mean she probably does, but I definitely do."

Silvana smacked him with a dish towel. "Take the platter out when you go," she said, her eyes shiny with laughter.

Darius turned me around to face him. "In a minute, Mum, I'm busy kissing my thief."

I gasped in mock indignation. "I'm not a thief."

"You stole my heart and have kept it in your back pocket since then."

I grinned at him. "So you're saying you like being on my good side?"

He laughed and kissed my nose. "You continue to steal the covers, my socks, and any shreds of dignity I pretend to have. But mostly, you've stolen my will to ever be without you."

He put his hand in the pocket of my new apron and pulled out a ring. "Anna Collins, my thief, my love – will you marry me?"

He slipped the most beautiful gold filigree band studded with seeds of Persian turquoise on my ring finger as I gasped, "YES!"

The room behind me erupted into cheers, and I realized his whole family had just shared in our engagement. And then I turned to see my sister there too, and I realized that this remarkable man had planned the perfect surprise. *He* was my honor – he was integrity and truth and his love gave me wings.

I shot kisses to Colette and wrapped my arms around my prince as all the butterflies in the world took flight and carried us up to dance on the wind.


*The End.*

# A NOTE FROM THE AUTHOR

"I love history, any kind of history, and even better if it's hidden, secret, or underground." Those are words time-traveler, Saira, says in book one of my Immortal Descendants series, *Marking Time*, and they speak directly to my soul. I can spend days down internet rabbit holes, researching historical facts to suit my stories, and my favorites are the anomalies that pop up between sources – those become the mysteries that my characters solve in my books.

The history of the Gardner heist, as presented by D (the reporter), and Crystal and Amber (museum docents) is, according to my research, accurate. I've never been to the Gardner museum in person, but I found the blueprints for it on the Library of Congress website, and with those I tracked down the annex and the hidden door. The photo of the crime scene, showing the open panel, is real, the music gigs and parties the guards held were real, and I found one blog post that mentioned the game of avoiding the motion sensors the night guards used to play throughout the museum, which I dubbed sensor tag. There was also one mention, buried deep in another post, about the *Madame Auguste Manet* having been out of the Blue Room for restoration on the night of the heist – thus, a plot was born.

My friend Christi flew to Boston specifically to visit the Gardner museum for me, and we spent an hour on Facetime as she walked me through the museum, finding the answers to questions I fed her through her headphones. As she approached the Blue Room, I spotted the decorative metal hook above it, which gave me a plausible way in for the thief. She's also the one who mentioned that there seemed to be fascinating little stories in the arrangements of art, so I gave them back to the character I named after her. Christi has my deepest gratitude for her generosity and willingness to listen to me babble in her ear as I worked things out.

Thank you to Agnes for inspiring Sophia, to Anna for inspiring herself, to Jen and Mahyad for their extraordinary generosity, and to my editors, Angela and Rebecca – there aren't enough languages in the world for me to thank you as thoroughly as you both deserve. Without you two and my husband Ed (who fed me and kept our family running), this book would not have been possible.

And finally, thank you Penny Reid, for your trust, your patience, your generosity, and your friendship. You've created a family with Smartypants Romance, and it's a sisterhood of support, laughter, connection, and love that stems from the stand you've taken in our community. You, and the readers who found you, are extraordinary.

# ABOUT THE AUTHOR

APRIL WHITE has been a film producer, private investigator, bouncer, teacher and screenwriter. She has climbed in the Himalayas, lived on a gold mine in the Yukon, and survived a shipwreck. She and her husband live in Southern California with their two sons, dog, various chickens, and a lifetime collection of books.

Facebook is a solid source of distraction for her, and therefore, her Facebook page, April White Books, is usually the first place to find news, teasers, quotes, and excerpts from her books. She also has a secret reader group on Facebook, called "Kick-Ass Heroines." If you'd like to get in on some of those conversations, you can request an add here: Kick-Ass Heroines.

Instagram is probably her favorite social media site because she finds so much inspiration for her plots and characters among other people's photos. Follow her there for books, travel, and the occasional profound observation.

Goodreads is another place to find her lurking around the stacks and spying on her friends' reading habits. Become her Goodreads friend so she can see what you're reading, too.

Marking Time was the 2016 Library Journal Indie e-book winner for Young Adult books, and was chosen by Library Journal for national inclusion on both the fantasy and young adult SELF-e Library Select lists on Biblioboard, The whole series is also available for libraries nationwide through Overdrive, and April is very happy to participate in any library (or bookish) events to which she's invited.

* * *

**Website:** https://www.aprilwhitebooks.com/
**Facebook:** https://www.facebook.com/AprilWhiteBooks/
**Goodreads:**
https://www.goodreads.com/author/show/6570694.April_White
**Twitter:** @ahwhite
**Instagram:** @aprilwhitebooks

Find Smartypants Romance online:
**Website:** www.smartypantsromance.com
**Facebook**: www.facebook.com/smartypantsromance/
**Goodreads:** www.goodreads.com/smartypantsromance
**Twitter:** @smartypantsrom
**Instagram:** @smartypantsromance

**Read on for:**
1. April White's Booklist
2. Smartypants Romance's Booklist

## ALSO BY APRIL WHITE

The Immortal Descendants Series

Marking Time

Tempting Fate

Changing Nature

Waging War

Cheating Death

The Baker Street Series

An Urchin of Means

The Cipher Security Series

Code of Conduct

Code of Honor

# ALSO BY SMARTYPANTS ROMANCE

## Green Valley Chronicles

### The Donner Bakery Series

*Baking Me Crazy by Karla Sorensen (#1)*

*Stud Muffin by Jiffy Kate (#2)*

*No Whisk, No Reward by Ellie Kay (#3)*

*Beef Cake by Jiffy Kate (#4)*

*Batter of Wits by Karla Sorensen (#5)*

### The Green Valley Library Series

*Love in Due Time by L.B. Dunbar (#1)*

*Crime and Periodicals by Nora Everly (#2)*

*Prose Before Bros by Cathy Yardley (#3)*

*Shelf Awareness by Katie Ashley (#4)*

*Carpentry and Cocktails by Nora Everly (#5)*

*Love in Deed by L.B. Dunbar (#6)*

### Scorned Women's Society Series

*My Bare Lady by Piper Sheldon (#1)*

*The Treble with Men by Piper Sheldon (#2)*

### Park Ranger Series

*Happy Trail by Daisy Prescott (#1)*

*Stranger Ranger by Daisy Prescott (#2)*

### The Leffersbee Series

*Been There Done That by Hope Ellis (#1)*